THE MAJOR IN A MAZE

As a good military officer should, Charles accepted the challenge implicit in taking the lead through the maze. He found it vastly interesting that the intrepid Lady Vanessa Rayne should turn fluttery and fanciful the moment she found herself alone with him. He suspected trickery.

A military engineer, he was an expert at finding his way through hostile territory. But he turned on his heel to discover he was alone. Of course. Lady Vanessa was probably halfway back to the house by now. Hell and damnation, but she was a difficult woman!

And yet . . . Her Arrogant Ladyship had not looked so gaunt this evening. The major reminded himself that when color flushed her cheeks, or on the rare occasions when she smiled, she was far more attractive than he had originally thought. Therefore, if she had escaped back to the house, he should consider the lady a true adversary. But if she were teasing him . . . if he should find her in the heart of the maze . . . Charles raised his head like a beast scenting his prey. Ah, yes, if he should find her waiting for him, then possibly they might be friends. And allies . . .

The Major Meets His Match

Blair Bancroft

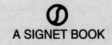

A SIGNET BOOK

SIGNET
Published by New American Library, a division of
Penguin Group (USA) Inc., 375 Hudson Street,
New York, New York 10014, U.S.A.
Penguin Books Ltd, 80 Strand,
London WC2R 0RL, England
Penguin Books Australia Ltd, 250 Camberwell Road,
Camberwell, Victoria 3124, Australia
Penguin Books Canada Ltd, 10 Alcorn Avenue,
Toronto, Ontario, Canada M4V 3B2
Penguin Books (N.Z.) Ltd, Cnr Rosedale and Airborne Roads,
Albany, Auckland 1310, New Zealand

Penguin Books Ltd, Registered Offices:
80 Strand, London WC2R 0RL, England

First published by Signet, an imprint of New American Library,
a division of Penguin Group (USA) Inc.

First Printing, August 2003
10 9 8 7 6 5 4 3 2 1

 REGISTERED TRADEMARK—MARCA REGISTRADA

Printed in the United States of America

PUBLISHER'S NOTE
This is a work of fiction. Names, characters, places, and incidents either are the
product of the author's imagination or are used fictitiously, and any resemblance
to actual persons, living or dead, business establishments, events, or locales is
entirely coincidental.

To my e-buddies in the Beau Monde, Clues-N-News, and WOWResearch networks, who provided such wonderfully detailed information on poison, Bath chairs, vinaigrettes, obscure forms of address, the measles, and that British landscaping trick, the ha-ha

Chapter One

"Charles! I say, Charles!"

Major Charles Tyrone, up to his waist in the ice cold rush of a Highland stream, failed to hear his assistant's shout. A veteran of the Peninsular campaign, he had thought seven years of war enough to make him indifferent to every discomfort. But with his bare feet precariously balanced on an uneven bed of granite and water of glacial temperatures threatening his most private parts in spite of his stout woolen trousers, visions of a hot Spanish plain in high summer were the only thing keeping him warm. Devil take all Scots, particularly those who wanted a bridge where nature never intended a bridge to go. And, more particularly, mad English engineers who thought they could build one anyway. And, very particularly, Devil take his personal decision as owner of the Tyrone Company of Engineers to build the blasted thing in the springtime when the water cascading down from the cloud-capped mountains above had been snow only a day or two before.

Charles gritted his teeth, scowling at the half-built bridge of stone and timber. Only from here, in the middle of the stream, could he truly judge if the foundations and their approaches were well balanced. Would the weight of the bridge be evenly distributed, assuring it a long life? Or would it be tilted, like the surrounding terrain, causing most of the weight to settle on one side?

So far . . . yes, it looked good. But he needed a wider panorama. With care, the former major slid his feet backward, toes curling over rounded stones, sinking into piles of pebbles. He kicked aside a tree branch stuck in an underwater crevice, kept moving back, a slow smile of satisfaction spreading over his ruggedly handsome features as he confirmed that the Tyrone Company's bridge was still looking straight and solid.

"Charles!"

The major had moved far enough downstream that his eye was finally caught by the violent wigwagging of his assistant's arms. Hell and the Devil, this was no time for conversation. Charles took another step back as he frowned toward shore. His right foot encountered nothing but water, a deep pool in the streambed. Arms flailing, he struggled for balance, undulating briefly on one foot, until with an oath he had not used since a particularly nasty incident at San Sebastian two years earlier, Major Charles Tyrone measured his length in the Scottish stream. Since he fell flat on his back, the swift-rushing water surged over and into his mouth and nose in a most unpleasant fashion. He came up sputtering and gasping further profanity which was fortunately drowned by the noise of the stream and the guffaws of the other members of the Tyrone Company of Engineers. Although the major was known to be a man of good humor and not at all starched up in his ways, the local bridge workers upstream thought it best to turn away to hide their laughter. As Charles struggled to his feet, he saw only a broad phalanx of shaking shoulders.

If that were not bad enough, as he splashed ashore dripping ice water from every pore, he spotted a vaguely familiar face standing beside Ian Hay, the eager and highly competent young man who had been his right arm through all the years of the Peninsular War and the first man chosen for Charles's fledgling engineering company. The newcomer seemed so terrified of being caught laughing that his cheeks were puffed out and his face turned red. Charles knew trouble when he saw it. Though eight or nine years had passed and the grizzled servant's name escaped him, the sight of a crested traveling coach stopped on the road above confirmed that this man came from Wyverne Abbey. The major's scowl deepened. Grimly, he took the hand his assistant thrust out to him and climbed up the bank. Although someone immediately threw a blanket about his shoulders, it was all Charles could do to keep his teeth from chattering as he turned to the messenger.

"Well?" he demanded. Whatever the news, he feared it was dire. Minions did not arrive by coach and four unless they expected someone to occupy the vehicle on the return journey.

"My lor—, Major, ah—sir," the servant stammered. "I've come from Wyverne Abbey with a message from the earl." He fished inside his jacket, drew forth a letter. "I'm Ned Burley, sir, groom to his lordship since I was a nipper. Might be you remember me from the time or two y've visited the Abbey." For a moment the older man stared blankly at the letter in his hand, then shook his head. "I know naught what he's writ to ye, sir, but the earl's took bad, he is. Like to die. And t'boy as well. And Lord Sherbourne gone already . . ." The groom drew breath, coming to the belated realization that in the urgency of the situation he had plunged ahead of his story. "I'm right sorry, sir. 'Tis a deal of bad news all at once. I'll clamp m'teeth over m'tongue, 'n let you read his lordship's letter in peace."

Charles rubbed his still dripping fingers against the blanket before taking a gingerly grip on a corner of the letter lest the ink upon it turn to unintelligible rivulets running down the page. The letter was short, eschewing details beyond the bare facts which were, in themselves, enough to justify dragging the owner of the Tyrone Company of Engineers from the middle of a Scottish stream. "An accident?" Charles questioned, as he finished the precise writing penned by his elderly relative's secretary,

James Prentice. "Sherbourne? He had the best pair of hands I've ever seen."

"Aye, sir," Ned Burley agreed, shaking his head. "The very best, he was. 'Tis a mystery, it is."

"The earl and Julian? How do they go on?" The major waved the letter with obvious annoyance. "This tells me little of their condition."

"His lordship was took powerful bad when he heard the news," Ned Burley told him. "An apoplexy it was. He can't walk, his words be slurred, painfullike it is to hear him. And 'is temper . . . ah, sir, I've never known him to be so crotchety, not in all the years I been at the Abbey."

"He has cause," Charles murmured. "And Julian?"

The groom's face, already solemn, grew more grim. "Ah, sir, he's bad, he is. Poor lad. Hasn't said a word since he was thrown from the curricle. Lady Vanessa swears he's opened his eyes a time or two, but none else has seen it. He just lies there—"

"How long?" the major demanded.

" 'Tis more than a month now since the accident, sir. That's why his lordship fears the boy may never wake up . . . or never be right in the head if he does."

Charles took a deep breath, his eyes turned inward, seeing his hopes and dreams for the Tyrone Company of Engineers disappearing as rapidly as the mountain water rushing under the bridge he took such pleasure in building. But all he said was, "Lady Vanessa? Do I have a cousin whose name I have not heard?"

"His lordship's ward, sir. Lady Vanessa Rayne, Rutherford's daughter. Come to us about the time you left for the Peninsula with Sir John Moore, must be seven, eight years ago now."

"It was a long war," the major said, voice grim with memory.

"Aye, sir. And his lordship kept us informed of all your doings. Right proud of you he was." Recollecting the subject of their conversation, Ned Burley added,

"Lady Vanessa's a right 'un, sir. A grand lady, to be sure, but since the accident, she's scarce left the boy's side. Tends him as if he were a brother."

Charles Tyrone, known for his supreme confidence in his ability to cope with any vicissitude, was struck by a rare pang of guilt. If he had called on his noble relatives after returning from the Peninsula, he might have become better acquainted with his distant cousins, Viscount Sherbourne and his son Julian. He might have met Lady Vanessa Rayne, this additional burden being thrust upon him. Yet he had been so far from the succession—and the society of noblemen so far from his thoughts or interest—it had never occurred to him to presume on his relationship to Sylvester Cecil Ashley Creighton Tyrone, the very wealthy and powerful Earl of Wyverne.

So now he was faced with the responsibility for a possibly dying earl, a nearly lifeless fifteen-year-old heir, and a duke's daughter. For these near strangers, for the earl's vast acres and hundreds of tenants, for the sake of the Tyrones and centuries of occasionally illustrious history, he was expected to drop everything and run to Wyverne's bedside. Hell and the Devil confound it! Was it his fault that he, a distant cousin, was next in line for the earldom? He was an engineer, by God. He had never expected to be earl. Was, in fact, appalled by the prospect.

But he was a Tyrone, and he would go.

Lady Vanessa Rayne lowered the *Morning Chronicle* from which she had been reading aloud, her voice trailing into a soft sigh. With the automatic precision of one whose mind is occupied by matters of considerable gravity, she folded the three-day-old newspaper and laid it on the quilted coverlet of the four-poster bed in front of her. "Julian," she pronounced, forcing herself to speak in the light, bantering tone she had so frequently employed in the past when speaking to the bed's occupant, "you should be rising up in indignation that I should dare inflict on you the latest *on dits*. You should castigate me for a mawworm, a gudgeon, a . . . a muttonheaded fribble. Even worse, I have read Minerva novels to you until my voice is worn to a thread, yet you've offered not one word of complaint about my sullying your ears with such farfetched nonsense. Ah, my dear Julian, what I would give if you would but rise from your bed and chase me from the room!''

Lady Vanessa paused, her small white teeth digging into her lower lip, tears threatening to obscure her vision. Julian Tyrone—since his father's death, Viscount Sherbourne—lay immobile beneath covers tucked up to his chin. Pale and thin, with long dark lashes lying over gaunt cheekbones, he was shockingly reduced from the happy, even boisterous, young man he had been only short weeks earlier. One arm lay above the covers, as Vanessa made it a practice to hold his hand each morning as she recited the news of the previous day at Wyverne Abbey. Yet the young viscount gave no sign he had heard her. Not so much as a blink of an eye, a turn of his head, or that most sought response, a squeeze of her hand.

On two occasions since the curricle accident he had opened his eyes, revealing irises of a fine clear gray, but he had stared straight ahead, unseeing, seemingly unaware of Vanessa's hopeful cries, her joyous greeting. In a matter of moments the long lashes had once again dusted his cheeks. Lady Vanessa, going so far as to shake her young friend's shoulder, had received no response. Though her disappointment was bitter, she clung to the slim hope that if Julian had opened his eyes once, he would do so again. Even when the next time brought the same unseeing stare, Vanessa refused to admit his case was hopeless.

Julian Tyrone was a handsome youth in the same devil-may-care style which had had London ladies pursuing his father both before and after his marriage to the beautiful but frivolous Lady Kitty Bainbridge. Since Julian was already showing signs of being yet another dashing Tyrone male, no one was surprised when Neville Tyrone chose his son to accompany him on a curricle race in which the stakes were two thousand pounds, not to mention the numerous side bets. Nor could anyone in the *ton*, including Vanessa, believe that their vital darling, Lord Neville Tyrone, a superb whip, member of the Four-Horse Club, could have met his end in a simple race—that matters could have gone so terribly wrong.

And, now, day after day, Lady Vanessa made the effort to rouse Julian from the world of darkness which had swallowed him, for he was the only brother she had ever known, just seven years of age when she had arrived at Wyverne Abbey, a frightened twelve-year-old. Julian's mother—Lady Sherbourne, known throughout the *ton* as Lady Kitty—had proved to be carelessly kind. A dazzling beauty garbed in exquisitely fashioned garments, she aroused awe in the young Vanessa's bosom. Neville and Kitty Tyrone had been gods who came down from the Olympus of London for occasional visits to Wyverne Abbey, spreading joie de vivre, *ton*-ish manners, and an astonishing air of sophistication in their wake.

Frowning, Vanessa took Julian's hand, squeezing the inert fingers between her own. In the weeks she had sat at his bedside, she had begun to see things which had never occurred to her before. Though she could never, of course, think it right that Lady Kitty had died in childbed four years earlier, it was perhaps best she had been spared the horrible grief that now beset them all. Kitty's high-strung, overly sensitive nature might have been overwhelmed, creating yet another invalid just as the Tyrone family needed stalwart members who could bear up under adversity.

This wayward thought Vanessa would later recall with much chagrin.

"I must go now," she told Julian, "as soon as Tabby arrives to sit with you. For your grandfather has said he will see me at three o'clock, though why he wishes to, I cannot say. My dear, you would not believe how crotch-ety he has become. You would scarce recognize the old gentleman. He is nearly as lifeless as you, you know. We must strain to hear his words, yet his tongue is as sharp . . . well, I assure you, 'tis past belief! He who was my dear guardian has become a growling bear. Laid low he may be, but his word is still law, and well may we quiver at it."

Vanessa patted Julian's hand, then gently tucked his arm back beneath the covers. She was a fool, she sup-posed, to continue to hope. Certainly everyone told her so. Truthfully, she dreaded her coming interview with the earl. What if he told her she must stop sitting with Julian, stop talking to him, reading to him? That she must give up all hope? She could not, simply could not, obey him. Yet the old man, even ailing as he was, had full control of her person and her not inconsiderable fortune.

"I am here, my dear," came a soft, fluttery whisper from the doorway. "I did not forget, you see. Indeed, I believe I am quite five minutes—" Miss Tabitha Halli-well, a female of uncertain years whose figure was as slight and wispy as her voice, broke off in mid-sentence. In her agitation one of her shawls escaped her grasp, trailing its fringe onto the Persian carpet. "Oh, child, I can see I should have come sooner. I *do* beg your par-don. You must go straight to your room and have Downes make you presentable. How you can get yourself into such a state when all you do is sit . . . but there's no time. You must fly. You know how agitated he gets if anyone is late." Vanessa's hands flew to her hair, quickly discovering that long strands of her straight, nondescript brown hair had escaped the black velvet ribbon tied at her nape.

"And I fear you are becoming as pale as poor Julian, my child," Miss Halliwell added. "If I did not know bet-ter, I would think you one of the Abbey's ghosts." Tabi-tha Halliwell's eyes fell on the folded newspaper. Should she chide her dear Vanessa or hold her tongue? Well aware of her anomalous position in the household, on most occasions Miss Halliwell carefully refrained from setting her will against her charge's. The twelve-year-old Lady Vanessa had taken one look at Lady Kitty, who had not a thought in her head beyond the next ball, and taken over management of Wyverne Abbey, easily brushing aside any tentative suggestions from Miss Halliwell, who truly had not the slightest notion of how to run a nobleman's household. Lady Vanessa Rayne, descendant of seven generations of Dukes of Rutherford, did. No matter that her companion—one of Wyverne's impecunious relations—was thirty years her senior, she had seized the reins at Wyverne Abbey and never let go.

And since Lord Sherbourne's accident and the earl's illness, Tabitha Halliwell had to admit, Lady Vanessa was all that was keeping the household from disintegrating. But Miss Halliwell had not forgotten where her duty lay, even if she exercised it infrequently. For the love of the Tyrones, as well as for Vanessa, she must make the effort to point the dear girl in the right direction before she, too, collapsed, leaving Wyverne Abbey with no one at the helm.

"My dear," she ventured, "you know Dr. Pettibone says you are only wearing yourself out by all this reading, that it does no good. And what, pray tell, will happen if you are stricken down as well? Lord Wyverne could not bear it. We will find him in the crypt next to poor Neville and Kitty and—"

"Enough!" Lady Vanessa declared. "I can manage without Downes, Tabby, for you are quite right, Uncle 'Vester will be quite put out if I am late."

Vanessa stood, indicating that her companion should assume the seat beside the bed. Then, scowling into a looking glass above a chest of drawers, she smoothed back the many strands of hair which had inexplicably escaped confinement, retying the black velvet ribbon with a defiant tug of her fingers. Lifting her firm chin and somewhat oversize patrician nose, she pinched her porcelain-pale cheeks to give them some color. Vanessa sighed. For once, just for a moment, she was not thinking of Julian. Tabby was right. She looked hagged.

Never a beauty, she knew her only truly fine feature to be her sparkling blue eyes, and at the moment they were as dull as the rest of her. She was, Vanessa granted, known for possessing more than her share of charm and ready wit. A young lady of outstanding countenance, everyone said. And, certainly, over the years she had discovered that Lord Wyverne was as susceptible to feminine charms as any other man; seldom had she encountered any more difficulty in managing him than the rest of the household. But since the tragedies of losing his son and heir, of seeing his grandson lie nearly lifeless, of suffering his own illness, the earl had become despotic. Quite impossible. Truthfully, life was much changed at Wyverne Abbey.

Lady Vanessa Rayne took one last peek at her image in the mirror, finding little improvement. With a sigh, she smoothed the skirts of her stiff black poplin mourning gown, then turned resolutely toward the door. Time to face the old, but far from toothless, lion in his den.

Chapter Two

A scant fifteen minutes later Lady Vanessa Rayne walked blindly out of Lord Wyverne's bedchamber, spine stiff, head high, controlling her rage only with fierce determination. With each step she took down the hall, her stride lengthened, her bearing grew more militant. By the time she reached Julian's bedchamber, she burst through the door on a whirlwind of fury.

"He has gone mad!" Vanessa cried to the startled Miss Halliwell. "Fit for Bedlam."

"Julian?" Tabitha Halliwell gasped. "Surely he would not keep you from—"

"Ah, no," Vanessa ground out with considerable sarcasm, "there were no edicts about Julian. It would seem the great Lord Wyverne has forgotten about Julian. His beloved grandson is cast aside like a broken toy." After a dramatic pause, seething with rancor, Lady Vanessa drew breath and announced, "He has sent for Major Tyrone!"

"Heaven be praised!"

"Tabby!"

"But my dear, what else should Wyverne do? He himself is incapacitated. Julian, even if he were whole, is but fifteen. The estate has great need of a vigorous man in the prime of life."

Lady Vanessa Rayne, who had thought she was managing remarkably well—with the aid of the earl's secre-

tary, James Prentice, and his steward, Tom Stebbins—
gulped back a cry of outrage. Swaying suddenly from the
culmination of weeks of intense emotions, she gripped
the back of a wing chair, turning her gaze toward the
empty grate of the green marble fireplace. *A stranger!*
After all she had done, Lord Wyverne was bringing in a
stranger, a man who had not set foot in the Abbey in the
eight years since her own arrival. What could a military
engineer possibly know about the earl's vast properties?
About the tenants, the villagers . . . those who lived
within the walls of the Abbey itself? About Julian . . .
or herself?

"Vanessa . . . my dear, you must not take it so to
heart. After all, Major Tyrone is a hero—"

"Hero?" Lady Vanessa sneered, without taking her
gaze from the depths of the fireplace. "Major Tyrone
was an engineer. No matter Uncle 'Vester maintained he
single-handedly won the war; I'm sure it was all a hum."

" 'Tis not as dashing as a cavalry regiment," Miss Halliwell conceded, "nor are the uniforms so elegant," she
added judiciously, "but Lord Wyverne has told us time
and again how often the major was cited for bravery—"

"Fudge!" Vanessa interjected, swinging round to glare
at her companion. " 'Twas all in his head. Major Tyrone
was undoubtedly groveling in some sapper's tunnel while
the fighting was going on."

Tabitha Halliwell sighed. "Nonetheless, my dear," she
ventured, "the major is coming to Wyverne Abbey. We
must make him welcome. Goodness knows he will have
enough on his plate without worrying his head over the
household, so you need not fear his interference."

"Fear?" Lady Vanessa scoffed. "A Rayne fear some
distant offshoot of the Tyrone family? An . . . an *engineer*
without the slightest idea how to go on in society? Indeed not!"

• "Vanessa . . . child, I feel it my duty to warn you to
go softly. The major is a military gentleman accustomed
to giving orders—"

"Orders? To me?" Seven generations of ducal Raynes stood behind Lady Vanessa's scornful challenge.

"Oh, my dear," sighed Miss Halliwell, picking at the folds of her shawl, "perhaps you are right. We are indeed going from the frying pan into the fire."

Except for one day of pelting rain, Major Tyrone rode beside the earl's heavy traveling coach on the long journey from the rugged Scottish Highlands to the gentle rolling hills of the Cotswolds. He had ridden, he told Ned Burley, all the miles from Portugal to Paris. Of a certainty, Rojo, his bay stallion, would curl his lip in a horse laugh if his owner took his ease inside a carriage. Therefore, the major and Ned Burley were riding in advance of the coach as the trees of the park thinned and Wyverne Abbey came into view.

"There she be, Major," the earl's head groom announced. "Too peaceful-like, I'm thinkin', for a place what's seen so much trial and tribulation."

Responding with nothing more than a curt nod, Charles pulled up his horse, allowing the coach to move ahead. Wyverne Abbey. His nemesis. A sprawling structure of soft yellow sandstone with mullioned windows set under Gothic arches, its unique beauty gleamed in the afternoon sun. New-built at the time Henry the Eighth broke from the Catholic Church, this architectural gem constructed by a wealthy abbey had been awarded to the king's faithful crony, Ashley Tyrone, created first Earl of Wyverne. Since that time, Wyverne Abbey had stood as a shining symbol of the wealth and power of the Tyrones. The thought that it one day might be his turned the major cold, even in the warmth of an afternoon in early June. The earldom of Wyverne was a responsibility, a way of life, he did not want. Gladly would he turn Rojo round and set him on the road back to Scotland. Any excuse would do. Any at all.

Yet why was he experiencing that odd frisson which had struck him all too frequently on the Peninsula, always before some particularly dramatic incident? A dangerous incident. Surely, there was no peril here. Trouble, yes. A challenge, yes. Something he faced with reluctance, yes. But danger? Surely the worst had already happened. Sherbourne dead; his son and heir bedridden, possibly forever; the old earl struck down. So what more . . . ?

Charles shook his head. It was not like him to be fanciful, yet it was his sharply honed instincts which had gotten him through the war. But that time was over; there was no danger here. What he was feeling was merely his distaste for what was to come. The earl expected him to stay, and some modicum of family feeling—which he would have sworn he did not possess—would force him to do as Wyverne wished. Mouth set in a grim line, the major resumed his ride up the drive to the Abbey. Perhaps, if the fates smiled on him, things would have improved dramatically since the penning of the earl's summons, and he could turn around and ride straight back to Scotland. Back to the active, productive life he had chosen for himself.

Unfortunately, Charles's hopes were short-lived. He took one look at the Earl of Wyverne's once imposing frame, now shrunk beneath the bedcovers to just another sick old man, and knew he was doomed to taking up the reins of Wyverne Abbey and all the responsibilities that came with it. Oh, there was still meat on the old gentleman's bones. And his heavy thatch of white hair topped a rotund pink face which had only partially gone to wrinkles. But the earl's once good-humored mouth was slack, his sharp gray eyes taken over by gloom. And it soon became apparent that his left side lay inert; his speech, labored.

Nonetheless, Charles had no difficulty understanding the earl's initial salvo of "So you're here at last, damn you. What took you so bloody long?"

"I was in the western Highlands, my lord," Charles

responded mildly, with respect for the old man's condition. "About as far north as one can get. It wasn't easy for Ned Burley to find me, and it was a long journey back."

"Humph!" the earl snorted, then paused, seemingly exhausted by his few words.

The major filled in the silence, giving the old man time to recover. "My engineering company was building a bridge up there, my lord. Truthfully, I worry that it is progressing properly in my absence. I hope to be able to do whatever you wish of me and return to Scotland as soon as possible." The moment the words were out of his mouth, Charles knew he had erred. Too late, too late.

Choler flooded the earl's face, turning it almost purple. "Return!" he sputtered. "Return, will you? You're here to stay, boy. You're needed, by God. This is your place now, and you'll not leave it!" The earl's man, Jarvis, rushed forward to stem the tide of words, shushing his master as only a longtime retainer can, proffering a drink from a glass filled with some mysterious milky liquid. The earl drank, coughed, slapped his right hand hard against the bedcovers. "Sit," the old man ordered. "Here, where . . . see you." Gingerly, Charles lowered his weight to the bed.

Suddenly, the earl's gray eyes were no longer dull and lifeless. They took on the gleam of a man caught up in a particularly pleasing scheme. "No need to fret, boy," he confided to Major Tyrone. "Got it all figured out right and tight. No need for you to work, you know. Make you an allowance and give you Vanessa as well. Fifty thousand pounds and a fine estate come with her. Then, even if the boy recovers, you're set for life. So . . . forget Scotland." The old man nodded, well pleased with himself. "You'll never need to work another day as long as you live."

As appalled as he was speechless, Charles recalled the frisson of warning he had experienced as he approached Wyverne Abbey. This, then, must be the danger. He was not only being coerced into taking over the earl's estates, he was to be forced into marriage with a woman he'd never met. *Impossible!* He wouldn't do it. Never. But what to say to a sick old man?

"My lord," Charles murmured, "you have worn yourself out. We will talk more of this tomorrow. I believe the best thing at the moment would be for me to see young Julian, to ascertain for myself how he goes on."

This seemed to satisfy the earl, who was lying back on his pillow, eyes closed, exhausted by the effort of imparting his grand scheme to Major Tyrone. A feeble nod was all the response Charles got. But as the door closed behind him, the Earl of Wyverne's mind was far from idle. For the first time since the accident he could see a bit of light at the end of the terrible dark tunnel. Charles Tyrone might not have a title, he might be a bit rough about the edges, but he was a *man,* by God. The earl settled in for a nap with a flicker of hope that was burgeoning into a warm glow. He could rest now, lay down his burdens. Major Tyrone would do. Oh, yes, he'd do very well. And as far as Vanessa was concerned? Well, that remained to be seen, did it not? Stubborn chit. Opinionated too. A man like Charles Tyrone would do her a world of good.

On this smug thought, the old man slept.

"My dear, that was not well done," Tabitha Halliwell declared, her sense of propriety outweighing her reticence to censure her headstrong charge, whom she found attempting to catch Julian's attention by reading from *Guy Mannering.* "You should have greeted the major upon his arrival."

"Uncle 'Vester wished to see him immediately." Lady Vanessa shrugged. "I instructed Meecham to take him straight up upon arrival. My presence, I assure you, was superfluous. Who am I to Major Tyrone? He has nothing to do with me."

"Oh, my dear," Miss Halliwell murmured, "I fear you

are mistaken. Not only should you have been present as hostess at the Abbey, but it seems certain Lord Wyverne intends to turn all his affairs over to the major. In fact, Mrs. Meecham confided that Mr. Ellington has been summoned from London. Indeed, what else can it mean?"

Frowning over the news that Lord Wyverne had sent for his solicitor, Vanessa lowered the open book to her lap. "He must, of course, change his Will in face of Neville's death . . . and Julian's illness," she suggested.

"He means to have the major act for him," Tabitha Halliwell countered in much stronger accents than usual. "Meecham and Mr. Stebbins are sure of it, and Mr. Prentice is quite put out, already complaining to any and all who will listen. Foolish little man—as if Wyverne would allow such as he to run the estate. Or so Bernice Meecham told me when I joined her for midmorning tea."

"Gossiping with the servants, Tabby?" Lady Vanessa chided softly, while her mind raced. How could Tabby know this startling news when she herself had not so much as an inkling? Quite easily, Vanessa had to admit. No one had dared mention it to her. Her fingers clenched around the leather-bound cover of Mr. Scott's latest novel. If only she could get as strong a grip on the many forces which suddenly opposed her.

For eight years she had ruled the roost at Wyverne Abbey. Even at age twelve, she had conducted a solemn consultation with Mrs. Meecham on a daily basis. In the last five or six years, as the earl began to show his age, she had taken on the burden of learning about the entire estate, from the local tenant farmers and villagers to the properties owned by the Earl of Wyverne in Lincolnshire, Yorkshire, and northern Wales. Most particularly, she had learned about the management of Beechwood, the fine manor house and good farming acres in Wiltshire which would one day be hers. She had, in fact, become so knowledgeable that, after the earl's apoplectic stroke, the reins of management had rested easily in her hands. Indeed, when she had time to think about it, she was quite proud of herself.

But the Earl of Wyverne had sent for Major Charles Tyrone. Who would . . . Vanessa paused, aware that neither sullen anger nor self-pity would serve. She should be magnanimous in her thoughts, grateful to the major for easing her burdens. Yet how could she—Lady Vanessa Rayne—play the simpering widgeon? Intolerable! Impossible! Major Tyrone would take over, squashing her like a bug if she got in his way.

"Now, Nessa, you must not fret so," Tabby urged. "We all know you have worn yourself to the bone trying to manage all by yourself. Just think, you may read to Julian as often as you wish, for you will not have to meet with Mr. Stebbins or Mr. Prentice or—"

"Major Tyrone," a breathless Meecham announced, having moved down the hallway at twice his usual pace, feeling the major breathing down his neck with every step.

"Good God!" came a disgusted voice from the doorway. "Is this a bedroom or a bat's cave?"

"This," Lady Vanessa announced most awfully, "is a sickroom. You will kindly keep your voice down, Major." Would she have been so bold if she had taken a good look at the man standing just inside the bedchamber door before she spoke? For a second look, from which she could not seem to break away, revealed a man whose thick shock of sun-streaked golden brown hair nearly reached the lintel. He had the broad shoulders and lean hips, the rough-sculptured features of a man of action, the sun-kissed skin of a man who spent most of his life outdoors. His eyes were deep set, the piercing gray common to the Tyrones. They were also eyes which had seen too much, eyes which would always see more than most people wanted him to see—of that Vanessa was certain. He was . . . overwhelming. A dynamic man who would plow his way to a goal, scattering peripheral people like chaff on the wind.

Or so it seemed. Certainly, at the moment, he was glowering, whether at the darkness of the room or at her less-than-polite greeting, Vanessa could not tell. With as much dignity as she could muster, Lady Vanessa rose to her feet, sketching a curtsey she felt more than adequate to a former major from the daughter of a duke. For her efforts she received an abrupt nod as cool as her curtsey.

Charles, furious at how neatly he had been caught in the old earl's trap—and feeling powerless to do anything about it—was in an exceedingly bad mood well before Meecham conducted him to his young cousin's bedchamber. The glimpse he caught of Julian's pale pinched face behind the two black-clad women was enough to bring seven years of war flooding back on a rush of horror. He'd spent some time in hospital himself, but never in such gloom. The smells in Spain and in Belgium had been worse, he conceded. No gangrene here, no piles of severed limbs. But the heavy draperies shut out hope along with the sunlight, trapping despondency along with the stale air. How anyone could endure such a place. . . . No wonder the poor boy showed no sign of recovery!

The major strode to the windows, pulled aside the drapes. Behind him, one or both of the women was protesting. No matter. If there was one thing he had learned during long years of war besides bigger and better ways to blow things up, it was the care of injured men. The locks on the casement windows took only a moment. Fresh spring air rushed into the room. Both women gasped. "That's better," Charles declared. "Now let's have a look at him." He strode back to the bed, where he stood staring down at young Julian, a faint frown creasing his brow. "He is like this all the time?" he asked.

"He has opened his eyes twice that I know of," Vanessa told him, "but he does not appear to see or hear anything."

"Then how have you kept him alive?"

"We—" Vanessa paused, realizing she had been so caught up in the efforts to care for Julian that she had

never questioned the things which had been successful.
"We slip a spoon between his teeth . . . and somehow
he swallows."

"Somehow he swallows," the major echoed. "Do you
realize how unusual that is?"

"Well, yes, now you mention it. I suppose that is one
of the reasons I have kept talking to him and reading to
him. For he is indeed able to swallow or else he would
have been dead long since."

Accustomed to assessing situations at a glance, Charles
had taken in Lady Vanessa Rayne the moment he
stepped into the room. Never a beauty, he'd decided, not
even when out of the sickroom. But endowed with
enough arrogance for a dozen duke's daughters. And
he'd seen fence posts with better figures. Yet now he
was forced to admit she possessed both steady nerves
and common sense. Else she would have made a run for
it or backed herself into a far corner as that wisp of a
woman who must be the companion had done long since.

Charles reached out, laid his hand on Julian's brow.
Odd—he had thought himself inured to suffering and
death, but somehow he was touched. This young man
was the little boy who had once grabbed him about the
legs and begged his big cousin to play a game of spillikins
with him.

Miss Halliwell screamed.

"See!" Lady Vanessa hissed, "his eyes are open." Eagerly, she seized Julian's hand.

"Julian!" the major commanded. "Julian, look at me!"
The young man continued to stare straight ahead.
Charles lowered himself onto the bed beside him.
"That's enough nonsense, boy," he declared. "It's time
to wake up. Look at me, Julian, and you'll soon be eating
rare roast beef instead of gruel."

Vanessa gasped; tears sprang to her eyes. "He
squeezed my hand, I swear it. He squeezed my hand."

Charles grasped Julian's shoulder, then slowly shook
his head, for the boy's eyes were once again shut, his

body beneath the covers as lifeless as ever. "Are you sure?" he asked Lady Vanessa.

"Yes. 'Twas the very first time," she got out around the lump in her throat. "Do you think . . . ? Oh, yes, surely this must mean that he is getting better!" Hope gleamed through her misted blue eyes.

The major gave the bedcovers over Julian's shoulder a pat, then stood up, looking thoughtful. "What does the doctor say?" he asked. "Has he given you no idea of what to expect?"

"He says," Vanessa imparted with scorn, "that some wake up, some do not. He says that *if* Julian wakes, he may be incapacitated. *Dicked in the nob* was, I believe, the rather inelegant expression he used. I fear Dr. Pettibone's idea of treatment for both Uncle 'Vester and Julian is bleeding. Since uncle seems to agree with the doctor, I do not argue on his behalf, but I cannot believe that bleeding can be anything but harmful for Julian. We have had some grand battles over it, I assure you." Vanessa pinned her gaze on Major Tyrone, causing him the first quiver of alarm that he might not be able to handle this particular responsibility. "Do *you* believe in bleeding, Major? For I fear we will be at daggers drawn if you say yes."

Since the major topped Lady Vanessa by more than six inches, he had no difficulty looking down his well-boned nose at his loftily patrician adversary. "I assure you, Lady Vanessa, I have seen too many men bleed to death to have any wish to see someone shed blood unnecessarily."

Caught with a sharp protest on her tongue, Vanessa settled for a curt nod instead. They would argue later about sunlight and fresh air. After all, these problems she could repair the moment the major left the room.

"I wish to speak with you after dinner tonight," Charles told her. "There is a certain matter which must be discussed." One lingering look at Julian, and he was gone.

Air gushed from Vanessa's lungs in a sigh of relief.

Miss Halliwell, who had sunk into an armchair in the corner, raised her head. "Do not say you told me so," Vanessa snapped. "Yes, he is formidable. Ten minutes, and already the battle lines are drawn. With more looming on the horizon." Tabby's only response was an elaborate sigh.

Vanessa, still holding Julian's hand, cocked her head to one side. "You know," she conceded, "he might have been worse. He is not entirely contemptible."

"Oh, my dear, no, of course not," Tabby burbled. "He is like to be Wyverne, you know. A Tyrone is always a gentleman."

Vanessa summoned a thin smile. "I believe it's past time for your preprandial nap, Tabby dear. Do go on. I'll stay with Julian a while longer." Murmuring her thanks, Miss Halliwell escaped, even while wondering how Lady Vanessa could even think of standing up to such a masterful gentleman as Major Tyrone.

For a long time Vanessa sat beside the bed, doing nothing, her mind at a standstill. Then, slowly, the tears began to fall. Julian might have squeezed her hand, but it was Major Charles Tyrone who had elicited this first distinct sign of life.

Not Vanessa. Not Vanessa who loved him. Who had tried so hard. She laid her head on the coverlet and burst into sobs.

Chapter Three

*D*inner that evening was marked by an occasional trumpeted commonplace interspersed by long minutes of awkward silence as none of the four diners, including Mr. James Prentice, the earl's secretary, could easily breach the distances caused by the sudden and mysterious growth of the table to a size fit for a banquet of twenty. A scant ten minutes after the ladies excused themselves, Major Tyrone laid his empty glass of port on the table with what might be called excessive force, excused himself to Mr. Prentice and stalked off to the bookroom. But not before a barked command to Meecham requesting Lady Vanessa to attend him at once.

Shortly thereafter, Charles's gaze swept over the young woman paused in the doorway, every inch the warrior queen prepared to battle to the death. Ah . . . if only she knew what war was truly like. For a moment he let her stand there while he examined this arrogant daughter of a duke with more care than he had been able to give while seated a full twenty-five feet away at the opposite end of the blasted dining table. She paid for dressing, he had to admit. Tonight he could actually catch a hint of figure beneath the high-necked black silk brocade. Unlike the ugly gown she had worn earlier, this one fell in soft graceful folds, softening her overly lanky body. And she'd pinched some color into her cheeks . . . or was that the flush of anger? Without a flicker of doubt crossing his grim-set features, Charles heaved an inner sigh. As if he didn't have enough worries without adding Lady Vanessa Rayne! Her color, he noted, was considerably higher than when she had entered; obviously, he had been staring too long. Ignoring the coziness of a burgundy leather settee, Charles waved her to one of two matching leather armchairs set before the cold hearth.

When she had arranged her skirts to her satisfaction, Lady Vanessa lifted her chin and looked him straight in the eye. "Well, Major?" she demanded. "What is it you wish to discuss?"

After flicking up the tails of his black evening jacket, Charles sat in the opposite chair. Their eyes locked, gray to blue; neither blinked nor looked away. "First," the major murmured, as if the matter were of no consequence, "perhaps you might tell me if it is truly the custom of the house to dine in such isolated splendor."

Lady Vanessa widened her eyes. "But you were proffered the earl's own place, Major. Was it not satisfactory?"

"I would have preferred the opportunity to converse, Lady Vanessa. To further my acquaintance with you, Miss Halliwell, and Mr. Prentice. Instead, I found myself confronted by a vast sea of mahogany." The major leaned forward, his voice still casual, his right hand suspiciously tight on the arm of the chair. "Tell me, Lady Vanessa, exactly how many leaves did you have added to the table?" *A flicker, by God!* He'd actually caused the haughty aristocrat to blink.

Yet she did not hang her head or wring her hands. Lady Vanessa Rayne glared straight back at him and said, "All of them, my lord. Every last one. I'm told it took the footmen a full twenty minutes."

Charles leaned back in his chair and once again allowed his gaze to roam over her, simply because he knew it would annoy her. He was rewarded by a fiery blush. "Your point is made," he told her, "and I quite willingly grant you the running of the household. However, Wyverne is determined on thrusting the reins of the estate into my hands. Therefore you will give me the same respect and obedience you owe to the earl. Do I make myself clear?"

"He will have to tell me so himself," Lady Vanessa retorted, beginning to rise.

"I am not done with you," Charles snapped in the same voice he used on raw and untrained troops. With a hiss of exasperation, Vanessa dropped back into the chair.

After a sharp glance to determine just how angry she might be—*seething* was his best guess—the major asked, "Have you consulted with a London doctor about Julian?"

Lady Vanessa's chin jutted into a militant angle. "Julian was seen by *three* London doctors. Perhaps you are not aware we were situated there for the Season when the accident occurred. All looked grave, shook their heads, and advised sending him home to the Abbey. Only time would tell, they each intoned—like some chorus from a Greek tragedy."

He should have remembered the race was from London to Brighton, Charles thought with some chagrin. Ned Burley had given him the details of the accident, at least as much as had filtered back to Wyverne Abbey. The major could not afford the slightest mistake with this headstrong chit. Give her so much as an inch and she'd take a mile. "Tomorrow you will send for Dr. Pettibone so I may consult with him," Charles announced. "I fear I am not pleased with some of his methods."

"He has been doctoring Julian since he was a baby—"

"This is a matter I must decide for myself. I will hear no more on this subject."

Vanessa gripped her hands together so tightly her knuckles turned white. The major was a hard-hearted wretch without an ounce of finer feelings. A beast, a monster, a . . . Her rioting thoughts shattered, falling with an almost audible plop onto the plush Aubusson carpet. "*What* did you just say?" she gulped.

Charles, seemingly unperturbed by her inattention, repeated his question. "I asked if you were part of this conspiracy to see us wed."

"*Wed?* You and I? You cannot be serious!"

"It was very nearly the first thing out of Wyverne's mouth," the major assured her. "And a second visit prior to dinner has elicited further details. A quite remarkable scheme the old gentleman has conjured up. Are you quite sure you have never heard of it?"

The surge of emotions which threatened to overwhelm her were so mixed, Vanessa was unable to pinpoint a single one. Her heart pounded wildly, then seemed to freeze. Her stomach churned, her body quivered. She, the strong one who always managed when other women were screaming and wringing their hands, felt a ringing in her ears; the candlelight flickered and went dim. She tried to jerk away as the major took her hand, but her fingers refused to move. Gently, he closed them around a small snifter of brandy, helped raise the glass to her lips. Though brandy was not unknown to her, she gasped, choked, making a further fool of herself. With calm indifference, the major set the brandy glass on a sidetable, then offered her his large white handkerchief. Vanessa wiped her streaming eyes, turned her face away to blow her nose as delicately as possible. Just when she had wanted to be at her strongest, her most dignified . . .

Charles Tyrone sat back down in the burgundy leather chair. "Very well," he pronounced, "I absolve you of knowledge of the old man's plans. I am curious, however, how it is that an heiress of such fine portions as yourself remains unmarried after—what?—three seasons."

"Two," Vanessa snapped. Only Major Charles Tyrone could add insult to injury without seeming to be aware of it. "We were in mourning for Lady Kitty before that. And this season was cut short by the accident." How was it possible that he had fixed unerringly on her greatest vulnerability? She was twenty years old and unwed, despite a dowry of a fine estate and fifty thousand pounds.

"You must have had a great many offers."

Better, Vanessa thought. The major was not unaware that he had been rude. "Yes," she conceded, "but Uncle 'Vester deemed them all fortune hunters, and likely he was right. As there were none who appealed to me, we did not argue the matter."

"You call him 'Uncle'. Are we related?"

"A courtesy title only. Lord Wyverne has been my only family since I was twelve. We long ago agreed that it was ridiculous to 'my lord' him when we were so closely associated each day."

"Ah." Charles's right index finger beat a tattoo against the burgundy leather. "I take it," he said softly, "that you find the concept of marriage between us as repugnant as I do." As soon as the fatal words were spoken, he knew he should have kept his tongue between his teeth.

Lady Vanessa Rayne sat tall in her chair, her eyes fixed somewhere over the top of Charles Tyrone's sun-streaked head of hair. "Indeed, Major," she responded, "how could I possibly feel any other way?" With that Parthian shot, she rose with great dignity and stalked from the room.

Charles, who had automatically risen when she did, stood looking after the Arrogant Aristocrat for some moments before slowly shaking his head. He poured a brimming glass of brandy, settled into his chair, and put his feet up on a padded leather stool. What few aristocratic women he had encountered in the last eight years had been married to officers on the Peninsula. He had ignored their romantic overtures, settling for the warm embraces of Portuguese and Spanish women who expected little more than a few coins and a smile. They were always willing, never scornful.

Unlike a certain ducal daughter whom he had not the slightest notion how to handle. There could be no doubt he had badly bungled his first private interview with the lady. And his chagrin, his regret over this uncomfortable state of affairs? What portion of his feelings was due to genuine concern . . . how much to a pragmatist's nagging dissatisfaction with his prideful rejection of a dowry fit for a princess?

The next morning, when Vanessa descended the sweeping curved staircase added by an eighteenth century earl and began to make her way toward the sunny breakfast parlor on the south side of the Abbey, she was brought up short as she passed the dining room. The vast expanse of polished mahogany had been reduced to its smallest dimensions. Vanessa had never, in fact, seen the imposing table without at least one of its many leaves, yet at the moment it was little more than a slightly elongated square. One word from Major Charles Tyrone and the faithful Meecham had deserted her. One word from a man who had not set foot in the Abbey for more than eight years and her rule of the household had been exploded into myth. Even as her fists clenched and her heart twisted, Vanessa castigated herself for her own foolishness. The major was a Tyrone; she, an outsider. When nip came to tuck, there was no question whose orders would be obeyed.

Common sense did not make the hurt any less.

Breakfast was a somber affair, with Lady Vanessa inclined to brood in silence while Tabitha Halliwell sent worried glances in her charge's direction. She, too, had seen the severely reduced dining table. The major, Meecham informed the ladies, had ridden out early with Tom Stebbins, the steward. Mr. Prentice had also dined early and was shut up in his study. "I believe he is preparing for the arrival of Mr. Silas Ellington," the butler confided. "He is expected on Wednesday, my lady."

"Thank you, Meecham," Lady Vanessa murmured, quickly turning her attention to her plate as the butler left the room. How kind of someone to inform her that a houseguest was expected, for Miss Halliwell's confidences from Mrs. Meecham scarcely counted as official notice.

"My dear," Miss Halliwell ventured, "you have spent so much time in the sickroom lately, it is almost as if you were not here . . ."

After a moment of silence in which not a teacup rattled or a spoon clinked against a plate, Vanessa said softly, "Yes, I can see that." But the slices of bacon lay on her plate untouched, and her soft-boiled egg peeking out of its porcelain eggcup seemed to take on Julian's pale features. Eschewing the jam pot, Vanessa attempted to nibble on some dry toast. She choked. Miss Halliwell rushed to pat her on the back.

"My lady," Meecham announced in formal tones. "The vicar and Lady Horatia are here. I have shown them into the drawing room."

"At this hour?" Tabitha Halliwell sputtered.

The butler cleared his throat, looking apologetic. "I believe, ma'am, they have heard about Major Tyrone's presence at the Abbey."

It was not fair that a day should go so badly, Vanessa thought, and all before nine in the morning! Not that she had reason to dislike Ambrose Tyrone, the vicar, except for his unwavering pursuit of her as a wife suitable for a clergyman who fully expected to be the Archbishop of Canterbury. Nor could she fault his mother, Lady Horatia, though that lady was a formidable dowager who never let anyone forget she was the daughter of a marquess. Lady Horatia Tyrone handled the responsibilities of the vicarage with such masterly competence that she had spared Vanessa many of the burdens of noblesse oblige customarily associated with the Abbey. Occasionally to the point where Vanessa had experienced certain qualms over the dowager's control of her son's parishioners, particularly among those who inhabited the vil-

lage of Lower Wyverne. But, as just emphasized so
neatly by Major Tyrone, Lady Vanessa Rayne was the
outsider. Duke's daughter or no, she was not a Tyrone.

Vanessa dabbed her napkin under her eyes to wipe
away her cough-induced tears and rose to her feet.
"Come, Tabby," she said. "I suppose we cannot blame
them for their curiosity, though they are bound to be
disappointed when they discover they have missed the
major in the flesh."

Lady Horatia Tyrone, like Miss Tabitha Halliwell, was
a lady of uncertain years. There the resemblance ended.
She was tall and stately, her dark hair undimmed by gray,
her equally dark eyes giving the impression that nothing
escaped her scrutiny. Lady Horatia possessed a bosom
Vanessa had, in lighter moments, likened to the figure-
head of a ship. Certainly, Lady Horatia's chest protruded
in a manner not considered at all fashionable, a fact duly
ignored in deference to the lady's rank and powerful
presence. Beside her, any proper gentleman of the cloth
should have paled into insignificance. Ambrose Tyrone,
however, was a chip off the maternal block. In addition
to hair and eyes which matched his mother's, he was a
tall man, who had added to his bulk by being a good
trencherman. In truth, the vicar was a solid block of a
man who looked more like a blacksmith or a burly
farmer than a potential archbishop—a cross his mother
bore with stoicism and which bothered the vicar not at
all.

"Is it true?" Lady Horatia boomed without giving the
Abbey ladies time for so much as a "Good Morning."

Vanessa saw no point in bandying words with the dowager. "Yes," she replied shortly. "Major Tyrone arrived
yesterday afternoon."

"Outrageous!" Ambrose Tyrone declared, cutting in
before his mother could voice her opinion, a feat he managed only from long experience. "Wyverne knows he can
always count on our support. Whyever would he send

for a stranger? Surely we were going on well enough without him."

Since these words were balm to her heart, Vanessa found herself more in charity with the vicar than she had been for some time. "I agree with you, of course—"

"A military man. An engineer," Lady Horatia interjected. "What can he possibly know of Wyverne Abbey. The history, the traditions—"

"The people, the farms," Vanessa added, not to be outdone. She broke off in sudden embarrassment as she realized only Lady Horatia was seated, the vicar having jumped to his feet the moment the Abbey ladies entered the drawing room. "Let us be comfortable," she said, and seated herself in a Sheraton armchair opposite Lady Horatia and her son. As was her custom, Miss Halliwell effaced herself to an obscure position against the wall, settling into an armchair, whose needlepointed seat and back had long been a favorite with her.

"Where is he?" Lady Horatia demanded as soon as everyone was seated. Her nose seemed to quiver, as if she sought to scent the major's direction.

"I fear you have missed him," Vanessa told her. "He is off with Stebbins, inspecting the estate."

"Encroaching," snapped the vicar. "What gives him the right—"

Oddly enough, Vanessa found herself doing something she would not have thought possible—defending Major Charles Tyrone.

"He is next in line to Julian," she stated quietly. "With things the way they are, I can understand why Uncle 'Vester sent for him. As much as I dislike the major's presence, he may very well become Wyverne. Though I am appalled by the thought that his succeeding to the title would only be through the deaths of those I love, I must face the fact that he has a right to be here. And that their deaths most certainly cannot be laid at his door."

"I recall him as a child," Lady Horatia sniffed. "A

rough and ready hey-go-mad boy who hobnobbed with the scaff and raff, completely oblivious to their class."

"I cannot like it." Ambrose Tyrone shook his dark head. "I fear your reputation is at risk, Vanessa, my dear. It would be best if we marry immediately. Yes, certainly," he continued in musing tones, "an excellent idea. I can post the banns this Sunday, and we may be married in a month's time. There can be no objection on grounds of mourning, for everyone understands the circumstances are—"

"Ambrose. Ambrose!" Vanessa was close to shouting in her attempt to penetrate the vicar's smug soliloquy. "I am not going to marry you. And I refuse to repeat all the formulas for polite refusal. Goodness knows I have used them all, and still you do not hear me." She paused for a quick breath, moving on before either the vicar or his mother could get in a word. "Even if we were not in mourning for Neville, I do not intend to marry you. In fact, I am at the moment so occupied with two people who may be sick unto death that I have no time to think of marriage at all. To you or anyone else." Vanessa gasped for air, plunged on. "My life is at sixes and sevens, and I know not when it may return to normal. I am unable to think of anything other than the two entrusted to my care. Do not, I beg of you, expect more than I can offer. Now, please, do go away. I assure you both invalids survive; Julian, unchanged; the earl heartened by Major Tyrone's arrival." Vanessa jumped up, strode to the bellpull, and turned to find Meecham already inside the door. Obviously, he had been eavesdropping.

"It is not proper," Lady Horatia declared, as she sailed by on her way to the door. "A rough soldier living under the same roof with Rutherford's daughter. And Miss Halliwell as much protection as a wisp of smoke! You'll rue the day, Vanessa. Take my word for it, you'll rue the day!" Lady Horatia swept out on a sniff of disdain.

Chapter Four

Mr. Silas Ellington, solicitor, arrived from London some two days later and was closeted with the earl for over an hour. Though half the household, including Miss Halliwell, found an excuse to pass by Wyverne's bedchamber during that time, not one sound was heard. Lady Vanessa, having declared herself far too proud to eavesdrop, did not hesitate to closely question Miss Halliwell when she returned to the cheery Ladies' Parlor at the rear of the house where Vanessa was perusing the household accounts. To no avail. The Abbey residents were forced to wait with bated breath until the following day.

Nor even then, when Major Tyrone was summoned to the earl's presence, was there an inkling of the old man's intentions. Not until midafternoon, after the earl's post-nuncheon nap, did he send for Lady Vanessa. With the Abbey staff peeping out from every nook and cranny and Tabitha Halliwell hovering in the hall, wringing the ends of her Norwich shawl, Lady Vanessa Rayne walked the length of the L-shaped corridor from Julian's room to that of the Earl of Wyverne. With every step her heartbeat increased; her hands were clammy, yet her mouth was so dry she feared she would be unable to speak. Surely she was being fanciful. The Earl of Wyverne might be her guardian, but she was the daughter of a duke. He could not force her to his will. Could he? He

was old and weak, unable to so much as feed himself . . .
Nonetheless, he was Earl of Wyverne. And sound of
mind. Sound enough to authorize Mr. Silas Ellington to
draw up whatever nonsense he wished.

*I asked if you were part of this conspiracy to see us
wed.* The major's words echoed along the empty corridor.
No, no, she wouldn't do it. They couldn't make her!

But, unknown to anyone including his solicitor, the
wily old earl had drawn in his horns. Since the major's
arrival, Lord Wyverne had taken a new lease on life.
Time enough to bend the chit to his will at a later date.
Today all she needed to understand was that Major
Charles Tyrone now held the reins of power to all that
the Earl of Wyverne possessed, including the guardianship of Lady Vanessa Rayne. Not that the boy appreciated the choice plum being tossed at his feet, the earl
grumbled to himself. But that would change. The girl
was far from a diamond of the first water, but
Beechwood and fifty thousand in the funds were not to
be sneezed at. Certainly not. If only the pair of them
would not stand there glaring at each other like two
cocks about to charge each other's throats.

"Get on with it!" the earl snapped, as Silas Ellington
finished his lengthy explanation of the complex document
which would give Charles Tyrone, engineer, all the power
of the Right Honorable the Earl of Wyverne, including
the guardianship of Lord Julian Blakeney Hayward Tyrone, Viscount Sherbourne, and Lady Vanessa Amelia
Courtney Rayne.

With labored concentration, the ailing Earl of Wyverne scrawled his name on three copies of the docu-
ments. James Prentice, Hollis Meecham, and Will Jarvis,
the earl's valet, stepped forward to sign as witnesses.
Lady Vanessa held her head high, staring blindly at the
elaborate embroidery which hung from the tester above
the earl's bed, so relieved no attempt had been to coerce
her into marriage that only pride held her up. A grim
Major Charles Tyrone wished he were back on the Pen-

insula, where the enemy was clear, the battle lines easily defined. Where the arrogant daughter of a duke did not cut him down with a glacial glare more lethal than a French cannonade.

"Julian," Vanessa asserted, her words ejected through thinned lips topped by eyes sparking blue lightning, "your grandfather is a sly old fox. Not one word to me about the major, not so much as a hint of marriage—as he knows full well what I would think of such a disastrous alliance!—but to the great Major Tyrone, the *hero,* he promises me as the pot of gold at the end of the rainbow. 'Do what I say, m'boy,' " Lady Vanessa mocked in a remarkably fine imitation of the Earl of Wyverne, " 'and you'll have your reward. Fine gal, my Nessa. Not much of a looker, but you're a soldier, lad. Know how to do what must be done. End justifies the means, and all that. Be glad enough to get what goes with her, I'll w-warrant.' " Vanessa choked to a stop. Not all the tea in China could remedy the situation in which she found herself. She was at *point non plus.* Having already used up nearly every ounce of backbone she had in dealing with the crises at Wyverne Abbey, she had little left for eschewing marriage to Major Charles Tyrone.

Reason began to creep back. She had rushed from the earl's bedchamber straight to the haven of Julian's room as if all the hounds of hell were after her. She had waved Mrs. Meecham out of the room with no explanation to that good soul, who deserved better. And here she was, feeling colossally sorry for herself, when all that had happened was that her guardianship had changed from a sick old man (whom she loved) to a ruggedly handsome, dynamic man of three and thirty (whom she was determined not to love). Uncle 'Vester and Julian were still bedridden; she, still the person most responsible for their care. Her own situation might be anomalous, but her problems would have to wait. For nothing had really changed.

What a fool she was! *Everything had changed.* The
Abbey fairly seethed with the major's presence. The
household had gone from stolid lethargy to the charged
atmosphere that preceded a powerful and cleansing
storm. Silence had been replaced by a rustle and bustle
of servants going about their jobs with a ready will. A
sea of grim faces had been transformed into smiles. And
all because of one . . . *engineer* who found marriage to
a wealthy heiress *repugnant*.

Merciful heavens, she had not thought it could hurt so
much! "You know," Vanessa confessed to Julian, pushing a lock of lank brown hair off his forehead, "neither
the major nor I wish to marry, but it is very lowering to
discover that even the dowry of a duke's daughter does
not tempt him." She refused, absolutely refused, to reveal the word *repugnant,* not even to a young man who
had been unconscious for six weeks. The pride of the
Raynes would not allow it. Then, again, Mr. Ambrose
Tyrone found her dowry delightful.

In his case, it was she who found the concept of marriage abhorrent.

Lady Vanessa's head snapped up, her face growing
thoughtful as an entirely new thought struck her. Marriage to the vicar was definitely repugnant. Yet her reaction to marriage to Major Tyrone was not the same.
Anger and resentment over the idea of being forced into
marriage, disdain for an ex-soldier who worked for a
living: yes, those feelings she could identify. Chagrin that
he did not find her attractive? Yes, that too. But repug-
nance? "Ah, no," she confided softly to the pale young
man in the bed. "It would seem I must watch my step,
Julian. Your grandfather is too clever by half." A Mona
Lisa smile animated her sharply patrician features. "I
wonder if the major has any idea how neatly he is being
maneuvered?" Vanessa, still smiling, picked up the copy
of *Guy Mannering* from the bedside table, found her
place, and began to read.

*   *   *

The major needed air. And not solely in reaction to the stuffy atmosphere in the earl's bedchamber. Wyverne Abbey was going to be the death of him. If not of his body, then of his soul. He was not cut out for pomp and circumstance, for waving a finger and having thirty servants jump to do his bidding. For worrying about wheat and barley, sheep, a dairy, and thrice-bedamned dams which gave way, flooding fields, and cottages. Nor did he want the responsibility of a whole village from vicar to miller to blacksmith to dry goods to little old ladies who lived down the lane. Yet he could not avoid the responsibility for a sick old man and a possibly dying boy. Nor for the difficult young woman he was legally bound to protect.

And marry off as soon as possible. He'd heard the vicar had an eye in that direction. Splendid! A perfect solution. Much more comfortable having the skinny hedgehog out of the Abbey . . .

But then who would oversee the care of the old man and Julian? Miss Halliwell would not last a day on her own. Mrs. Meecham had the running of the entire household. Very well, Charles sighed, the Arrogant Aristocrat had her uses. So long as she kept to the sickroom and did not order the leaves back in the dining table, he and she could manage to rub along together. At least for a short space of time. Which was all he was willing to grant. Surely the earl could not possibly expect him to give up the engineering company he had dreamed of through all those long years on the Peninsula, the company he had worked so hard to launch this past year. Was that why the old man was pushing the girl on him, figuring marriage would tame him enough to get him to settle down at the Abbey until Julian came of age?

His brain still smoldering with conflicting emotions, Charles trotted down the drive toward the gatehouse. What he needed was a good gallop to clear the cobwebs, to make him feel he was his own man again and not a slave to the situation which had been thrust on him. Spy-

ing a path which wound off into the woods, on a whim
he turned Rojo off the drive. Someone—he could not
remember who—had mentioned this path, recommended
it as a fine ride over the southern portion of the park,
with a fine view back over the expanse of the Abbey.
As Charles was swallowed up in the shade of the spinney,
he kept the big bay to a trot, enjoying the leafy shade,
the simple feel of the woods. An enormous copper beech
had marked the entrance to the path. Now all around
him was the wonder of solid English walnut, elm, maple,
even a rowan to two. Nearly all with the north sides of
their trunks greened by moss, a phenomenon he had not
seen in Spain's dry climate. The birds, not the least intim-
idated by a big man on a large horse, continued their
songs with only the veriest flutter to mar the major's
passing. Charles drank it all in. A whole year since his
return to England, and he still could not get enough of
the rolling green hills, towering trees, and lush gardens
which assured him he was far from the hot, dry, and
yellow-brown plains of Spain and the bloody carnage that
was Waterloo.

And all this . . . all this might one day be his. *Never!*
With sunlight ahead, outlining the end of the woods,
Charles broke into a gallop. He did not want the Abbey.
He wanted the world. To roam free, building bridges and
fine buildings, structures that would last for hundreds of
years. Perhaps something which might, like Stonehenge,
endure for thousands of years.

Charles and Rojo broke out of the woods, charging
across an expanse of scythed grass which slanted up a
slight rise. Leaning low over the bay's neck, the major
urged his stallion on. This was what he needed, by God.
A powerful horse and the wind whistling in his ears. And
no feisty woman to mar his peace.

If the major and his faithful charger had not spent so
many years in the rugged Spanish countryside, they
would have died on the spot. As it was, the major's daydreaming was abruptly cut short as he felt Rojo gather

his hindquarters for an unexpected leap. For at the top of the rise the ground simply fell away into a six-foot drop to a sheep pasture beyond. Charles had only seconds to castigate himself for a daydreaming fool. Not that Rojo hadn't saved his neck countless times in the past, but never because his rider had not been paying attention!

The great bay hit hard, stumbled, went to his knees. Charles, who had only been thrown once before in his life—by the explosive blast of close cannonfire—went flying over Rojo's head, his last thought before he hit the ground being: Damnation, he refused to break his neck and let that arrogant chit rule the roost!

Once again, gloom, silence, and long faces prevailed at the Abbey. Hushed voices, tip-toes, heartfelt sighs. Dr. Pettibone went straight from Major Tyrone to the earl, Lord Wyverne having suffered a severe setback at news of the major's accident. Lady Vanessa had the vicar and his mother turned from the door. Her plate was full. She could not even find an ounce of satisfaction in the major's downfall. How *could* he . . . on top of everything else! She told herself she was glad he had not broken his neck, but only so she could wring that part of his anatomy for herself. Of all the idiotic, incredible, ridiculous things to have done!

Calmer reflection, however, indicated she had not appreciated how much more pleasant the Abbey had become in the past few days until the house was once more plunged into doom and gloom. Having absorbed all the doctor's admonitions and instructions—and suffered another outpouring of his ire because she would not allow his leeches anywhere near the major—Vanessa seated herself in a comfortable armchair near the window in the major's bedchamber, took a deep breath, and settled in to wait. The sheep pasture had had more than its share of stones, Ned Burley told her when they brought the major home on a hurdle. No doubt about it, the major's head had encountered one of them. Dr. Pettibone pulled a long face and repeated words that were all too familiar. The major was severely bruised, but would he wake up? Only time would tell.

Several hours later, Charles opened his eyes to the dim light of a single candle and the acrid odor of medicines, instantly flooding his senses with memories of tents filled with so many cots the doctors could scarcely wind their way between them. Of wounded men and dying men. Screams and blood and smells far worse than medicines. *No!* He couldn't be back there again! He started up, only to fall back as pain shot through his head, echoing into every part of his body. He swore softly and fluently in English and in Spanish.

A hand touched his brow. He hurt too much to identify the hand with a face, but it was cool and comforting. He liked it. Something wet splashed onto his cheek. Rain? He would have sworn he was indoors. The bed sagged as it took someone's weight. This time the wetness fell straight onto his mouth. He put out his tongue and tasted it. Hm-m-m. Salty. He told his right arm to move and, amazingly, it did. Straight up to the hand on his forehead, which jerked back as if it had been scalded. "No!" he protested, still without opening his eyes. "Like it."

The bed bounced as a body was removed. "I daresay you like it because you are a bit feverish, Major," said a voice as cool as the hand now lost to his brow. "I shall get a wet cloth for you."

The ducal daughter. This was Wyverne Abbey, not Spain. And, naturally, his weakness was being flaunted in front of his rival for power. What else had he expected? Her Arrogant Ladyship had him right where she wanted him. Charles grimaced, quite unnecessarily, as a cool wet cloth was spread over his forehead. Truthfully, it did such wonders he was able to open his eyes. "Rojo?" he inquired. Lady Vanessa frowned, obviously not understanding his question. "My horse," he added shortly.

"Ah-h. Both Ned Burley and your man Lund have assured me your stallion will be fine. He has scrapes and bruising, very much as you yourself have, but with time he will recover."

"Thank God," Charles murmured, once again closing his eyes. "Rojo and I have been through a great deal together."

"Rojo?"

"Spanish for 'red,' " Charles told her. "I fear we soldiers have little imagination."

Making no attempt at a reply, Lady Vanessa studied her toes with great interest. Was it possible, Charles wondered, that she felt even the smallest qualm over the antagonism which had marked their relationship from the moment they met?

"I fear we have not been at our best with each other," Charles said. "Were you . . . were those tears I felt?" He shouldn't have mentioned it; those drops must have been all in his head. Lady Vanessa gave a minimal nod. Very likely this rapprochement was hurting her as much as it was him. "Did you let that old fool bleed me?" the major asked, shying away from sentiment.

"As a general rule I am not at all squeamish," the lady, at her most lofty, told him. "But the very sight of leeches turns me queasy. I refuse to go near Uncle 'Vester when those horrid things are around. Though I admit he seems easier afterwards," she added.

"Because he's too weak to be difficult," Charles growled. "Leeches are an abomination."

"Yes, well, I must agree. I told the doctor I would not let him near you with those things."

"Thank you," the major intoned with considerable fervor.

"Pettibone informed me that if you were to go off in a high fever, it would be my fault."

"You may tell the scoundrel that if he ever tries to use those things on me, his next meal shall be a nuncheon of roast leech!"

Vanessa giggled, clapped a hand over her mouth. It was not possible she was exchanging humorous badinage with Tyrant Tyrone. "I believe you are going to survive all on your own, Major."

"I may succumb to mortification," Charles admitted, "but I shall survive all else. I'm too tough an old soldier not to. But how I could have ridden off a ha-ha . . . that's what it was, was it not?" Vanessa nodded. "A novice's mistake. If not for Rojo, you'd be sitting by my coffin, my lady, instead of plying me with wet cloths and tears."

Lady Vanessa turned her face away to hide the horror his words inspired. Another death at the Abbey would be past all bearing. Relief swept her as Jake Lund, the major's batman, entered the room. "I will leave you in good hands, Major," Vanessa said, adding with a sincerity which surprised her, "I am greatly relieved to see your injuries are not as serious as we had feared. Goodnight."

Both men allowed their eyes to linger as the ducal daughter sailed across the room and out the door. "A real lady, sir," said Jake Lund. "Could be a royal duchess, she could."

Best to leave that one alone, Charles thought, at least until he was feeling more himself. "Jake, my friend," the major declared, "do you think you could commandeer a bit of rare roast beef?"

A few moments later, Vanessa stood beside Julian's bed, gazing down at the pale thin face lit by the flickering light of her candle, which refused to hold still. She was not given to bouts of nerves, she assured herself. The candle's tendency to shake was solely due to exhaustion. Her day had been wearing, to say the least.

Liar! Her heart had had no trouble standing still when

the men walked past her, carrying the major's inert form. She had felt like Lot's wife, turned to a pillar of salt. It had taken every ounce of courage she possessed to turn and follow the procession upstairs. She could not tolerate the man—his soldier's manners, his calm assumption of authority, his interference in every nook and cranny of her life. Or so she thought until she saw him laid out so still, his vitality snuffed, his aura of authority whisked away as if it had never been.

They needed the dratted man! How dreadfully lowering to have to admit it. Before his arrival, she had been on the verge of collapse. Since then . . . since then, her spirits had been almost as thoroughly rejuvenated as Uncle 'Vester's. Perhaps, Vanessa mused, it had been the challenge of her constant sparring with the major.

Or perhaps it was something more.

"Julian," she confided, heedless of Mrs. Vance, the viscount's old nurse, who sat near the window, calmly knitting by the light of a partially shuttered lantern, "I think we must be kinder to the major. We seem to be caught in a plague of accidents at the moment. I do believe a strong hand might not come amiss. Not that I shall not fight him tooth and nail if I disagree with him," Vanessa added judiciously, "but I believe he may do. And you, young man," she said, on a less reflective note, "you might well heed his example. He threw off his injury with remarkable alacrity. Let me assure you that you could do worse than emulate his example. Julian? Julian!" Vanessa repeated more sharply. "Wake up, my dear. We need you, too!"

Surely this time . . . But the young Viscount Sherbourne never moved.

"You've had a bad day, my lady," Sally Vance said with considerable sympathy. "Off to bed with ye, there's a good girl. You mark my words, one of these days the boy will open his eyes and declare he's starving. Until then, there's naught you can do but pray."

Since Mrs. Vance had been a solid rock of common

sense in the midst of a storm of anguish, Vanessa had learned to heed her advice. Nanny Vance and Neville Tyrone's valet, Fielding, had shared the nighttime vigil over Julian ever since Lady Vanessa had brought his broken body back to the Abbey. At times Vanessa had been tempted to throw herself on the older woman's ample bosom and cry the rivers of tears she seldom let fall. As for Fielding, he seemed as dazed as the rest of the family, automatically turning the full measure of his devotion to Julian, learning to care for a sick boy instead of a top-of-the-trees Corinthian.

As she herself had done, Vanessa thought. She had turned her back on the *ton*, on balls and routs, Venetian breakfasts, musical evenings, the opera, and the theater. On her all-too-eager suitors, their determinedly smiling faces, and their greed. On an instant, her world had been reduced to an old man and a boy, to the small enclave that was Wyverne Abbey. Until Major Charles Tyrone splashed into it, like a giant frog in the midst of a very small puddle.

Vanessa, head bowed, hands clasped tightly in front of her, let out a heartfelt sigh. Sally Vance was right. They had survived another day at Wyverne Abbey without a death. The way things were going, they could only count their blessings and hope to muddle through as well tomorrow.

Chapter Five

The following morning, Lady Vanessa was on her way to one of her twice-daily visits with the earl when she heard a commotion in the vast entry hall below. A few steps back along the corridor brought her to where she could see over the gallery railing. The sight which met her eyes was daunting. Lady Horatia Tyrone stood like an avenging angel facing the Apocalypse, arms crossed, bosom quivering, as she directed a parade of footmen carrying in luggage while, at the same time, fending off Meecham's protests with a basilisk stare. The butler, who was far from a doddering old man, was as close to losing his temper as Vanessa had ever seen. Mrs. Meecham came scurrying into the black and white marbled entry, took in the scene, clasped her hands beneath her chin, and raised her eyes to the heavens.

Dignity forgotten, Lady Vanessa Rayne charged down the staircase with the speed and determination of a brigade of light horse. "Mrs. Meecham, find Mr. Prentice," she ordered, as she flew past the flustered housekeeper. Vanessa drew a deep breath, smoothed her agitated features, and addressed the vicar's mother. "Lady Horatia, what a pleasant surprise! Won't you join me in the Yellow Salon?"

"I am not paying a call," the vicar's mother declared, wearing her consequence like a suit of medieval armor. "I am come to stay. You cannot be allowed to live here with *that man* without a proper chaperone. Now that you are here, you may tell your footmen where to place my luggage."

"By all means," Vanessa answered graciously. "Jenkins, Fisher," she said to the Abbey footmen, "you will return Lady Horatia's cases to her carriage. She is not staying." Out of the corner of her eye Vanessa caught her butler's smirk. Her lips quivered.

"Ah, good morning, Lady Vanessa, Lady Horatia," said James Prentice, striding into the fray. A man of medium build and innocuous features which made him look years younger than his true age of nearly forty, Mr. Prentice had been the earl's secretary for close to twenty years. A fixture at the Abbey, he resented Major Tyrone's authority almost as much as Lady Vanessa did. He was, in fact, her devoted slave. At times more worshipful than she could like. Nonetheless, Mr. James Prentice had his uses. As Wellington had used his reserves on the Peninsula, so Lady Vanessa was using Mr. Prentice. With Lady Horatia, reinforcements were frequently necessary.

"You may go about your business, Prentice," declared that lady. "We have no need of you here."

"Merely passing through the hall, my lady," he told her. "Obliged to pay my respects, don't you know."

"You are an idiot," Lady Horatia told him roundly. Mr. James Prentice, long accustomed to the vicar's mother, did not so much as blink.

"I believe we should discuss this in the Yellow Salon," Lady Vanessa repeated, in the steel-edged ducal tone she had learned at her father's knee. Somehow Lady Horatia found herself moving through the entry hall with Lady Vanessa on one side, James Prentice on the other, and Meecham bringing up the rear. They were trailed, at a safe distance, by Tabitha Halliwell, who had been hovering at the edge of the hall, hidden under the shadows of the gallery.

Though Lady Horatia continued to sputter about her

cases, she soon found herself seated on a sofa covered in gold satin brocade, facing a perfectly composed Lady Vanessa, who took a matching chair opposite her. James Prentice chose to stand. Miss Halliwell scurried for the confines of the tallest wing chair, set some distance from the others. Meecham bowed himself out, then put his ear to the crack he had carefully left between the door and the jamb.

Lady Horatia got in the first blow. "Your reputation will be in shreds, Vanessa," she declared most awfully. "A man like that. You cannot possibly—"

"Major Tyrone is an officer and a gentleman," Vanessa heard herself say. He was also considerably the lesser of two evils. In a choice between the major and Lady Horatia, she would gladly suffer Charles Tyrone under the Abbey roof. In fact, the thought of the vicar's mother ruling the roost at Wyverne Abbey made Charles Tyrone look like a gift from the gods.

"Major Tyrone is a rough soldier. Everyone knows Wellington's troops got up to every sort of vile—"

"Mother!" Ambrose Tyrone barked from the doorway, where he had had to push aside two footmen and Meecham in order to enter the room. "I told you this was a mad scheme. I do not wonder that Lady Vanessa cannot like it." He turned to his hostess. "My apologies, Vanessa. I am quite certain Mama did not mean to impugn your virtue, nor that of Major Tyrone. She was merely, ah—concerned."

"So concerned she would move in, bag and baggage, without consulting me!" Vanessa fumed, losing the precarious hold she had attempted to place on her temper. "It is outside of enough! Let me tell you, Ambrose, I fear your mother's nose grows too long."

"Hussy!" Lady Horatia declared. "Lower Wyverne could not do without me. And you, Vanessa Rayne, are a fool. How that common soldier could be next in line, before Godfrey and my darling Ambrose, I shall never know. A mistake I was certain the good Lord would rectify. All those years of war . . . and he comes marching home unscathed. As healthy as if he'd spent his years in London! It is unfair. Shockingly unfair!"

"How true," came a voice from the doorway. "I wanted to have a talk with the College of Arms myself."

"Sir!" the vicar choked out, his horrified gaze fixed on the major's attire.

"That man is not dressed!" Lady Horatia gasped.

No, he wasn't. And he shouldn't be out of bed. Nonetheless, Vanessa was very much afraid she was going to laugh. Schooling her features to some semblance of polite manners, she said, "Lady Horatia, Ambrose, may I present Major Charles Tyrone? He suffered an injury yesterday and is supposed to be confined to his bed. But I believe you will agree his robe is more than ample cover." The major's robe was of coarsely woven wool, faded to various shades of gray. The hem was tattered, a few unraveled strands dangling onto the carpet; a hole could be seen in one elbow. "Major, this is Lady Horatia Tyrone and her son, Ambrose. He is our vicar and second in line as your heir, I believe."

"Heir?" Charles echoed, obviously puzzled.

"To the title," Vanessa explained. "To the Abbey and the earl's entire estate. After you is Godfrey and then Ambrose, each of you cousins in some obscure degree."

Major Tyrone studied the burly vicar with some interest. "We are all so remote from the title that the matter is surely moot," he returned softly. "Now, if you please," he said, scanning the various people in the room, "would you be so kind as to explain why Mrs. Meecham came flying up the stairs to summon me?"

A cacophony of voices struck him, causing his headache to explode into a blinding stab of pain. "Enough!" he roared, waving his hand. "Enough," he echoed, his voice faded to a whisper. The major didn't really need an explanation, for Mrs. Meecham had quickly sketched the problem. Which was what had prompted him to charge downstairs in his robe, knowing full well the sensation he would cause. Somehow rescuing the fair maiden, no matter how much of a termagant she might be, seemed imperative. Now—Charles looked down at his tattered robe, at the white cotton nightshirt peeking through the slits and from under the ragged hem—now he had to prove he could be a man, even when he looked a perfect looby.

"Lady Horatia," he said, looking that formidable dowager straight in the eye, "your intention was admirable. Your commission of it without speaking to Lady Vanessa or to myself was abominable." He threw up a hand, halting the lady's indignant protest. "Lady Vanessa is well protected in this household. We have no need of your services. Mr. Tyrone," the major said to the vicar, "you will please help your mother back to her carriage and see her safely home. You are both welcome to call whenever you wish news of how we go on, but the Abbey is not accommodating guests at this—"

"Indeed I am not a *guest*!" Lady Horatia burst out.

"Quite so," said the major. "I am so glad you agree. Mr. Tyrone?"

If he put that kind of steel into his buildings, Vanessa thought, they should stand forever.

"Come, mother," Ambrose Tyrone murmured, crossing the room to take Lady Horatia's arm and detach her from the sofa. She was still sputtering as her son led her from the room.

"Oh, my goodness gracious," Miss Halliwell wheezed.

Vanessa rushed to Charles as she saw him sway. Throwing an arm around his shoulders, she held him tight. "Jenkins, Fisher, see the major back upstairs immediately." Very softly, for the major's ears alone, she told him, "Thank you."

Not that she could not have handled the matter herself. She and James. Yet . . .

It was a highly thoughtful young lady who climbed the stairs for her delayed visit with the Earl of Wyverne.

*   *   *

Vanessa, conscious of the earl's frailty, had bitten her tongue and avoided controversial topics over the five days since the major's arrival. But since she also knew there was no love lost between Lord Wyverne and Lady Horatia, she did not hesitate to entertain him with a detailed account of the scene just passed in the Yellow Salon. The old man chortled, chuckled, and wiped his face as tears of glee dripped down his rotund pink cheeks. "Routed, by God! Told you the major was a right 'un, girl."

"I had the situation well in hand," Vanessa protested automatically, knowing perfectly well that the major had spared her a good deal of brangling and unpleasantness.

The earl ignored her. "A good man," he declared, his gray eyes at their most piercing, as if attempting to penetrate her innermost defenses. "You remember that, young lady. Rutherford's daughter or no, you could do far worse than Charles Tyrone."

As if she had not an inkling of his purpose, Vanessa raised her eyebrows and lifted her strongly patrician nose into the Rutherford stare, an intimidating look perfected by her grandfather and successfully imitated by her father. It was a look designed to quell the slightest pretension, the least encroachment, the tiniest intimation that someone dared consider themselves equal to a Rayne. Even an earl of the realm. "You cannot possibly be suggesting a match," she intoned.

"Aye, that I am. And you can come down off your high horse, my girl. A better man's not to be found. And he's like to be Wyverne within the year, so don't be so hoity-toity! And where else will you look, pray tell? There's like to be two more deaths soon enough. By the time you're out of mourning, you'll be so well fixed on the shelf the *ton* will see you as a wrinkled old prune."

"My lord!" The thought of his death—and Julian's— might haunt her in the wee hours of the night, but that the earl should come right out and say the fateful words was a most unpleasant shock.

"So, tell me," the earl barked, showing no distress over anticipation of his own demise, "how do you go on with the major? From what I've heard, this morning's stand, shoulder to shoulder against the evil witch, is a rare concordance. Well, child, let me have the story with no roundabout'tions."

Vanessa ducked her head, searching for a way out, but unless Meecham made an appearance, announcing a second unexpected caller, or someone shouted "Fire!" she could not squirm out of a reply. "We get on well enough," she ventured. "We have had a few differences over the running of the household." The old devil was smiling. Undoubtedly, someone had regaled him with the story of the expanding and contracting dining table. "I—ah—cannot agree with the major's ideas about Julian's sickroom. I shut the windows and draperies as fast as he opens them. Indeed, 'tis a wonder the slamming up and down has not penetrated to your chamber."

"Tales of it have," said the Earl of Wyverne. A peep from under Vanessa's lashes revealed the old man was scowling. "Has it not occurred you," he demanded, "that the major has had a vast deal more experience in dealing with young men than you have, child? That if you live to be a hundred, you will never know as much about injuries as he has learned in these many years of war?"

"But—"

The earl waved his one good hand. "No! I have not stopped your reading to the boy, as futile as it seems, for it cannot harm him. But you will allow the major his way—"

"Dr. Pettibone also condemns the major's high-hand—"

"And how many times have I heard you castigate Pettibone as a charlatan and a fool?"

Vanessa inhaled sharply, gulped, and was still. If she were of age, she would leave this place, go somewhere far away from illness and death. She would make a new life for herself. Yes, why not?

And then there was Julian. He was as dear to her as if he had been born of her own flesh and blood. She could not leave him. And Uncle 'Vester? Angry as she was with him at the moment, he had raised her with all the privileges of a princess and a kindness few princesses were ever privileged to see.

Swallowing the bitter pill of defeat, Lady Vanessa stood. "I am not unmindful that the major did me a favor this morning," she declared, very much on her dignity. "I will make an effort to come to cuffs with him less frequently. As for Julian . . . the thought that he might catch his death from the night breezes freezes my bones, but perhaps we may work out some compromise for the daytime."

"It is June, child," Wyverne pointed out.

Vanessa sighed. "I will attempt to understand the major's methods," she conceded. "I promise to discuss the matter with him." It was as far as she could go.

And the earl, who had had the raising of her for the past eight years, knew it. "Very well," he nodded, "but I will quiz you both on this subject in a few days." Lady Vanessa sketched a curtsey and turned to go. "Remember, girl," he called after her. "Even if Julian were perfectly sound, we'd need the major. Julian is a boy and I'll not leave this bed again—there's no sense denying it. You *will* make an accommodation with Charles Tyrone."

Lady Vanessa, who had turned back toward the bed as the earl spoke, put a hand to her mouth and fled from as painful an encounter with her guardian as she had ever had.

The Earl of Wyverne settled into his pillow, not at all displeased by the normally unflappable Lady Vanessa's display of emotion. An almost gleeful smile spread slowly over his face as he pictured Major Charles Tyrone in his scandalously ragged robe confronting the outrageously prideful Lady Horatia Tyrone in the Yellow Salon. Ah, by God, but the boy was a match for that nasty tartar!

A match for his Nessa too. He himself might be crippled and weak, but he still had his wits. They were born for each other, the pair of them, whether they liked it or not. The major was one of the few men he had ever known who might be able to keep the ducal daughter from running off with the reins. He'd see them wed if he had to . . . Well, he'd think of something. But right now . . . a nap seemed in order. Plenty of time for schemes when he felt more the thing.

Vanessa glowered at the major over the low arrangement of cream and yellow roses she had created for the much-reduced dining table. All nagging twinges of guilt over the realization that she had not yet expressed more than a simple two-word thanks for his charging to her assistance that morning had flown out the window when Charles appeared in the salon where the family customarily gathered before dinner. Although he was, thankfully, fully dressed, his black and white evening wear did nothing to diminish the quite splendid expanse of his shoulders. That she had noticed anything so personal about the major further shortened a temper exacerbated by genuine concern. To Vanessa's scold—which sounded shrewlike even to her own ears—the major had merely raised one eyebrow and offered her a gentle smile. How could Wellington have won the war, he asked her, if his officers took to their beds after every little blow? His aches and pains would be the better for moving around. By morning he'd be right as a trivet.

Recalling some of Dr. Pettibone's more dire predictions about head injuries, Vanessa was all too aware that by morning Charles Tyrone could be dead. Yet, in all fairness, perhaps he was right. The major had survived all those long years on the Peninsula; it was unlikely he would be brought low by a ha-ha in the Cotswolds. Nor did she wish to pursue her scold before Tabby and James. If she had not been so startled by the major's appearance at table, she would have held her tongue. Indeed, she took her promise to Uncle 'Vester seriously.

Nor, Vanessa had to admit, did she care to have the major see her as a shrew. No woman would, she assured herself, as she took a small sip of sorrel soup with eggs. Truthfully, there was nothing personal in her feelings about the major. She cared not a whit more what he thought of her than of James Prentice's opinion.

Very well . . . she was a liar as well as a shrew.

Two courses later, Lady Vanessa picked at her chicken cutlets in béchamel sauce, which might as well have been horses' hay for all the enjoyment she was getting from the dish. She could not put it off any longer. She owed the major something more than a breathless "thank you," even if her lack of breath was due to the size and searing warmth of the shoulders she was clutching at the time. She opened her mouth.

"Was it you who sent the robe, my lady?" Charles Tyrone asked, keeping his voice carefully neutral. The robe which had arrived via Jenkins, the footman, was a splendid creation—heavy black silk, piped in white, with some exotic-looking designs, oriental in flavor, embroidered along the hem.

Charles regarded Her Arrogant Ladyship with considerable interest. For a woman of iron nerves and tart tongue, she certainly blushed easily. He wondered if ladies felt as hot as they looked when they turned that particular shade of red. "I must thank you, then," he told her, accepting the fiery blush as a "yes." "It is very fine. I admit to being attached to my old rag—it saw as much of the war as I did—but your point is well taken. It was not fit for display in genteel company." This time it was Miss Halliwell who blushed.

"I would suggest, major," Lady Vanessa sniffed, "that *no* robe is fit for display in genteel company." For a moment she glanced down at her plate. "It was Neville's," she added in a small choked voice.

"Ah!" Charles swallowed his chagrin. "Then I am doubly appreciative of the gesture, Lady Vanessa. Lund has already taken off my old one—to be burned, no doubt." A strangled sound came from Miss Halliwell, who had been extremely fond of Neville Tyrone, as much a willing victim of the Corinthian's easy charm as every other lady of the viscount's acquaintance.

"Major," Lady Vanessa declared, with what Charles would later interpret as a strong attack of duty, "I have not properly thanked you for jumping into the fray this morn—"

"Undoubtedly, you feel you could have managed well enough on your own."

Lady Vanessa considered, head tilted to one side. "I might have," she told him, "but truthfully Lady Horatia and I manage our relationship by seeing as little of each other as possible. You saved me a goodly number of difficult moments." She paused, lips curling at the edges. The quite lovely blue eyes she suddenly raised to his brimmed with unexpected mischief. "Indeed, I would not have missed her face when she saw you in that robe for anything in the world. I think, rather than burning, we should have it bronzed."

Miss Halliwell uttered a squeak of shock. James Prentice swallowed his wine the wrong way and fell into a fit of coughing. The footman who was clearing the table stumbled, a fork and an uneaten sauce-covered cutlet plopping onto the richly patterned carpet. Lady Vanessa clapped a hand over her mouth. Charles hid his face behind one broad hand, shoulders shaking. When he dared a peek at his usually arrogant adversary, he caught her peeping at him above her fingers. Their eyes met, and suddenly she succumbed to a fit of the giggles. Charles gave up the struggle, leaned back in his chair, and roared with laughter.

Meecham, poised like a statue in the doorway while
supervising the footman's cleansing of the carpet, felt a
suspicious rush of moisture to his eyes. It had been a
very long time since there was laughter at the Abbey.

Later, the four diners, recovered from their hilarity, were
enjoying a raspberry trifle when pounding feet were heard
upon the stairs. "Major . . . my lady!" gasped Peter Fielding, Julian's valet, as he burst into the dining room. "Mr.
Julian's took bad, right bad. Mrs. Vance fears he's dying!"

Chapter Six

Charles barked a command to Meecham to send for Dr. Pettibone, then followed Vanessa's run up the staircase. The appalling scene in Julian's bedchamber brought them up short. The viscount's youthful face was twisted in pain; his body, which had not moved of its own volition since the accident, thrashed about the bed, as if attempting to escape from the agony gripping it. Neither Charles nor Vanessa doubted the boy was in extremis. The why of it could wait. Action was imperative. The doctor would be too late.

As Fielding ran to the boy's side, attempting to keep him from rolling off the bed, Vanessa raised stricken eyes to the nurse. "Nanny?" she begged. The motherly old woman had to know what to do, for surely no one else did.

"Food poisoning," declared Mrs. Sally Vance. "Can't be anything else."

"A seizure?" the major challenged. "That's not uncommon with head injuries."

"I've seen a good many convulsions in my time, Major," Nanny Vance asserted. "This is from something he ate. I'd stake my life on it."

"But how—"

"No time for how!" The major cut off Vanessa's question, without taking his eyes from Mrs. Vance. "What must we do?"

"There's water in the basin," the nurse instructed. "Work up a good suds, pour it into the pitcher, then bring it here." She placed her hand on Fielding's shoulder, indicating with a few low words that he should go round to the far side of the bed.

"Major, stand at the head of the bed and hold him from this side," Sally Vance ordered. "Lady Vanessa?"

"I'm ready." Vanessa gripped the heavy pitcher of soapy water in both hands as she approached the bed. "Is there no other way?" she burst out as Mrs. Vance took the pitcher and the two men got a good grip on Julian's shoulders.

"We can leave him to die," the nurse tossed over her shoulder. "Meecham," she bawled to the butler who was fixed in the doorway, "come here and open his mouth."

The stalwart Meecham looked as close to quailing before disaster as Vanessa had ever seen him, but he inserted himself between the major and Mrs. Vance, his long slim fingers prying open the young viscount's mouth. "You'll drown him!" Vanessa cried as the soapy liquid poured forth, some down Julian's throat, considerably more onto the bedcovers and the four people struggling round the bed. Julian coughed, choked, let out a moan of protest. Nanny Vance gave him a moment's rest, then poured another flood of soapy water into his mouth.

"Swallow, damn it!" the major snapped.

"Come on, lad, there's the boy," Meecham muttered. "Get it down."

"My lord, you must drink!" Fielding urged, even as he was forced to lie flat across the broad bed to keep Julian from jerking away from the waterfall of soapy water.

"More!" the major ordered, while Vanessa clapped a hand over her mouth to keep from protesting.

Nanny Vance poured again, emptying the pitcher. The occupants of the room held their breaths. There was little doubt that on the last two attempts Julian had swallowed a goodly amount of the pitcher's sudsy contents. It was Lady Vanessa who suddenly gasped and ran for the basin, returning with it just in time as, with agonized paroxysms and hideous retching, Julian began to empty the contents of his stomach.

The major and Meecham, suddenly galvanized into action, dragged the poor viscount out of bed, lowering him to his knees on the floor as Fielding shoved a large porcelain chamber pot under the boy's nose. Only in retrospect did Vanessa recognize the ghastliness of the scene. At the time they were all too relieved to see Julian casting up the poisonous contents of his stomach to be revolted by what was happening. When the worst was over, Vanessa judged the young viscount looked like a painted effigy on All Hallow's Eve, but it was weakness—thank God—not pain, which was casting shadows on his pale cheeks.

By the time Dr. Pettibone arrived, confirming their diagnosis of poison and forcing Julian into another round of vomiting by the judicious use of ipecac, the boy had little left of whatever had caused him such agony. His young lordship would live, Pettibone pronounced, but he'd surely like to know how the boy ended up in such sore straits.

"So would we," the major sighed, exchanging a significant look with Lady Vanessa. "My lady, we must talk, I believe. Meecham, tea and sandwiches all around, as soon as your staff may manage it. Lady Vanessa and I will take ours in the bookroom. Pettibone, if you would be so good as to join us?" The doctor's nod of assent was remarkably grim for a situation where the patient had just been pronounced out of danger.

The major turned to the others. "You have all given exemplary service tonight. Well done!" Nanny Vance, Fielding, and Meecham looked as if they were about to come to attention and salute. Or so Vanessa later told Miss Halliwell. If the major had offered gold sovereigns—which the earl undoubtedly would—the trio could not have been more pleased.

Charles turned to Vanessa. "Come, my lady, there's

nothing you can do here but put the boy to the blush. And do not protest. As you have so often pointed out, we have no idea what he understands. Leave him to Fielding and Mrs. Vance. Meecham, ask Jenkins or Fisher to give them a hand." When the major looked back to Lady Vanessa, she offered no protest, allowing him to lead her from the room.

"To be blunt," the major said, as he seated Lady Vanessa in the depths of the comfortable burgundy leather settee in the bookroom, "I would prefer brandy."

"I, also," Vanessa echoed faintly.

Without so much as a look askance, the major poured a generous measure for both of them. "A restorative," he murmured, as he handed her a snifter.

"I doubt anything will help," Vanessa returned. In spite of the warmth of the evening, a shiver wracked her body.

The major hastened to pour a tot of brandy for Elijah Pettibone as the doctor entered the bookroom. Pettibone sank into one of the armchairs grouped before the cold grate, placed his black bag onto the floor, and accepted his snifter with alacrity. Charles, already well aware of the doctor's proclivities, stood by with the brandy bottle, refilling Pettibone's glass as soon as the first brandy disappeared in one long swallow.

After being fortified by his second glass, Pettibone slowly shook his head. "A bad business," he muttered. "Can't think how it could happen. Mrs. Meecham runs a clean kitchen. Eat from the floors, the woman brags, and I believe her."

"The boy eats nothing but gruel and liquids, does he not?" the major asked. "Spoiled food seems unlikely. Even soured milk will not produce such a reaction."

Dr. Pettibone's sigh was closer to a groan. "Indeed, no." Silence filled the bookroom, slim threads of doubt stretching out with it, lurking in the shadows, working their way into the minds of the three persons present.

"Are you suggesting this was not an accident?" Lady Vanessa whispered, horrified.

"I believe that is exactly what the doctor is attempting to tell us," the major confirmed.

"I would suggest arsenic," Pettibone told them. "Oh, I know I am nothing but a country doctor, but many's the time I've seen the results of rat poison, and not all of the dead were rats. Not by a long shot." On this cryptic note, Elijah Pettibone took up his bag and stood. "My thanks for the brandy," he said. "I'll be by in the morning to check on the boy. I've instructed Sally Vance to get as many fluids down him as she can. Other than that, a few prayers wouldn't hurt."

"I know I need not tell you not to speak of this matter," the major said. "This is an incident of grave concern, and I wish to keep the nature of it close." Charles walked the doctor to the door, thanking him profusely for his services.

A stunned Lady Vanessa raised anxious eyes to Charles as he returned from seeing the doctor out. "It's true, isn't it?" she said. "Someone tried to kill Julian."

Charles sat heavily in a chair across from her, a whoosh of breath escaping in a long sigh. "It would appear so."

"But who would do such an appalling thing?"

"I believe," Charles said, swirling his brandy in its snifter as if his only interest were in the shining amber color illumed by the wall sconce, "that I am the mostly likely culprit."

"*You?*" Vanessa was shocked at how loathsome she found this particular thought. Impossible. Not the major. Even though they were adversaries, she could not believe it.

"In the eyes of the world, the earldom of Wyverne is considered a great prize. Indeed, it *is* a great prize. Men have been murdered for far less."

"You would not—"

Charles tossed off his brandy, plunked the snifter onto

a sidetable. "No, I would not. I do not, in fact, have any interest in the earldom at all. I consider it a burden. But I fear there will be few who believe that."

"Dr. Pettibone must be mistaken," Vanessa asserted. "This has to be an accident."

"As Sherbourne and Julian met with an accident," Charles murmured. "As I met with an accident." Abruptly, he rose to pour himself another brandy, leaving Vanessa to stare after him in consternation.

"You cannot think . . . you cannot suspect . . ." she whispered.

"I think Sherbourne's accident needs further investigation," Charles told her. "And as for myself, someone told me of that ride through the spinney, someone recommended it to a stranger who could not possibly know there was a sudden six-foot drop onto a pasture with granite outcroppings."

"Who?" Vanessa demanded.

"Ah, if only I could remember."

"Devil!" she accused. "You are making it up."

"Alas, no," Charles told her. "Unfortunately, before the ha-ha incident, I had ridden the estate for two days straight, talking to villagers as well as tenants. I must have spoken with well over a hundred people. Small wonder I cannot remember." The truth was, he did remember, but this was scarcely the time to throw accusations at a faithful family retainer. Especially when a veteran of the Peninsula could have been expected to handle any sudden emergency with no consequence other than a moment's annoyance. The whole disaster had been infinitely embarrassing. Major Charles Tyrone laid low before the Arrogant Aristocrat. To his body, nothing but a few aches and pains. To his mind, a thoroughly humiliating experience.

"Fielding must take Julian's food straight from cook," Vanessa declared.

"And how well do you trust Fielding?" the major asked. "Has he been with the family long?"

"Good God, you cannot—" The major raised a speaking brow. "He was not with Neville long," Vanessa said, frowning. "His former valet was pensioned, and Neville acquired Fielding at the start of the London season. But his loyalty is unquestioned," she asserted. "He has been wonderful with Julian, amazingly devoted."

"Quite so," Charles murmured.

"You are abominable!" the ducal daughter declared. "Is everyone suspect?"

"Better than myself," the major replied, at his most provocative.

Lady Vanessa Rayne rested her chin on clasped hands beneath her chin. She eyed Major Tyrone balefully. "Are you always so outrageous?" she inquired.

"It helped on the Peninsula," he told her. "No sense sitting around brooding on what cannot be changed."

"Charles . . . Major, what are we to do?" Vanessa regretted the anguish revealed by the distinct quaver in her voice.

"I preferred the 'Charles,' " the major said, before swiftly adding, "I think we must have Mrs. Vance supervise the boy's meals. I believe we can agree that no harm will come to him from that direction." Vanessa nodded, eagerly seizing on this sensible suggestion. "Other than that, we must begin to make a list of those who might wish Julian harm."

"But how could anyone—"

"Sherbourne is dead; his son, on the very brink tonight. That we were successful in saving him was close to a miracle. My accident may have been planned— though quite subtly, I have to admit. And we must remember that the earl was an old man who could be expected to be struck down by an apoplexy on receipt of tragic news. It is possible that, too, was part of someone's dastardly scheme." Vanessa could only stare, rendered speechless by what struck her as the outpouring of a deranged mind. "I may be wrong, I may even be a damn fool," the major continued, "but I think we must plan for the worst and be pleasantly surprised if I am making the proverbial mountain out of a molehill."

Lady Vanessa nodded, thoughts racing. Surely he was mad, but if there were even the slimmest chance of Julian's poisoning being deliberate, they would have to go on as if it were true. "If Mrs. Vance is to work days," she said, "we will need someone to be with Fielding at night."

"A most reasonable conclusion," Charles agreed.

"You really believe it, don't you?" Vanessa whispered. "You actually think someone has contrived these incidents."

"I think it a possibility which must be considered." Their eyes met—challenging, adversarial—enemies who unaccountably found themselves on the same side. "And in your planning," Charles added, "you must make sure I am not alone with the boy either."

"Then you acquit me of any motive?" Lady Vanessa asked. "I am one of the true blue?"

"As far as Neville, Julian, and the earl are concerned," he replied, with only the faintest twitch of his lips. "As for myself, let us say you might not have mourned too greatly if I had broken my neck. However, since we have scarcely been on speaking terms these past few days, I can acquit you of suggesting a ride containing a ha-ha."

"Thank you . . . I think."

With the brilliance of a flash of lightning, the major displayed a smile, one so dazzling and unexpected it took her breath away. "You and Nanny Vance I would bet my life on," he told her. "As must Julian." Charles reached out, took her hand in his. "Is that too much to ask, Lady Vanessa? More responsibility than I have a right to expect?"

She shook her head. "No, of course not," she murmured, but her head was awhirl and she scarcely knew of what they were speaking. "I-I will make the necessary arrangements." Withdrawing her hand from his, she stood. "I must make sure everything is all right with Julian," she said, and fled, passing Meecham with a tray of tea and sandwiches on her way to the door.

The major poured brandy into his tea, absentmindedly munching on the sandwiches during a long ruminative vigil in which his agile mind contemplated the ramifications of his burgeoning suspicion. Clearly, the lady thought him mad. And how easy it would be to dismiss his fears as chimeras haunting him from his long years at war.

A candle flickered and went out, plunging the bookroom further into gloom. He could almost feel the long bony fingers of centuries of Tyrone ancestors reaching out, demanding his presence, when all he wanted to do was mount Rojo and escape to Scotland, cleansing the contamination of this aristocratic nightmare in the clear waters of a Highland stream.

But, of course, Major Charles Tyrone could not leave the Abbey. He could not abandon the earl, Julian . . . not even Her Arrogant Ladyship, now crushed and forlorn. Frightened. And more overburdened than ever.

Hell and the Devil! Charles reached for another sandwich.

Vanessa woke to brilliant sunshine peeking through the draperies and the twittering of birds so cheerful she was tempted to throw a slipper at the partially open window. The previous night, so perfectly awful, flooded into her mind like a cascade of nightsoil from a medieval window. *Julian!* Vanessa's feet hit the floor. Jamming her feet into her slippers and grabbing her dressing gown from the back of a chair, she rushed into the hallway, tying her sash as she went. *Dear God, let him be all right!* She would have been called if anything had gone wrong; of course she would. It was, after all, only a few short hours since she had given Mrs. Vance her new instructions and made sure that Jenkins had been added to duty in Julian's room. The Jenkins family, she knew, had served the Tyrones for five generations. If anyone could be trusted, it was Tom Jenkins.

The serenity of Julian's bedchamber struck her the moment she opened the door. Fielding was asleep in a deep wing chair, but Tom Jenkins bounded to his feet the moment he saw her. " 'Morning, my lady." His grin faded, his eyes sweeping up to a point well over head. "All's well. Missus Vance went off to bed three hours since. Said Master Julian—um, his lordship—be doin' well, and she must be up in time for breakfast. A spry old lady she is, my lady. No doubt about it."

The young footman was babbling, Vanessa realized. He was also blushing. In a flood of embarrassed revelation, the ducal daughter realized it was her own dishabille which had so discomforted the young footman. In calm tones at odds with her inner mortification, Lady Vanessa thanked him for his report and fled the room. But not before slamming shut and locking the casement windows and closing the draperies with a snap. Obviously, an early morning visit by the major had preceded her own.

When she returned to Julian's chamber after breakfast, she was assured by Mrs. Vance that the dear boy had managed a bit of clear broth. The windows and draperies were open.

Mrs. Sally Vance cast a concerned glance at Lady Vanessa's face. "The major's been keeping a close eye on the boy. An outdoorsman, the major. A great believer in fresh air and sunshine, he is."

Vanessa drew a deep breath, her gaze fixed on the view through the wide-open windows. The formal gardens, the dark intricacy of the boxwood maze, the expanse of park sloping down to a stream almost broad enough to be called a river. It *was* a perfectly lovely June morning. "Perhaps fifteen more minutes," she conceded. "I will take care of closing them, Mrs. Vance. No reason why you should encounter the major's wrath."

"My lady." Sally Vance dropped a swift curtsey and took her favorite chair near one of the windows. Fielding and Jenkins had gone to their much deserved rests.

Vanessa lowered herself into her customary chair beside Julian's bed, her gaze fixed on his beloved face. Oddly, he looked little the worse for his terrible ordeal. She grasped his hand. Last night it had been cold and clammy, as if death had already taken him. This morning it was firm and warm, as if giving promise the lively boy still dwelt somewhere inside the lifeless shell before her.

"You frightened us nearly out of our wits, young man," she told him roundly. "We were certain we had lost you. I have not seen you that sick since you got into Neville's sherry." Leaning forward, she laid her fingers on his hollow cheek. He had been such a vital young man, gay, fun-loving, a bit loud. A bit naughty. He'd been in London for the Season because he had been sent down from Eton. Neville had simply laughed, slapped the boy on the back, and invited him on a race to Brighton.

Vanessa reached for the *Morning Chronicle* and began to read, a routine task to keep the nightmares at bay. But London was thin of company in the summer, and even Lady Vanessa Rayne was soon bored with the column of *on dits*. Somehow they no longer seemed to have any relevance to her life. "Ah, here's something," she declared with forced enthusiasm. "It would seem my cousin Rutherford is taking a wife at last. He offered for me, the beast. Did I tell you that, Julian? He had the nerve to tell Uncle 'Vester that since I inherited so much of the estate's funds, he saw no choice but to marry me to get it back. That was four years ago. I suppose you were too young for me to mention it. Uncle 'Vester put a flea in his ear, let me tell you. Sent him off so cowed we've had no contact with him since. And now he's found an heiress who'll have him. Caldicott, Caldicott? Can it be she's a cit? What a coup, nabbing a duke!"

"Lord, Nessa, must you natter on so? It's enough to give a fellow the headache. I say, was I sick in the night?

Tell me I wasn't fool enough to get into the sherry again? Nessa, come to think of it, what *are* you doing here? I'm not dressed yet. Even I know that ain't proper."

Vanessa opened her mouth. Nothing came out. A pain shot through her chest, stabbed up her throat. Her breathing stopped. Vapors. She must be having an attack of the vapors. The room faded, but the mist was pierced by a pair of clear gray eyes as penetrating as the major's. Just not so many wrinkles at the corners, she noted irrationally. A hand closed over her shoulder. Nanny Vance. Kind, reliable, practical . . . *unflappable* Nanny Vance.

Lady Vanessa Rayne summoned the backbone of seven generations of Dukes of Rutherford and looked straight into the Viscount Sherbourne's inquiring eyes. "Julian?" she said. "What was it you asked me?"

"Silly," Julian Tyrone chided gently. "What you're doing here, of course. And why the devil do I feel like death warmed over?"

"Master Julian!" Nanny Vance scolded through her tears. "How often have I told you not to swear?"

It took the most heroic effort of Vanessa's life to keep from bursting into tears herself. But during the moments Mrs. Vance took Julian's attention, she got herself in hand. Turning a brilliant, if watery, smile on Viscount Sherbourne, she said, "Well, my dear, it's quite a tale I have to tell. Perhaps Mrs. Vance will be good enough to find you some food while I explain." The two women exchanged beaming smiles of pleasure and relief. "I'm sure she will know exactly the right thing to please a queasy stomach."

Oh, dear God! Vanessa thought as the door closed behind Sally Vance. He doesn't even know his father is dead. For a single desperate moment she closed her eyes before turning back to Julian Blakeney Hayward Tyrone, Viscount Sherbourne.

Chapter Seven

"**I** had to tell him," Vanessa repeated yet again to Major Tyrone. She had found him in the bookroom, and the whole incredible tale came pouring out. "When I told Julian of the accident, he immediately asked about his father." She raised anguished eyes to the major. "I could not lie to him, truly I could not."

"Of course you could not," Charles soothed. "The boy had to know."

"I did not mention the other incidents," Vanessa added hastily. "Nor our suspicions. I told him he was sick last night from spoiled food."

"Good girl," the major approved. "Does Wyverne know?"

Vanessa's rather plain face was transformed by a lovely smile. "Oh, yes, I went directly to him after speaking with Julian. He cried. He has never done that before, Major, not even when Neville was killed."

"Surely we must be on Christian name terms by now?"

Startled, Vanessa looked into eyes nearly identical to Julian's. But with depths the boy would not have for many a year. Did she wish to acknowledge this *engineer*—this little better than a cit—as a close member of the Tyrone family? As an intimate acquaintance?

How could she not?

"Very well . . . Charles. If you wish." Vanessa's words were directed toward her lap.

"Good." In typical military fashion, the major did not dwell on this new aspect of their relationship. "Mrs. Vance is with the boy?" he asked.

"And Jenkins. Both of them with tears in their eyes."

"Then I will go up. I confess I would like to see this miracle for myself." Charles stood, looking thoughtfully down at his nemesis. "It would seem I failed to mention last night that you, too, have given exemplary service. Noblesse oblige goes only so far, Vanessa. You have exceeded the limits of anything that might have been expected of you."

"They are my family!" she protested.

"Nonetheless, there are many who would not have given of themselves as you have. I wish you to know I am aware of your sacrifice."

" 'Twas no sacrifice!" she declared hotly.

Charles sighed. "Termagant," he taunted softly, and with a smile. "I wish to speak with you further on a number of subjects . . . Nessa." He thoroughly enjoyed the sight of her speaking blue eyes widening at this further familiarity. "We are at the long evenings leading to Midsummer's Eve, and I think it's time you got some fresh air." *Ah!* How those blue eyes sparked at this open reference to their continuing battle. "Plan on taking a walk with me after dinner tonight. Perhaps you would care to show me the maze?" When he received no answer, Charles raised his brows in silent question.

The lady's chin was set, lips thin, the blue eyes gone to ice. "Somewhere less private, I think," she countered, every one of her ducal ancestors arrayed at her back.

"But privacy is exactly what I desire," the major murmured provocatively.

He'd done it again, Vanessa fumed. Lured her in with his handsome face and gracious words, then shocked her by his boorish lack of knowledge of what was right and proper. She jumped to her feet and headed for the door.

"Nessa," he called after her—even with her back

turned, she could *hear* his grin—"I shall expect to see you after dinner. Be sure you have a shawl. I'm told on excellent authority that the evening breezes, even in June, can be cool."

If she'd had a sword, she would have run him through. Truly she would. Except that honesty forced her to admit Major Charles Tyrone would have disarmed her in a matter of seconds. Therefore, her only response was an exceedingly childish slamming of the bookroom door.

Charles stared blankly at the solid mahogany door. What had he just done? He could not possibly have put himself in the position of being alone with the Arrogant Aristocrat, the woman who waved her ducal ancestors in his face like a battle flag. The Abbey had driven him mad. He was touched in the upper works. His brains had been baked too long under the hot Spanish sun. She was the last, the absolute last, woman in the world on whom he cared to fix his interest. And he'd just invited her to wander through a maze on a night as close to Midsummer's Eve as made no difference.

No matter. She would be pleased if he changed his mind. Pleased? Her Arrogant Ladyship would shout "Hallelujah."

The devil she would. The lady would go with him if he had to drag her. He was her guardian now, was he not? He controlled her manor, her golden dowry . . . her person. . . .

He was an officer and a gentleman.

And the lady was no temptation.

Having come to these grand conclusions, Charles Tyrone climbed the stairs to Julian's room well pleased with himself.

He sent no message canceling his walk with Lady Vanessa Rayne.

The major paused in the open doorway to Julian Tyrone's bedchamber. The young viscount was propped up on pillows, in the act of pushing away Nanny Vance's hand, causing some of the gruel in the spoon she was holding to slop onto the bedcovers.

"No!" the boy muttered, his voice wan but determined. "I'm heartily sick of that pap. No more, I tell you!"

A vivid recollection of sending Jake Lund to the kitchen for rare roast beef surged through Charles's mind. He could scarce blame the boy for rejecting invalid food, however unwise a decision that might be. A few short steps brought the major to the bed, where he laid a hand on Mrs. Vance's arm. The nurse promptly responded to a nod of the major's head, effacing herself in her favorite chair by the window.

He looked down his full height at the boy in the bed. "I am your cousin, Charles Tyrone," he pronounced. "I'm pleased to see you looking so much better." He held out his hand, was gratified to find Julian's grip remarkably firm.

The boy's eyes went wide. "*Major* Tyrone?" he burbled. "Boney's engineer? By Jove, I am pleased to meet you. Nessa said you was here, but I wondered if it was all a hum. I mean, never seen hide nor hair of you since I was a pup."

Charles sat in the bedside chair vacated by Nanny Vance. "Yes, well, I seem to remember a boy grabbing me about the legs and begging me to play spillikins and—ah, yes—insisting that I watch him put his pony through his paces." The major shook his head. "A long time ago, I fear. I apologize for being away so long."

"But you were with Wellington," Julian said, eyes shining. "Grandfather and I read the dispatches together. You were a hero."

"Scarcely that," Charles demurred. "But I promise we'll talk of the war another day. Right now we have a few things to discuss, man to man." If the major felt a frisson of guilt over using the boy's hero worship to manipulate him in the right direction, he did not show it. With the patently eagle eye of a military inspection, he took his time examining the uneaten contents of the bedtable set over Julian's lap. "Firstly," said Charles, "I assume you have some recollection of the time you have lain here?"

"A bit, sir. Vanessa's voice . . . it was always there. As long as I could hear her, I knew I wasn't dead."

The major sucked in his breath. "Did you tell her so?"

The young viscount looked stricken. "No, sir. We spoke of . . . other things."

"Understandable," the major murmured, "but I believe you should tell her your remembrances as soon as possible. She was a most faithful caregiver."

"I will, sir," Julian promised, looking suitably solemn.

Charles rearranged his face to military sternness. "And you seem to recall eating endless bowls of gruel?"

"By Jove, I should say I do. Nasty stuff, that!"

"And do you recall last night?" the major inquired with deadly calm.

Julian, no fool, was instantly thoughtful. "You mean when I cast up my accounts?" he ventured.

"To put it mildly," Charles replied grimly. "Do you think, young man, that a stomach which has suffered such a severe upset is ready to digest a joint, a leg of lamb, even chicken fricassee?"

Viscount Sherbourne hung his head, though it was apparent he was regarding the bowl of gruel with loathing. "No, sir, I would suppose not, sir."

Charles lifted a spoonful of gruel to Julian's mulish lips, raised his brows. The boy opened his mouth and accepted the food, but not without making an horrible face as he swallowed. Since the major was wise enough not to beat a dead horse, he said nothing, merely bringing another spoonful to the viscount's mouth.

"I can do it," Julian grumbled, seizing the spoon.

"Fine," Charles declared. "Then I can open the windows and get some fresh air in here."

"Vanessa don't like—"

"I am well aware of the lady's opinion," the major cast over his shoulder as he jerked back the draperies. "And I know you love her dearly, but a growing boy needs sunlight and fresh air as much as the plants in the garden and the trees in the woods."

Julian, whose mouth was full, merely nodded. Whatever Major Charles Tyrone decreed was as good as a pronouncement from on high.

"Sherbourne, you poor dear boy!" exclaimed Ambrose Tyrone as he pushed past Meecham, leaving the butler with his mouth open to announce this visitor to the sickroom.

Since everyone at the Abbey had carefully refrained from addressing Julian by his new title, knowing it could only remind him of his father, there was a moment of awful silence. The major scowled, Nanny Vance jabbed a knitting needle into her ball of wool as if she wished it were the vicar's chest. Julian paused, a spoonful of gruel halfway to his mouth.

"We must, of course, praise God for this miracle," Mr. Tyrone intoned. "Crippled though you are, my boy, you are back with us at last."

Charles forced his fisted hands to stay at his sides. The urge to evict the vicar of Lower Wyverne from the room was nearly overwhelming. When he looked at Julian, he discovered the boy's eyes were fixed on himself, demanding answers. Inwardly, Charles winced. He was the hero, was he not? The miracle worker. The boy expected him to wave some magic wand and make all right.

"I am sure we are all grateful for any prayers you might offer, vicar," the major said. "But Julian's limbs were moving quite nicely just last night. I believe we will find he is merely weakened by his long days in bed."

"That's not what I heard," Ambrose Tyrone sputtered, frowning as if Charles's reassurances displeased him.

"As you have noted," Charles replied evenly, "we are delighted to have Julian among us again. That it may be some time before he is up and about is understandable, considering his long days in bed." The major dared not look at Julian, who was being strangely silent for such a voluble young man. "Although Julian is not strong enough for company at the moment," Charles added, "perhaps you would care to lead us in a prayer before you go."

It was a hint the vicar could not ignore. After a ponderous rendition of the Twenty-third Psalm, he took his departure. He had not, Charles noted, extended good wishes from Lady Horatia. Probably because there were none.

"He's right," said a small voice from the bed. "I cannot move my legs, major. Pettibone tried to get me to do so this morning."

"He wiggled his toes, he did," declared Nanny Vance from across the room. "Indeed, I saw him to do it."

Charles fixed his young cousin with the superior stare which had never failed to silence junior officers, nor even hardened troopers. "Last night," he pronounced, "I saw your legs moving every which way. The circumstances were dire; nonetheless, they moved. I do not believe you will be a cripple, Julian. Nor," he added judiciously, "do I think you will be up and about in a fortnight. It may take a good deal of time and effort, but I believe you will mend. Only despair will stop you. Do you understand me, Julian? Your mind is as important in this task as your body."

As the major lectured, the viscount's gray eyes sparked back to life. "Yes, sir," he responded, squaring his shoulders. "I understand."

The major gave an abrupt nod. "Right now," he declared, "your job is to finish your food. Time enough to work on your legs when you've gotten some meat back on your body."

"I can't get any meat on my body—"

"Yes, yes," Charles interjected, grateful for a chance to laugh, "I know. You cannot get any meat on your body if you have to eat gruel all day." He turned toward

Mrs. Vance. "Perhaps some toast, Nanny? And a soft-boiled egg?"

With an indulgent smile, Sally Vance stood and pulled the bell rope.

"I must get up!" the Earl of Wyverne fumed. "I must see the boy, I tell you. Else I'll not believe it. You are coddling an old man, pulling the wool over my eyes. Nessa, girl, I've got to see him!"

"Hush, hush," Vanessa crooned, frantically signaling Will Jarvis to bring the earl's medicine. "I swear to you it's true. He's talking away nineteen to the dozen, Julian to the life."

"My lady, he's been like this ever since you told him this morning," Jarvis said. "Nothing will do but he see the boy."

"Uncle 'Vester," Vanessa stated slowly in the tone usually reserved for recalcitrant children, "you are not fit to get out of bed. Julian is not fit to get out of bed. But the major has already ordered a specially constructed Bath chair. As soon as it comes, we will bring Julian to you—"

"Mine!" the earl roared. "I'll ride the infernal contraption. Don't want the boy disturbed. For me, it don't matter. What little time I've got left don't signify."

"Uncle 'Vester," Vanessa declared severely, "I assure you Julian is in far better twig than you are. He will use the Bath chair and come to you."

The earl's agitated response was cut off as Jarvis tilted the contents of a glass between the old man's teeth. Vanessa, well aware that the earl would not calm down while she remained, dropped a kiss onto his puckered brow and left the room, softly closing the door behind her.

James Prentice was hovering in the hall. "It's true, then?" he asked. "Julian—I mean, Lord Sherbourne—is awake?"

Happily, Lady Vanessa regaled the earl's faithful secretary with the details of the viscount's miraculous recovery. "Dr. Pettibone is uncertain about Julian's legs but assures us all else is fine. It appears he will live to inherit the Abbey, after all."

"Then the major will be leaving us?" Mr. Prentice responded swiftly. Too swiftly. Eagerly, in fact.

Vanessa was surprised by her surge of anger. Almost, she snapped at him. "The way I understand it," she replied with studied calm, "Major Tyrone will be needed for some time. The earl is frail, Julian six years short of his majority."

"We managed quite well without him—"

"We endured, James. We endured. We must, I think, be reconciled to the major's presence."

"But—"

"Enough, James! We may still be engaged in a battle of supremacy during the occupation, but I do believe we have lost the war. The major has triumphed."

After leaving Major Tyrone and James Prentice to their port that evening, Vanessa ordered the candles lit in the music room. She rummaged through the chest of music until she found a challenging Mozart sonata which would require her entire concentration. If not for the Abbey's industrious housemaids, the pianoforte's keys would have been dusty, for every time she had tried to play since the accident, she had dissolved into tears. Therefore, she was sadly out of practice. Fortunately, Miss Halliwell did not have a fine ear for music and would not be bothered by her mistakes. Placid as always, that lady seated herself in front of one of the tall windows overlooking the gardens and, taking advantage of the summer sun which was still well up over the trees, devoted her attention to her embroidery.

Vanessa, grimacing at dissonances Mozart had never intended, threw up her hands, frowned at the music, and began again. More slowly this time. Perhaps she should have settled for some simple country tunes. But they reminded her too much of happier days. Of long summer evenings when Neville and Kitty had actually spent a month or two at the Abbey, exclaiming with delight at Vanessa's progress on the pianoforte, praising her needlework, her horsemanship, even going so far as to teach a very young Julian and herself the dance steps they would one day need. They might have been careless parents, seen only on rare occasions, but they had been kind. And loving. Neither she nor Julian had ever had reason to complain.

Vanessa discovered her hands were still, lying idle on the white and black keys. The notes on the music rack might as well have been Aristotle in the original Greek. A tear welled up, dripped down her cheek. How perfectly foolish! Tonight she had every reason to rejoice, and she felt . . . She could not name what she felt. Confusion, perhaps. A soupçon of fear. Nostalgia . . . yes, certainly that. A yearning for . . . something. Freedom? Was she so devoid of character that she rebelled against the responsibility thrust upon her?

No, that could not be true. She would never begrudge the time spent with Julian and Uncle 'Vester. In fact . . . it was the lessening of the burden which seemed to be bringing her pain. *Confusion, thy name is Vanessa.* With a sigh, she settled to playing a Bach invention, long since memorized. Though not as precisely fingered as she would like, it was certainly an improvement over the Mo—

"Ah, there you are!" the major declared. "Hiding, were you?"

Exactly. But he might have been gentleman enough not to point it out. Lady Vanessa Rayne sat on the needlepointed tabouret with her back straight, her hands positioned in her lap. She nodded stiffly. "Major."

Charles turned to Miss Halliwell. "Dear ma'am, I trust you will forgive my removing Lady Vanessa from your company, but she has promised to show me the gardens, you see. I am sure you will agree she has spent far too much time indoors in recent weeks. Some fresh air will put the bloom back in her cheeks."

Bloom in her cheeks! Vanessa fought to keep her hands from crashing onto the keys. The devil! How dare he? Her cheeks were perfectly . . . Oh, very well, her cheeks were close to the color of the Abbey sheets fresh out of the bleach bath. She was hagged, pinch-faced, and dour. Without a single attribute which would inspire a gentleman to invite her for a walk in the shrubbery. And, to top it all, black did not become her. She was a ghost face topping a vulture body. The major could not possibly wish . . . it was all a mistake . . . he was making fun of her.

He was thinking of her dowry.

He was standing beside her, holding out his arm. "Shall we go, my lady?"

His smile was gentle, almost as if he knew how flustered she was. Vanessa was ready to sink. Miserable man. She cast a desperate glance at Miss Halliwell, who surely should have been protesting the lack of chaperonage for such an outing. But Tabitha Halliwell's eyes were fixed on her embroidery, as if she had not a care in the world that her charge was being swept off into the intimacy of the gardens . . . and the maze.

With a purposeful display of reluctance, Lady Vanessa Rayne unglued herself from the tabouret. Nose in the air, eyes fixed straight ahead, she ignored the major's arm, marching out the music room door like Caesar at the head of his legions. Charles, torn between annoyance and admiration, allowed her a few steps advantage. Princesses needed their pride. And he'd have no trouble catching her up. No trouble at all.

Long after the major and Vanessa exited the room, Miss Halliwell sat, embroidery forgotten, staring out the window. The gardens were so lovely, the setting so romantic. She sighed. When Vanessa's dark-clad figure appeared on one of the neatly bricked paths, alone, she frowned. But, there! The major's powerful form was just behind . . . now beside her, inserting her arm through the crook of his elbow. Tabitha Halliwell emitted a heartfelt sigh, composed of equal parts of relief and satisfaction. A tiny smile curved her lips as she watched the couple stroll through the rose garden, past the perennial borders, moving ever closer to the dark shadows of the maze. Not until the two distant figures disappeared within the towering walls of boxwood did she turn her work to the light and continue her stitchery.

Miss Halliwell was smiling.

Chapter Eight

$\mathcal{V}$anessa did her best to avoid the maze, but short of pulling away from the crook of the major's arm and running back to the house, she could not sway the inevitability of Charles Tyrone's steps. He *would* see the maze, and she was to venture in with him. How else would he find his way out? he inquired, gray eyes wide and innocent. Vanessa began to form a plan.

The pathways inside the maze had been designed to accommodate two persons walking abreast, but it was the time of year for surging plant growth, and the boxwood cooperated beautifully with Vanessa's plan. The new growth had gotten ahead of the gardener's shears, reaching out to snag the major's jacket of dark blue superfine and poke at the tender flesh exposed by the skimpy bodice of her evening gown. Of soft black silk in a finish which shimmered in candlelight or sunlight, Vanessa's gown was decorated with narrow black velvet ribbons falling from the small puffed sleeves and accenting a décolletage worthy of a London salon. It was quite the most flattering of her mourning gowns, one Vanessa had ordered from town, rather than sending garments she already owned to the dye vats in the Abbey cellars.

She had donned the gown quite intentionally for this walk through the gardens, disgusted with herself even as she did it. But she had failed to anticipate just how private a place a maze could be. For years it had been her shelter, her place of escape where she could be completely alone, where she could contemplate the fragile thoughts of a growing girl—and later, the wonders, the anguish of the adult world. Frequently, she had shared her maze with a series of phantom heros—knights on white chargers, cutlass-wielding pirates, masked highwaymen. But she had failed to conjure the reality of sharing the close confines of the maze with a large and dynamic gentleman of flesh and blood. One who raised her heartbeat as easily as he raised her temper. Yet, here she was, alone with Charles Tyrone, what little figure she had fully exposed to his observant eyes, for—idiot that she was—in her pique she had left her shawl behind.

The air around them seemed to pulse with awareness. Whatever the spell that surrounded them, making her forget Charles Tyrone's less-than-sterling origins, it must be broken. Vanessa uttered an exaggerated squeak of alarm as a boxwood branch brushed against her shoulder. She dug in her heels, forcing an abrupt halt. "You go ahead, Major," she said. "I vow these branches are like tentacles in some enchanted wood."

As a good military officer should, Charles accepted the challenge implicit in taking the lead. He found it vastly interesting that the intrepid Lady Vanessa Rayne should go all fluttery and fanciful the moment she found herself alone with him. He suspected trickery. Undoubtedly, the lady knew every twist and turn of the maze. He did not. The lanky minx was looking forward to his making a fool of himself, he'd stake his reputation on it. Well, he'd show her that military engineers did more than dig siege tunnels and blow things up. He was an expert at finding his way through hostile territory. If she wanted him to lead, so be it. Charles strode off down the path. Too proud to even hesitate at the next boxwood wall where the path abruptly offered a choice of either left or right, the major swung left at close to quick-march tempo, for his well-honed sense of direction knew the center of the maze lay to the left.

When the path he had chosen turned suddenly right, trapping him in a dead end, Charles knew he had been outfoxed by an expert. He turned on his heel, to discover he was alone. Of course. Lady Vanessa was probably halfway back to the house by now. Hell and damnation, but she was a difficult woman! Charles glared down at the shining leather of his evening shoes. If he'd been this careless on the Peninsula, he'd have been dead long since and out of this disastrous coil that had been thrust upon him.

And yet . . . Her Arrogant Ladyship had not looked so gaunt this evening. Her gown, for all its ugly color, was the most flattering he had seen yet; the single strand of pearls adorning her aristocratic neck the perfect adornment for a maiden of quality. The major reminded himself of the many good qualities he had observed in the lady . . . and that when color flushed her cheeks, or on the rare occasions when she smiled, she was far more attractive than he had originally thought. And once or twice, between the slamming of Julian's windows and the whoosh of closing draperies, he thought he had caught a glimpse of humor.

Therefore . . . therefore, if she had escaped back to the house, he should consider the lady a true adversary, possibly permanently hostile. But if she were teasing him . . . if he should find her in the heart of the maze . . . Charles raised his head like a beast scenting its prey. Ah, yes, if he should find her waiting for him, then possibly they might be friends. And allies.

More than that? Resolutely, the major put aside speculation, dealing in military fashion with the challenge of the moment.

It took him fifteen minutes, a record far superior to most. But, expecting better of himself, Charles's temper was a bit frayed by the time he stumbled onto the grassy area in the heart of the maze. The grassy area with a pair of curved marble benches around a predominantly undraped statue of a female whose charms were so shockingly exposed he judged her to represent Venus. Good God, if that statue had been acceptable to the earl's ancestors, the inhabitants of his own century had deteriorated to a bunch of namby-pambies.

The grassy area also harbored Lady Vanessa, who was seated on one of the marble benches, hands folded meekly in her lap, eyes demurely lowered. Avoiding Venus, was she, the minx!

Ignoring the empty bench, separated from Vanessa by the towering near-naked goddess, Charles walked straight up to her, hovering silently, saying nothing. Neither heard the twittering of the birds, the chirps of the garden's many insects. They were completely alone. And like to stay so. How many women, Charles wondered idly, had found themselves as undraped as the statue in this isolated spot? Perhaps that thought struck the lady at the same time, for, quite suddenly, she lost her air of smug triumph.

"Are you angry?" she asked, blue eyes clouded with anxiety. "I only meant to tease. It seems so very long since . . . since there was fun at the Abbey. I thought, with Julian's recovery, it was not so terrible to—"

"Hush," Charles told her, as he daringly laid aside a fold of her skirt to make room for himself on the bench. He paused, giving her an opportunity to jump up and walk away. "Truly, I am only chagrined that it took me so long to find you. I frequently had occasion to act as a scout in the army. I fear I pride myself on my sense of direction. This maze, I must admit, is very cleverly laid out. Are you cold?" he added as a shiver shook her.

"Oh, no," Vanessa demurred. Indeed, it was not the evening breezes which were causing the frissons running up and down her spine. Nor the warmth that flushed her cheeks. Nor the palpitations she had heard described by others but never thought to experience for herself.

"Nonetheless . . ." Charles said. Peeling off his jacket, he placed it around her shoulders, then sat down beside her. He found it interesting that her mouth opened, ostensibly to thank him, but no words came out. Flummoxed, by God! This round was his. He supposed he should have felt more gratified.

Taking pity on her, he swiftly moved to a neutral topic. "Tell me, Vanessa, were you present when Neville and Julian had the accident?"

Obviously startled, she shot him a look which appeared to be gratitude. "No, I am sorry to say. I waved them off at the start of the race—there was quite a crowd. But the accident was in a village some miles from the center of town. I am told there was a difficult turn around a market post, followed by a plunge down toward a bridge across a river. There was a surge of the crowd into the street. Reports varied. Some said a child, some said a vendor chasing a thief, some said they simply could not tell what happened. But something caused Neville to swerve. He could not compensate in time. The team hit the bridge abutment. They say he died instantly. Julian was thrown clear."

Blast the man! Vanessa mourned. How could he force her to remember what she had tried so hard to forget? And yet . . . the warmth of his hands as he'd placed the jacket around her shoulders had felt like fire. Certainly, it had lit a conflagration inside her that was not easily put out. And then he had found the one topic which would quench the flames as easily as a flood. All day she had quivered with anticipation over this meeting, castigating herself for a fool even as she did so, and the reality of it struck a hard blow. They could not have been in a more romantic situation, and the major wished to discuss Neville's accident.

But of course he did. Why else would he wish to be in private with Lady Vanessa Rayne? Obviously, even her dowry was not enough to tempt him. The thought was a severe blow to her pride.

"Who was actually present?" the major asked. "Who would be most likely to give an accurate account?"

Vanessa kept her head lowered to hide the emotions

chasing over her face. "Neville's groom was riding behind. He jumped clear, I'm told. Got off with naught but a few scratches."

Charles pounced on the information. "Where is he now?"

Vanessa frowned, trying to remember. "He was one of the best," she mused. "Neville always said Rankin was a good part of the reason he was chosen for the Four-Horse Club. Rankin came to me, quite upset, after the accident. Said he had had a great many offers but felt disloyal asking to leave service to the Tyrones. I assured him he had a right to pursue his trade where he might be of use, rather than cooling his heels with nothing to do. I believe he went to Lord Camville. Although his seat is in Yorkshire, he spends a goodly amount of time in London, so Rankin could not feel he was hiding his light beneath a bushel. And, of course, Lord Camville is also a member of the Four-Horse Club."

"Rankin," the major nodded. "You're sure he went to Camville."

"As sure as I can be, Major. I was not at my best at that time."

"Forgive me," he murmured. "And my name is Charles."

Charles, the engineer. Charles, the reluctant guardian. Charles, the insensitive oaf. Charles, the Tyrant, Tyrone.

"I'm off for Scotland in a few days' time," he told her. "I'll find this groom as I pass through Yorkshire."

"Scotland . . . but you can't!" Vanessa cried.

"I must. The bridge I am building will not wait."

"But the accidents," she sputtered. "Julian! You cannot raise so many suspicions, then go trotting off and leave us alone."

"Indeed, I fear I must take the earl's ponderous carriage, as Rojo is not up to trotting off anywhere," the major replied blandly.

"Charles!" she wailed. The welter of words on her tongue tripped her into silence.

Looking as innocent as the devil on the prowl for a new soul, he purred, "Why, my dear Vanessa, I thought you would be delighted to see the back of me."

"It is Julian who concerns me," she sniffed. "You say someone is trying to kill him, and then you go chasing off to Scotland. A fine guardian, I must say!"

"I have sent for three of my best soldiers. Good men who have not found life easy since they left the army. I will not leave until they arrive. Their sole job will be to guard the boy, including making sure he takes no food from any hand but Mrs. Vance's."

"Oh." Startled by the intensity of her emotions when she thought Charles Tyrone was leaving for good—that one inarticulate word was all Vanessa could manage.

"There is one thing else," Charles said. "You may rest easy, I believe. If someone truly wishes to kill Julian, he will not attempt it while I am gone. And thank you for frowning so delightfully," he added, lips curving upward in satisfaction. "It is gratifying to realize you do not suspect me of wishing to do away with the boy."

"Good God, of course not!" Vanessa clapped a hand over her mouth, eyeing the major with considerable consternation at her unaccustomed lapse into strong language.

"That's right," Charles nodded. "No serious villain is going to go after the lad when I am not here to take the blame."

"But no one thinks—"

"Oh, yes, they do," Charles murmured. "Lund has already heard the rumors at the Bull and Bear. And if Lady Horatia has not been filling your ears with the nonsense, 'tis only because you've barred her from the door."

"Not well enough," Vanessa sighed. "She has put her suspicions in writing, spewing out the most vitriolic nonsense about your intentions. I did not credit it, I assure you."

Why was it, Charles wondered, that the lady had taken

on such an attractive glow? Long lashes fluttering above
eyes the color of a lake under a summer sun, skin so
porcelain pale it could rival the Abbey's finest dinner
plates, a nose large enough to give character to what
might otherwise have been an insipid oval. A mouth . . .
a mouth which he should not be staring at as if . . . *Do
something, you dolt, before the blasted woman turns into
a raving beauty before your very eyes!*

Charles straightened his back, squared his shoulders.
How he'd leaned in so close to the lady he could not
imagine. "Forgive me," he apologized, falling back on a
cushion of formal good manners. "I did not mean to
frighten you. Truthfully, I will be gone no more than
a fortnight. I would never leave you to cope with all
this alone."

Ah, but he was a smooth-talking devil! Vanessa's jumble of mixed emotions at the moment did not bear close
scrutiny. Yet, what she had seen, just for a moment.
What she had thought!

"This is a good time," the major was saying. "Now
that Julian is back among us, I do not feel so guilty
about going away. But you must understand that building
things is my life. I do not plan to give it up. It was a
great relief to me when I discovered I was not to inherit
the title and all the responsibilities that go with it."

Why tell her this? Vanessa wondered. The idle conversation of friends? A warning? *Foolish girl!* As if there
were any possibility the major's future and hers would
ever coincide. If he had any interest in her direction, it
was solely because of her dowry. Nor would she consider
a man so far beneath her in rank.

Yet . . . if only Charles Tyrone would, just once, look
at her as if he saw a woman and not a lump of
charcoal . . .

The major raised his head, examined the sky. The sun
had fallen below the level of the boxwood, casting dark
shadows around them. The Venus statue was now

cloaked in a modest gray haze. "I believe we must go," he said, rising and holding out his hand. "Else even you might have difficulty finding your way out of here."

"I did it blindfolded once," she told him, "though I confess I peeked a time or two." She accepted his help to rise, hoping her delight in the renewed warmth of his hand was not reflected on her face. Keeping a tight grip on the major's hand, she moved with confidence along the one path which was not a dead end. She might wish to discover what would happen if she and Charles Tyrone were benighted in the maze, but she was Lady Vanessa Rayne, and ducal daughters never allowed themselves to get into such a fix.

But his hand was more than warm. It was powerful. And comforting. Surely, this was quite the most delicious moment of her life, Vanessa thought as she took the lead, with the major following so closely on her heels she could feel the warmth of his breath on the back of her neck. At least that was the excuse she made for the heat which suffused her body as they wound in and out among the walls of boxwood . . . as the shadows deepened, and the soft glow of a summer dusk turned the labyrinth of the boxwood maze into a land of enchantment.

Near the final twist in the path their footsteps slowed. Had she felt a slight pressure from his hand, urging—at least coaxing—her to halt? Suddenly, as awkwardly shy as a country girl who had never known the sophistication of the *ton*, Vanessa ducked her head, appearing fascinated by the pebbled pathway beneath her feet.

"We are friends now, are we not?" the major inquired, his voice scarce above a whisper. "Allies?" he added more strongly. Dissatisfied with the barely visible nod of her head, he tilted up her chin, spent some moments staring down into her solemn face. Somehow in this special moment Lady Vanessa Rayne seemed transformed. The sharp facial features of a harpy became the regal beauty of a queen, the modest curves of her too-thin body, more appealing than the voluptuous women who usually caught his eye.

Impossible! He was overwhelmed by the magic of a midsummer night, by shadows which obscured the Lady Vanessa's imperfections, both of face and of temperament. Time to move on, to break out of whatever cloak of enchantment had trapped them here.

His thoughts met his resolve. His actions did not.

"I will not be gone long," the major assured her. "And I have no doubt as to your ability to carry on in my absence." He then spoiled this perfectly proper speech by leaning down and brushing a kiss across one porcelain cheek. Charles jerked back, dropping her hand. "I beg your pardon!" he burst out.

His horror over his action was so obvious Vanessa could only drop her head, pick up her skirts, and run. For a moment, just for a moment, she thought she had seen something in his eyes. Admiration, warmth . . . desire? Undoubtedly, her imagination. It was much too dark to have seen any such thing, no matter how much she might have wished it.

Wished it? The more the fool, she! They had both succumbed to the romance of the moment. A man, a woman, a maze, and a summer night. It had been inevitable. How fortunate the major was leaving soon. By the time he returned, this moment would be forgotten.

Unless, of course, he was truly having second thoughts about her dowry.

Vanessa entered the Abbey via the door from the terrace which led into the bookroom. She removed the major's jacket from her shoulders, carefully hanging it over the back of a chair so it would not wrinkle. Then, not wishing to meet anyone at the moment, she took the servants' stairs to the upper floor. After some moments standing in the dimly lit rear hallway, she felt herself sufficiently composed to bid Julian goodnight.

The major found a bench in the garden overlooking

the green expanse of lawn which sloped all the way down to the stream, whose gurgle sounded more clearly as the birdsongs died away and dusk settled into night. By what incredible aberration had he found Lady Vanessa Rayne beautiful? Appealing? Gallant? Truthfully, he couldn't stand the chit. She was arrogant, head-strong, sharp-tongued, so determined on having her own way that they could seldom pass two sentences without brangling. Besides having the sharp features of a witch and a body which might be mistaken for a fence post.

Oh, very well, he grumbled, that last was an exaggeration. As he put his jacket around her shoulders, he had not played the gentleman, averting his eyes. He had, in fact, caught a glimpse of a more intriguing figure than he had previously noticed. Or had his standards changed, along with his perceptions of the lady? Blasted woman. It was a demmed good thing he was going away. When he returned, he should be back to normal, once again able to look at Her Arrogant Ladyship with the cool impartial head of an outsider.

And if he still found the lady attractive . . . ?

A moot point. Charles sighed, as darkness settled over him, leaving nothing but the distant rush of the stream over a natural waterfall of tumbled granite. The lady would never believe his interest lay in anything other than her manor house and her fifty thousand pounds.

And perhaps that's all it was. Why else should he have found his nemesis transformed into a woman of surprising appeal? Charles scooped up a handful of pebbles and threw them as hard as he could. If only he could continue to live his life in a world comprised solely of men! The army, his construction company . . .

Liar! Beside the challenges lurking at Wyverne Abbey—most particularly, Lady Vanessa Rayne—bridges in Scotland, and even the Peninsular War faded to obscurity.

Two days later, Major Charles Tyrone climbed into the Earl of Wyverne's coach with eager step. Lady

Vanessa Rayne, watching from a window above the drive, scowled. Yes, she had imagined his interest. It was plain to see he could scarcely wait to get away. And who could blame him? Fixing a pleasant smile on her face, she set off to see the earl. He would wish to know that the major was safely embarked on his long journey to Scotland.

Chapter Nine

"I say, Nessa, do you know what engineers do?" Julian burbled some days after the major's departure. "Of course you do not," he continued with scarcely a pause, as Vanessa raised her eyes from the book she had hoped was amusing him.

"Build bridges," she pronounced, knowing quite well this statement of the obvious would set him off. At this point in Julian's recovery, Vanessa would have stood on her head if she thought it might incite the young man's enthusiasm. For his mind raced so far ahead of his capabilities, producing flare-ups of frustration and temper, that she occasionally thought of the earlier days of his illness with wistful nostalgia.

"They have to scout out campsites suitable for a whole army," he informed her, "then supervise the setting up. Everything from tents, kitchens, stable areas, where to put the gun limbers and the la—" He sucked in a sharp breath, his pale cheekbones flushing pink. "And, well, other facilities an army needs."

Lady Vanessa considered that last, finally realizing Julian was right. She had not considered the more intimate details of army encampments. Nor did she wish to. "What else?" she inquired briskly.

"Charles—he said I might call him so," Julian assured her. "Charles rode ahead of the army, sometimes deep into enemy territory. It was also his job to make maps and charts, you see. And he had to choose the spot to set up the cannon for artillery barrages—so they'd have the right trajectory," the young viscount added, well pleased with his correct use of a military term. "And, of course, if fortifications were needed, he had to design the plan and supervise the building—indeed, Charles supervised a section of the lines at Tôrres Vedras," he proclaimed. "That's how he first drew Boney's attention."

"Merciful heavens," Vanessa interjected, refusing to be impressed, "I thought military engineers just blew things up."

"Gudgeon," Julian crooned. "Charles had a whole slew of men who could do anything from spanning rivers to digging tunnels."

"And laying explosives," Vanessa murmured.

"Well, of course, silly. Did you know the major was once trapped in a tunnel when the blast went off too soon?"

"*He told you that?*" Vanessa was stunned. Somehow she could not imagine the reticent major imparting all this information to a young man barely able to sit up in bed.

"Oh, no. Simmons did."

"Simmons?"

"One of my guards, Ness. Don't you know their names?"

Guards. There Julian lay, helpless in bed, fully knowledgeable about the three stalwart ex-soldiers who took turns guarding his door day and night. And who, obviously, made their way inside the room on occasion as well. It was not knowledge she wished him to have.

"Yes, of course I know their names," she responded brightly. "I merely forgot for a moment. You have enjoyed talking with them, I take it?"

"I should say! They're great guns, I can tell you. It was Simmons who saved Charles's life. They were checking the explosives in a tunnel dug by their sappers, you see, when an artillery shell exploded nearby, collapsing the tunnel around them. Charles was hit on the head by a falling rock, but Simmons was in this small air pocket. Somehow he managed to dig them both out. Told me that's how he got his promotion to sergeant," Julian concluded triumphantly, while Vanessa struggled with a vision of Charles Tyrone buried alive.

The three former soldiers from Major Tyrone's engineering battalion had caused some consternation in the Abbey household. While on duty outside Julian's door, they wore their shabby Peninsular uniforms—perhaps at the major's orders or perhaps because their personal garments were even shabbier, Vanessa was unsure. But their faces—lined by seven years of war which had cut more ravages than the relentless Iberian sun—set them apart from the other Abbey residents. As did the set of their shoulders, the sureness of their stride. They were men resurrected from postwar poverty by their former major, and there was no doubt they would still follow him to the death. The ex-soldiers were not, however, favorites with the Abbey footmen, as the maids had taken one look at the major's stalwart trio and the fluttering below stairs had assumed earthquake proportions. When off-duty, Luke Simmons, John Hart, and Hugh Davies led pampered lives. And if they were doing more than standing guard outside Julian's door, Vanessa could not fault them for it. Keeping Julian amused when his legs refused to function and words seemed to wave before his eyes when he tried to read was surely the hardest job she had ever tackled. She welcomed all the help she could get.

"Do you miss him?" Julian's gray eyes were uncomfortably penetrating.

"The major?"

"Of course, the major," Julian grinned. "Do you miss him?"

"I had not thought about it," she lied.

"Like ruling the roost, do you?" the viscount taunted. "Daresay you've gotten rather used to it over the years.

Mother was never here much, and Lord knows Aunt Tabby gets lost in the woodwork." Vanessa glared at him in the manner usually reserved for siblings. "The major was quite a shock, was he not?" Julian added, eyes dancing. "I must say I miss the parade back and forth to the windows. The two of you practically wore a path in the rug, opening and slamming, opening and slamming. The constant whisk of the draperies back and forth was like the hissing of a snake. What did he finally threaten you with, Nessa, to get you to let in the light?"

Vanessa gave up on the book she had been attempting to read aloud, laying it down on the table beside the bed. "He told me you wished it," she admitted, expressionless. "And, if you will recall, I asked you to confirm it. Since I should have questioned some of Dr. Pettibone's notions much earlier, I acquiesced."

"But not at night."

"No, I admit I still have doubts about insidious humors in the night air. I will take no chances on your suffering an inflammation of the lungs." Or of someone climbing the walls in the dead of night.

Julian settled back into his pillow. "Don't fight with Charles, Nessa," he murmured as his eyes closed. "He's a hero . . . we need him."

With her hands clasped tightly together in her lap, Vanessa studied the newly made viscount, who was already sound asleep. He was so young, so vulnerable . . . a tug upon her heartstrings. He was all the family she had except for a cantankerous old man whose life had hung by a thread until Julian showed signs of recovery. And now . . . now the thread had strengthened to perhaps the thickness of one of Nanny Vance's strands of wool. It was, however, still far from the firm thickness of a sailor's lifeline. Her responsibilities weighed heavily on her shoulders. She could not have been closer to either Tyrone if they had been joined by ties of blood. In fact, she knew many blood relations who were more enemies than friends. Indeed, Lady Horatia's tirade against

Charles Tyrone still rang in her ears and haunted her at night, casting insidious tentacles of doubt over the rapport she had begun to establish with the major before he left.

"The boy was poisoned, was he not?" Lady Horatia had shrilled two afternoons earlier, when good manners dictated that Vanessa offer her unwelcome visitor tea, even though she steadfastly refused to allow the vicar's mother into the sickroom. "Do not trouble to deny it, Vanessa. Everyone says so. 'Tis the scandal of Lower Wyverne, and I've no doubt it's spread over the whole county by now," Lady Horatia continued, much aggrieved. "There's never been scandal attached to the Tyrone name. Well . . ." she stumbled to a short pause. "There have been some wild oats sown by a few Tyrones, I'm sure, but poison! My dear, we have never had any Borgas in the family, I assure you."

Vanessa did not attempt to correct Lady Horatia's misnomer nor that lady's assumption of the Tyrone family as her own when she was, in fact, an Ashburn until her marriage. From long experience Vanessa knew that Lady Horatia in the full flow of her vitriol was well nigh unstoppable. It would take . . . it would take a Major Charles Tyrone.

"But with the coming of this *engineer*"—the older lady spat out the word—"you have allowed riffraff to enter the Abbey. A man capable of anything, I'm sure. What could be easier than getting rid of a poor defenseless boy and an old man with one foot in the grave already? You mark my words, Vanessa, you have a viper in your midst. Best you should have Meecham bar him from the door when he attempts to return."

A sudden vision of Meecham standing at the front door, barring the entrance of Major Charles Tyrone, took Vanessa's breath away. The concept was so ludicrous, her sense of humor nearly overcame the shock of Lady Horatia's accusation. Meecham, even with the backing of Jenkins and Fisher, stood about as much chance against

Major Tyrone and his three battle-hardened Peninsular veterans as toothpicks caught in a flooding stream. Not to mention that Charles Tyrone had been declared the legal master of Wyverne Abbey.

"You are mistaken, Lady Horatia," Vanessa declared firmly. "The major is here solely out of duty to the family. He is anxious to return to his engineering work as soon as possible."

"Nonsense. He will be fixed here for years. If Julian does not find himself taken off now, be assured he can never let down his guard. *That man* will find a way to be rid of him."

At that point in Lady Horatia's tirade, Lady Vanessa Amelia Courtney Rayne had summoned the regal backbone of her ducal ancestors and asked her visitor to leave and not return until she could keep a civil tongue in her head. Or words to that effect. In truth, Vanessa was unsure what she had said, but Lady Horatia Tyrone had unfolded from her chair at a deliberate pace, shaking her head in pity at the obtuseness of young chits who would not see what was before their very eyes. "It's on your head, child," she declaimed. "If the poor boy is murdered in his bed, the fault is yours for not insisting Wyverne throw the major out on his ear. Never say I did not tell you so, Vanessa. When dear Julian is dead and gone, you will know I was right." With that Cassandra-like prediction, Lady Horatia had finally departed, leaving a shaken Vanessa behind.

That awful woman. How could she possibly accuse the major of such a dastardly crime? And when had her own opinion of Charles Tyrone diverged so greatly from those of the vicar and his mother? Vanessa had not gone so far as to acknowledge that she missed him . . . but now, she began to suspect the major's absence was the cause of the inexplicable doldrums which had settled on her after his departure. Julian was doing well; the earl was doing well . . . so what other explanation could there possibly be?

Well, why not? She had had sole responsibility for the Abbey for so long, why should she not welcome someone willing to share the burden? And the struggle for power between the major and herself had been . . . stimulating. Yes, that was the word. After each burst of anger faded, she had been left with a glow of satisfaction in her ability to hold her own against what no one could deny was a powerful personality. Major Charles Tyrone, a worthy adversary. Not a man who could make his presence felt and not be missed when he left.

Yet, an adversary was all he was, Vanessa told herself. Though having someone to talk to—even when they were brangling—was a vast improvement over the isolation of the long weeks since the accident.

With a decisive nod of her head, as if reassuring herself there were no other emotions connecting her to the major, Lady Vanessa stood up. Julian was serenely asleep, Mrs. Vance patiently knitting in the chair near the window, Corporal Hart standing guard outside the door. Time to go about the many tasks involved in assuring the smooth functioning of life within Wyverne Abbey. Perhaps she might even find time for a ride this afternoon.

As Vanessa walked toward the sweeping staircase leading to the ground floor, she saw Meecham making his stately way up. Something about the firm set of his shoulders, the rigidity of his back—in fact, the alert posture of his entire body—gave her warning that his errand was something more than the usual. She awaited him at the top of the stairs, noting with interest as he drew to a halt in front of her that his eyes were gleaming with news.

"Visitors, my lady," Meecham announced. "Sir Godfrey Tyrone and Miss Arabella. I have put them in the drawing room. I have not yet instructed Jenkins and Fisher to bring in their luggage," he added, as if that were a most natural action to be taken by a country house butler.

Between shock over the arrival of unexpected guests and an incipient attack of the giggles over Meecham's refusal to unload the visitors' baggage, Vanessa had some trouble finding her voice. "I will go to them at once," she finally managed. "And I fear they must stay the night, Meecham. It is too far to expect them to drive back to London today."

"Yes, my lady." Meecham radiated his disapproval.

For a moment their eyes met in commiseration. "I cannot imagine what they are doing here," Lady Vanessa confessed, "but we must manage. Please inform cook there will be two more for dinner. And, Meecham," she added, as the butler turned away, "I will inform Lord Wyverne *after* I have discovered the reason for Sir Godfrey's visit. Meanwhile, I would prefer that his lordship not be disturbed."

"Of course, my lady." Meecham bowed a little lower than usual, as if, Vanessa thought, he were reaffirming her authority in the household. She was suddenly infinitely grateful that the servants, at least, knew who ruled the roost at Wyverne Abbey.

A strong attack of Rayne pride forbade running to her room to set herself to rights before greeting the most fastidious of the Tyrone cousins. Sir Godfrey must accept her as she was—chatelaine of a household wrapped in mourning and beset by a double bout of severe illness. If the London dandy expected to see the confident and exquisitely turned-out daughter of the aristocracy he had known in town, he was fair and far out. Nonetheless, Vanessa did go so far as to grimace as she smoothed the front of her gown. Truthfully, the somewhat uneven charcoal achieved by the Abbey's laundress when she had dyed one of Lady Vanessa's muslin morning gowns made her look like a complete dowd. Which might be an advantage, she considered thoughtfully, for Sir Godfrey had never been known to fix his interest on any female until this past Season, when he had suddenly begun to follow her about like a puppy dog.

When Vanessa had expressed her discomfort over this state of affairs to Neville, the viscount had gone off in gales of laughter, assuring her Godfrey's pursuit could not be serious. The baronet wasn't such a nodcock as not to recognize Lady Vanessa Rayne would have his hide for breakfast if they were riveted, Neville added. Nor were Godfrey's pockets to let. He had no need to marry her fortune. His grandfather had made enough blunt to acquire a title in return for his generous contributions to the old king's coffers. So better Godfrey, the man milliner, should practice his first serious flirtation within the family. However, if the boy became too troublesome, Viscount Sherbourne had added with an avuncular pat on Vanessa's shoulder, she must tell him, and he would give Godfrey a sharp setdown.

But there had been an odd gleam of speculation in Neville's eyes when he made his assertions. Vanessa, who had not been as sheltered as some young ladies, drew her own conclusions, and thenceforward handled Sir Godfrey's attentions with light humor and considerable grace. He was, after all, a fashion leader; a young man of wit, charm, and exquisite taste; the darling of hostesses, as he never failed to dance with the shyest, most inarticulate, or least well-favored of the young ladies brought to London by their hopeful mamas. But as a houseguest at this particular moment, particularly when accompanied by his sixteen-year-old sister, for whom there could be nothing of interest in a house of mourning, the London dandy left a great deal to be desired.

Lady Vanessa Rayne threw back her shoulders, lifted her chin. Her unexpected guests would get short shrift. One night only . . . then it was back to London for Sir Godfrey and Miss Arabella Tyrone.

The Tyrone family had not been prolific for several generations, not since the days of Julian's great-great-grandfather, who had fathered five sons. Charles Tyrone was descended from the second son of that time, Godfrey

from the third, Ambrose from the fifth. The fourth son
and his wife had produced only females. Yet the title
had somehow managed to survive in the direct line
through the one boy born to each succeeding generation
of earls. Only now, in the present crisis, had it been
necessary to consider the descendants of Julian's grandfather's grandfather. Vanessa was well aware that neither
Godfrey the exquisite nor Ambrose the vicar considered
this long-ago order of birth a fair or equitable method
of deciding the succession. It was, however, the law of
the land. She could only hope Godfrey was not going to
be difficult. As an acknowledged arbiter of London fashion, he had developed an occasionally sharp tongue. She
had no desire to have it turned upon herself.

Lady Vanessa Rayne paused outside the drawing room
door, gathering positive thoughts from the deep recesses
of her mind. A regal nod to Jenkins. The footman threw
open the heavily carved oak door.

Chapter Ten

"*V*anessa!" Sir Godfrey cried, rising from the depths of Kitty Tyrone's favorite lavender silk brocade chair with a nimble grace few could emulate. He glided across the room, seizing Lady Vanessa's hands in his own, which were, she noted wryly, more perfectly cared for than her own. "My dear girl, we have come to support you in your hour of need." He turned toward the sofa, from which had risen a lovely, if very youthful, young lady. "And here is Bella. Gone from child to lady since Christmas, has she not?"

Indeed she had, Vanessa thought, as Miss Arabella Tyrone dropped a deep curtsey, her eyes firmly fixed on the reds and blues of the Aubusson carpet. Unfortunately, Sir Godfrey's words brought back a vision of the drawing room seven months past. The warmth of the two vast fireplaces matched by the gaiety of the extended Tyrone family. Uncle 'Vester, Neville, Julian, Godfrey, Arabella, and Ambrose. Not even Lady Horatia had been able to dampen the festivities. Lady Clorinda, the perpetually ailing mother of Godfrey and Arabella, who seldom ventured out of her townhouse on Portman Square, had not been present. The Abbey drawing room had rung with chatter, laughter, the music of carolers from Lower Wyverne, the smell of pine and . . .

"Nessa, my dear, do you feel quite the thing?" Godfrey, still holding her hands, was staring at her in genuine concern. Without waiting for an answer he steered Vanessa toward the sofa, gently seating her beside his sister. "Ah," he pronounced, looking down at her with a frown. "I, who pride myself on my facile tongue, should not have mentioned Christmas. Indeed, I should not. My apologies, my dear. Not another word on the subject, you have my humble promise."

"Oh, do sit down, Godfrey," Vanessa told him, waving him back to his chair. The thing which most disturbed her about Godfrey Tyrone, she had decided long since, was that it was impossible to stay angry with him. No one could doubt he meant well. It was only when he dogged her heels that frissons of warning ran up and down her spine. Beneath his supercilious air he really was a good soul . . . if *different*. "Now," Vanessa declared, consciously fixing her lips in a pleasant smile, "perhaps you will tell me how you happen to be in the vicinity of the Abbey."

They were dazzling, she had to admit, these two youngest of the Tyrone cousins. Even though Vanessa had known them both since Bella was a child in the schoolroom and Godfrey was a mincing fop of sixteen without an ounce of nous to match the extravagance of his clothes, the two of them together never failed to take her breath away. Although separated by eight years, they could never pass as anything but brother and sister. Each was slim and willowy, moving with a natural grace which was the envy of all who saw them, particularly females who had been forced to walk endless hours with books on their heads. Their hair was a matching shade of golden blond, falling into soft curls which framed faces of exquisite beauty. Indeed, some of the more sharp-tongued ladies in the *ton* did not hesitate to remark that Sir Godfrey could easily pass for a girl, for his height, alas, was less than average. Their faces were oval, both blue-eyed with perfectly formed noses which showed not a hint of the prominent ancestral appendages that gave character to Lady Vanessa's face. Even Charles Tyrone boasted a nose more similar to Wellington's famous prominence than to either of his London cousins.

And their clothes . . . Vanessa hid an inward sigh. Even as a child, Arabella had always been neat as a pin. Her pinafores remained pristine, her golden curls in order, fingernails clean and neat, half boots unscuffed. Neville had laughed and told Vanessa not to worry. It was Arabella who was missing out on the joys of being a child. Fortunately, because she worshipped the fun-loving Viscount Sherbourne, Vanessa had believed him. Which did not keep her from being aware that not even seven generations of ducal ancestors would ever make her as beautiful as Arabella Tyrone.

And Godfrey? Godfrey Tyrone had gone from being a boy awkwardly dressed in the latest fashions to the most likely candidate to replace the sartorial eminence of Beau Brummel, whose debts had recently forced him to flee to the Continent. Everything about Sir Godfrey Tyrone was perfection, although he tended to enjoy color a bit more than the Beau. His golden curls fell onto his brow just as his valet had placed them and for some mysterious reason did not seem to stray, even when Godfrey was tooling his high-perch phaeton. His shirt points were high, but never so high he could not turn his head; his cravat exquisitely tied in a series of knots which had the younger men of the *ton* begging for his secrets. His jackets fit without a wrinkle; his waistcoats were the envy of all but the most dour of older gentlemen, and the creativity of his buttons a wonder to behold. His pantaloons fit as tightly as his gloves, revealing thighs and calves of lithe grace and symmetry. Godfrey's boots were the shiniest in London, some sporting white tops, others boasting tassels of silver or gold.

In short, these two scions of the London Tyrones went a long way toward brightening up the drawing room at Wyverne Abbey. Even though they had obviously dressed in deference to the occasion; Arabella in half-mourning of lavender softened by bands of lace, Godfrey with a black armband over his jacket of suitably dark blue superfine. Which was more than Ambrose had done, Vanessa thought. The vicar's black armband had disappeared in less than a month, as she recalled.

"As I said, my dear," Godfrey informed her, "we have come to support you. Lady Horatia wrote mama about Julian's miraculous revival, and knowing full well how difficult boys can be in convalescence, she has sent us to you. Bella, after all, is Julian's age—"

"I am *sixteen*," Bella asserted, sounding aggrieved.

"Pish-tush," said Godfrey. "You are of an age, the two of you."

Vanessa, who had opened her mouth to protest Godfrey's unwarranted assumption, snapped her jaws over her tongue. Was Julian not driving her to distraction? Had he not thrown Scott's *Waverly* across the room, barely missing Nanny Vance and nearly shattering one of the panes in the mullioned windows? And had not the major blithely gone north to look at a bridge just when he was most needed?

A tiny smile flitted over Lady Vanessa's face as she contemplated the possible consternation caused by a prolonged visit from the London Tyrones. Lady Horatia and her son would be incensed, considering Godfrey another rival for her hand. And the major? Truthfully, she could not even imagine what Charles Tyrone would make of his exquisite cousins, particularly Godfrey. Suspecting they had never met, she looked forward to the initial encounter with something closely akin to glee.

"You should know," Vanessa said to Sir Godfrey, "that Major Tyrone rules here now. And quite legally, for Wyverne has signed over his powers. Therefore, you are welcome to stay until his return in a sennight or so, but after that, I cannot say. I must warn you that he has taken most of his notions from the long years he served in the army. You will not find him easy."

"A-ah!" Godfrey raised his perfectly plucked eyebrows. His beautiful long-lashed blue eyes shone with interest. "I look forward to meeting him," he murmured, before adding more briskly. "Then we may stay for the nonce?"

"Indeed," Vanessa nodded. "Unless I discover the excitement too much for Julian, your visit may be just the thing." She rose and pulled the bell rope. "I am certain Meecham has had your usual rooms prepared. If you will excuse me, I will inform Uncle 'Vester of your arrival." Head high, she exited the drawing room, leaving her guests to be conducted upstairs by the butler. Truthfully, as she climbed the stairs, Vanessa's feelings were ambivalent. In a fashion not too different from some of her encounters with Charles Tyrone, she was not sure if she had carried the day or been thoroughly routed.

Major Charles Tyrone had had too many tedious days shut up in the earl's coach and too many nights on lumpy mattresses in strange inns to be able to avoid the serious company of his own thoughts. The worst of the revelations which assailed him was that he could detect a certain animation, almost an eagerness in himself, which increased with every mile he grew closer to Wyverne Abbey. Cautious contemplation of this phenomenon brought the reasonable conclusion that he found civilian life sadly flat. Wyverne Abbey and its inhabitants presented a serious and intriguing challenge.

And building a bridge in Scotland did not? his inner voice jeered. *Operating a fledgling engineering company did not?*

In truth, neither was a matter of life or death, Charles was forced to admit. The problems at Wyverne Abbey, however, might be exactly that. Not to mention a certain stimulation he experienced during contretemps with a particularly disdainful ducal daughter.

He could not possibly have an interest in that direction, he repeated at frequent intervals as the coach's wheels moved inexorably south. Nor if he did, would that difficult young lady believe his interest genuine. If she

were beautiful, Charles speculated, Lady Vanessa might
have accepted that a man could woo her for herself. As
it was . . . as it was, no man who was not rich as Croesus
would ever win the Lady Vanessa Rayne.

Not that he could live with such a termagant! And
that night in the Abbey maze, when he'd suddenly found
himself confronting an attractive, desirable woman, he
himself did not know how much her dowry had affected
his vision. Yet, Charles was nearly certain the emotions
which tended to sneak up on him at the oddest moments—just when he thought he had everything properly
analyzed and sorted out—had nothing to do with wealth
and privilege. When he thought of Vanessa, he thought
of defiance, pride, arrogance, loyalty, faithfulness,
family . . . love. *Enigma, thy name is Lady Vanessa
Rayne.*

Hell and damnation! All right, he'd admit it. He missed
her. Though how a man could miss a thorn in his side
he could not imagine. It was absurd. Yet his heart beat
faster with each mile closer to the Cotswolds, and it was
not merely the thought of possible evil hanging over the
Abbey that was striking sparks off his soul.

Feeling guilty because he had not been able to put
thoughts of the Abbey behind him, Charles had compen-
sated by staying an extra three days in Scotland. It was,
therefore, more than a fortnight after his departure
when the earl's coach pulled up in front of the imposing
Gothic edifice known as Wyverne Abbey. The major,
in his eagerness, scarcely waited for the steps to be let
down before he was striding toward the front door. This
time, having grown accustomed to the efficiency of the
Abbey servants, he was not surprised when the huge
metal-studded front door swung open and Meecham
welcomed him with no attempt to repress a broad
smile.

He could become accustomed to all of it, Charles

thought uneasily, as Jenkins and Fisher tugged their fore-
locks on their way to the coach to retrieve his luggage.
Deliberately, the major squared his shoulders, took a
deep breath, rearranged his features into a scowl. He was
a soldier. This . . . this blatant luxury was not at all what
he liked. Acres of black and white marble, suits of armor
complete with pikes and swords glowering in the shadows
along the walls, a roast-an-ox fireplace, and ancestral por-
traits in ornate gilt frames eight inches wide. Chinese
vases and enormous flower arrangements sprouting from
marqueterie tables. *Bloody hell!* The value of any single
item could keep his engineering company solvent for a
year.

Reflecting the major's scowl, Meecham's smile faded.
"The family is in the dining room, sir. I am certain they
will not mind your joining them in your traveling
clothes."

Grimly, Charles strode toward the dining room. Just
let Her Arrogant Ladyship raise a dust over his clothes
or how long he'd been gone. He was hungry, by God,
and wasn't about to waste time with a bath and change
of attire. It wasn't as if this were London, after all.

And, besides, he'd had a picture in his head . . . that
mysterious woman in the maze. The pretty one. He had
to see if it was all a hum—

Charles stood stock still in the doorway to the dining
room. He did not see the red satin walls flocked in gold.
He did not see the rainbows sparkling from the crystals
of the chandelier. He did not see Mrs. Meecham or the
two maids who had scurried in to serve when the major's
coach had been spotted coming up the driveway, thus
freeing Meecham and the footmen to wait upon the Master of the House. Even Lady Vanessa Rayne occupied
his attention for only a fraction of a moment before the
major took in the unexpected, the faces which should
not have been there.

Good God! His eyes flicked over James Prentice, Miss

Halliwell, and a pretty but very young lady, to settle unerringly on the dandy whose head had been bent close to Vanessa's. Dammit, the two of them were still chuckling.

"Major!" Vanessa smiled, very much the lady of the house. "Welcome home. May I introduce your cousin Sir Godfrey Tyrone and his sister Arabella? My dears, this is the missing Charles Tyrone. No, no, Bella, you do not need to get up. You must practice being a lady instead of a schoolgirl."

Sir Godfrey, however, rose from his chair, extending his hand. Charles clasped it with caution, fearful of breaking it. This man milliner was his cousin Godfrey? The major's opinion of Ambrose Tyrone's bluff heartiness rose several notches. Charles pictured what the advent of Sir Godfrey Tyrone might have done to Wellington's officer corps on the Peninsula. The thought was appalling, though the major was not quite sure if they would have hanged the exquisite baronet or killed him with kindness. Made him a pet, perhaps. Rather in the nature of one's favorite hunting dog.

Since no one but himself had dared sit in the old earl's place at the head of the table, Charles was soon seated in his customary place opposite Vanessa, noting with satisfaction that only two additional leaves had been added to accommodate his cousins. The story of his London cousins' unexpected arrival and their efforts to help Vanessa entertain Julian was soon told.

"Indeed," Vanessa said, "they have been of immense help. I fear Julian dislikes being confined to bed."

"What happened to the Bath chair?" Charles demanded. "Has it not arrived?"

"Yes, but—" Vanessa and Godfrey spoke at once. Miss Halliwell pulled her shawl high around her neck. James Prentice could not quite stifle a groan. Arabella's eyes went wide.

"Well?" The major was far from pleased by the invasion of the household. An additional unexpected problem was not to be tolerated.

"I fear Ambrose has not been helpful," Lady Vanessa murmured.

"And what has Ambrose to do with Julian's Bath chair?" Charles's tone had grown ominous.

"He . . ." Vanessa paused. She simply could not say the words.

"I fear, Major," Mr. Prentice began, "that the vicar is overly influenced by his mo—"

"Perhaps I should attempt the explanation," Godfrey offered. Neither Charles nor Vanessa missed the gleam in his eyes. Sir Godfrey was enjoying himself. The wilds of Wyverne Abbey had not provided enough scope for his occasionally viperish talents. Charles's cousin leaned back in his chair, daintily patted his lips with his napkin. "It would seem that Lady Horatia is convinced that you wish to harm young Julian. She has, of course, inflicted her radical notions on her son—who, as vicar, should of course know better. And, alas, since my sister and I are now resident here, dear Vanessa can no longer claim that Julian is unable to have visitors. Therefore, the poor boy has had Ambrose and his mother inflicted upon him nearly every day. And never does that remarkable harridan refrain from harping on your desire to do away with Julian and become heir to this great pile of stone and all that goes—"

"She *what*?" Charles bawled, throwing his napkin onto the table in the midst of his minted lamb.

For a moment everyone talked at once, attempting to make excuses. Suddenly, silence reigned. Charles looked straight down the table to a pair of stricken blue eyes. Into the face of the vulnerable, appealing woman who had made a miraculous appearance in the maze. Distracted, he lost his terrifying grip on the anger which consumed him.

"Forgive me, cousin," Godfrey said, "but let me tell you the whole. Then you may be angry with my blessing. I'll not fault you for it." Sir Godfrey paused, organizing his thoughts. His appearance might be effeminate, but

his brain was first class, his agility of thought as superb
as his fencing, at which he was a master. "Julian adores
you, Major. You are his hero, but a steady diet of Lady
Horatia and Ambrose can be wearing. They have been
telling him that the Bath chair—which was ordered by
you—is an instrument designed for his destruction. That
it is a device not to be trusted, particularly in the hands
of what she terms the three ruffians you have brought
into the house."

"Truthfully," Vanessa interjected, "I did not make
a huge effort to intercede. I felt it best to wait for
your return. I believe Julian has allowed himself to
hesitate simply because he fears getting out of bed.
Fears he will be in a Bath chair forever. He needs
your reassurance, Major, for Godfrey is right—you
are his hero. I doubt he believes a word of the
nonsense Ambrose and Lady Horatia have been pouring into his ears."

"And now you may be angry," Godfrey told him.

But Charles did not hear him. His return to Wyverne
Abbey was so at odds with what he had pictured that his
head was in a whirl. He'd gone off a hero and returned a
villain. He had looked forward to seeing the woman of
the maze, only to surprise her gazing fondly into the face
of the king of all fops. Major Charles Tyrone was an
outsider again, a guest in the household in which he was
supposed to be master.

"We will leave you gentlemen to your port," Vanessa
announced, rising to her feet. "Major, I trust I may have
a private word with you before you retire. In the library
at half after nine?"

"Yes, of course," Charles nodded, watching almost
blindly as the table cover was rolled back and a crystal
decanter of port and matching gold-rimmed glasses were
set upon the table.

"Not the most pleasant homecoming," Sir Godfrey
murmured to the air. "Shall I pour?"

"No," the major snapped, coming to himself. "Let us

begin as we mean to go on." He poured three glasses, handed them to James Prentice and Sir Godfrey, who had joined Charles at his end of the table. "To the King." The major and his cousin emptied their glasses. Charles poured out more.

"To Prinny, the spendthrift blighter," Sir Godfrey suggested, straight-faced. After a brief pause for Mr. Prentice to assimilate his shock, they drank.

"To the Tyrones," Sir Godfrey offered, when the glasses had once again been filled.

"And to the continuity of the direct line," Charles added grimly.

The three men drank.

"And to N-nessa," stuttered James Prentice, who was attempting to keep up with two gentlemen with far better heads for liquor than himself. "A prize of a woman."

A brief frown crossed Charles's face. He shrugged and drank. Sir Godfrey, fascinated, smiled. And drank. Almost as good as a play, this was. He could manage a bit longer in the wilds of the country. Bella, after all, was worth his deprivation. If she couldn't attract the boy, there was always the major. The major. Ah, yes, the major. Godfrey heaved a sigh. After setting the stopper firmly into the decanter, he watched in appreciation as Charles Tyrone hauled James Prentice to his feet and urged him to go up to bed. The ladies would manage an evening without him, the major assured the earl's secretary. With a nod and a vague smile, Mr. Prentice tottered off to bed.

Charles turned to his younger cousin, nodded toward the decanter. "Ah, no," Godfrey demurred. "I would never enter into a bout of drinking with a man who outweighs me by three stone."

"Ah, but you already did," the major noted, "and fared rather well."

"You do not expect to have to carry me into the drawing room then?"

"Nor anywhere else," the major added with a certain emphasis.

"Unfortunate." Godfrey heaved an elaborate sigh.

"Come along," Charles laughed, "before I begin to like you."

Chapter Eleven

$\mathcal{A}$s the ormolu clock on a Chippendale console chimed half after nine, Vanessa rose from her place behind the tea tray, smiling graciously as she asked Arabella to take her place. Flushing with pleasure, that young lady immediately inquired if Miss Halliwell would care for another cup. When Vanessa slipped out of the drawing room in Charles Tyrone's wake, she paused to look back at the scene behind her, well satisfied to see Arabella solemnly pouring a third cup for her brother as well. Not for the first time, Vanessa noted that Godfrey—though still well disguised behind his supercilious façade—occasionally displayed a kind heart as well as a sharp mind. She particularly found him more likable now that he seemed to have abandoned his pursuit of her. Although why his marked attentions had ceased so abruptly, she had no idea.

A brace of wall sconces cast a mellow glow over the bookroom where the major stood with his hands resting on the back of one of the burgundy leather chairs. "My lady," he murmured stiffly as she sat down in the same chair from which she had confronted him in the Battle of the Table Leaves.

"Tell me what you learned from Rankin," Vanessa burst out. It was only when the major's formidable scowl continued unabated that she remembered Charles Tyrone might have cause for grievance.

"Perhaps you would care to tell me how you and Julian came to believe me a villain." His voice was soft but deadly. He remained standing.

Vanessa's stomach churned. "We do not!" she asserted. "I am certain Julian has told you so as well."

"Ah, yes," Charles murmured, steepling his fingers, "some faradiddle about my inspecting the blasted thing before he would be willing to trust himself to it."

"Well?" Vanessa challenged.

"Well, indeed—if the boy had not turned flame red even as he spoke."

"He is a boy," she protested. "Little more than a child. An invalid whose world has fallen in around him. You cannot expect him not to be shaken when his own vicar— the cousin he has known all his life—spouts warnings, no matter how nonsensical they may be."

The major looked down the full length of his hawk-like nose, gray eyes piercing her to the bone. "And you?" he demanded. "What excuse can you have for going along with this calumny?"

"I never believed you wished him harm," Vanessa declared hotly. "But what do I know of Bath chairs? It seemed best to wait until you returned."

"Ha!" Charles snorted. "Let the old battleaxe frighten you, did you? I thought you had more bottom, girl."

"I do!" Vanessa ducked her head, suddenly wondering if he were right. "It's just . . . well, it seemed best to let an engineer look at it first."

"My men are all expert mechanics," Charles pointed out, unforgiving.

"Yes, of course." Could she possibly have made a greater fool of herself? Later, in the privacy of her room, she might be able to understand why she had let Ambrose and his mother spew their malevolence into Julian's ears, offering reassurances of Charles's character only after the vicar and his mother were safely departed. *No.* She had to face it now. The truth was . . . she was worn down, worn out. Exhausted. She had fought all the fights that were in her. If Charles had not been coming back, she supposed she might have been able to dredge up some last ounce of gumption, but, truthfully, she had counted on him to pull them out of the terrible mire into which they'd plunged.

She had depended on Major Charles Tyrone to take the burden from her.

Facing the stark reality of this admission was such a blow to Lady Vanessa Rayne's pride that all color faded from her porcelain cheeks. The word *coward* had never before been associated with the Raynes—the many generations of ducal Raynes. It was an infinitely lowering reflection.

"Charles," Vanessa declared, slowly and deliberately, her face bravely raised to his. "I never believed a word of Lady Horatia's nonsense. But I was brought up to respect my elders. Nor am I truly a Tyrone, merely a cuckoo in the nest, as Lady Horatia delights in reminding me. I just . . . I fear I simply left the problem for you to deal with." She attempted a smile. "You are supposed to be a hero, you know."

For a moment Charles stared at her, as if he could not have heard her correctly. Then, abruptly, he turned on his heel, pacing behind the earl's broad mahogany desk to gaze out the double glass doors which overlooked the terrace and the last lingering traces of midsummer dusk being swallowed by night. God help him, he believed her. He should tell her so, but the words would not come. Julian had made a gallant effort to recover his hero worship. And failed. Even Wyverne had looked at him with eyes that held the tiniest hint of skepticism. Only his own men—and Lady Vanessa Rayne—had stated their faith in him. Something that should never have been necessary. He had always said he did not want to be a hero, but this . . . this situation was abominable. What could he do or say to regain the trust that had been lost?

What, indeed?

He could point out he had sent for combat-scarred

veterans of the Peninsular War to guard young Julian. And Lady Horatia and her son would allege that he had sent for assassins in his designs against a fifteen-year-old helpless boy.

He could bar the vicar and his mother from the house. And convince the entire village of his infamy.

He could take his men and go. Leaving the field free for whoever was attempting to do away with the boy.

He could do what Arthur Wellesley had done in the early years of the war when it seemed as if the British army could do nothing but retreat. He could hang on and wait. Guard what had to be guarded, and hope that time would prove him to be the protector, not the villain. But it was hard. The role of murderer sat so ill upon his shoulders that he was swept by waves of revulsion as well as fury.

Yet, how odd that his sole ally was his nemesis, the ducal daughter. Perhaps those few magical moments in the maze had not been as one-sided as he had thought. Perhaps that tentative friendship—and an elusive something more—still lingered, wafting a breath of hope through the heavy and sullen air of the Abbey.

Charles took his gaze from the stars which were brightening in the sky outside, turning back toward Vanessa. "Rankin says it was a pig, chased by a dog, with a man pounding after both of them, yelling at the top of his lungs." The major shrugged. "You can make of it what you will. An unkind trick of fate . . . or a cleverly staged accident. I have decided to send someone to the village to ask questions—to discover if the man is known there; if so, have there been other incidents of his pig escaping."

"Then you think it might be true?" Vanessa said in a whisper. "Someone arranged Neville's accident—"

"Hoping to get Julian as well. And possibly forgetting that I, too, stood in the way of the title."

"Having expected you to die in battle long since."

"Very likely," Charles nodded. "But when I turned up, safe and sound, a new strategy was necessary—"

"You had to be blamed!" Vanessa exclaimed.

"It would appear so."

"But that means," she declared slowly, raising stricken eyes to his, "that means you suspect Ambrose or Godfrey."

"They have the only motive that I can see," Charles admitted. "Only the three Tyrone cousins—Ambrose, Godfrey, or myself—have anything to gain."

"But was not poisoning Julian too obvious?"

"Not if Julian had died and the blame could be turned on me. And even though Julian survived, the blatant nature of the attack works all too well to discredit me. In any future incident I shall be the first suspect. I am, after all, the boy's heir."

"It is abominable!" Vanessa cried.

Charles found her indignation adorable. "I shall not argue with you." Striding to Lady Vanessa's chair, he took both her hands in his and raised her to her feet. How he loved it when he could make the ice maiden blush! "Thank you, my dear, for believing in me. Frankly, I would have expected you to be leading the cry against me." Maybe it was the dim light from the wall sconces where several candles had burned down into puddles of hot wax, but the lovely lady of the maze looked back at him. A creature of glowing blue eyes and promised warmth backed by intelligence, dignity, and an admirable sense of responsibility. How very strange to have to admit that he liked her.

And, just perhaps, she liked him as well. Although, when morning came, they would likely be back to brangling over one thing or another. Charles squeezed her hands, bent forward to place a light kiss on her high, aristocratic forehead. "Goodnight, my dear. Sleep well, for I fear all our problems will crash down upon us in the morning."

Vanessa could not move. She was a marble statue destined to decorate the bookroom of Wyverne Abbey forever. She had endured a number of ardent scenes during her Seasons in London and at a variety of country house parties, all of which she had handled with ease, having no difficulty attributing the aberrant moments to the gentlemen's greed or an excess of punch. Their hot breaths and practiced groping had produced nothing more than anger and distaste, while the merest brush of a kiss from Major Charles Tyrone could cast her into a mindless daze. Vanessa found herself in the hallway, her feet moving toward the stairs. She had no idea how she had got there. Had Charles ejected her bodily from the room? No, of course not. Her dignity was still intact. Was it not?

Behind her, in the bookroom, Major Charles Tyrone poured himself another brandy. Then stretching out on the burgundy leather settee, he raised his snifter in salute to a gallant lady. Unfortunately, the tilt of his lips just before he drank was just a wee bit smug.

The following morning, after enjoying a short ride on Rojo, who seemed eager to demonstrate he was now in fine fettle, the major was pleased to find Lady Vanessa, Miss Halliwell, Sir Godfrey, and Arabella at the breakfast table. James Prentice, he assumed, was already hard at work on the vast correspondence needed to keep five far-flung estates running smoothly. After a round of polite greetings, Charles declined the newspaper Sir Godfrey promptly offered him, concentrating instead on filling his plate with a selection of delectable items he had not enjoyed since leaving the Abbey nearly three weeks before. Only when he had assuaged the sharpest pangs of his hunger, with true appreciation for the Abbey cook, did Charles raise his head and address his companions.

"Sir Godfrey," he declared, "I believe you and Miss Arabella would enjoy a trip to the village today, a bit of shopping, followed by lunch at the Bull and Bear. Or

perhaps a longer drive? I hear there's a fine prospect
from Houndstooth Hill, some five miles west. I am happy
to put the barouche at your disposal."

Godfrey Tyrone might never have been in the army,
but he knew an order when he heard it. "An excellent
suggestion, cousin," he agreed, daintily stifling a yawn,
"though I am still struggling to deal with your country
hours. At home—"

"At home," Arabella interjected saucily, "he is still
abed at noon."

"True," Godfrey conceded, "but I am certain all this
fresh air and country charm must be doing us both a
great deal of good. We will, of course, be happy to ex-
plore the countryside at your orders, Major."

Charles ignored the faint gasps which echoed from
Vanessa and Miss Halliwell at this blunt acknowledgment
that Sir Godfrey and his sister were being hinted away
from the Abbey that morning. "Meecham," the major
called to the butler, who was standing just inside the
servants' entry, making sure that the sideboard never
lacked for any of the delicacies necessary for a proper
country breakfast, "we are not at home to visitors today.
Not to *any* visitors," he emphasized, exchanging a significant look with the sympathetic Meecham.

The major turned to his next targets. "Miss Halliwell,
I suggest you attend to your correspondence or your embroidery in the Ladies' Parlor this morning. Lady
Vanessa, you will be good enough to meet me in Julian's
room at ten o'clock."

Somehow Vanessa expected to hear the roar of cannon, the rumble of charging cavalry, the clash of sabers.
Major Charles Tyrone had encountered the enemy and
was going into battle, on the attack. A glow of satisfaction stole over her, her resentment of the major's high-
handed machinations fading into abeyance. Sir Godfrey,
she noted, seemed to be struggling with inner amusement, and Arabella . . . Miss Arabella Tyrone, age sixteen, was regarding the major with glowing admiration.

Oh dear, Vanessa groaned to herself. That was all they needed—a schoolgirl *tendre* on top of everything else.

She promptly pushed back her chair. "If you will excuse me, I must see Uncle 'Vester now." Vanessa turned to Charles. "Until ten, Major," she pronounced, at her most formal, before sweeping out of the room.

Ah, where had the magic gone? Charles sighed to himself. He could swear her nose was an inch longer than it had been the night before. No matter. There were more important problems to be dealt with at the moment. But as the major took a second helping of eggs and gammon, he recognized his lie. The Abbey's problems must take precedence, but the thought of peeling back the flinty layers surrounding Lady Vanessa Rayne was an intriguing challenge. The lady was an intricate, occasionally lovely puzzle which he was more drawn to solve with each moment he knew her.

If there were a solution . . . if a lowly engineer dared tackle an enigma which floated so far above his head the lady might as well have been the moon.

If he were Wyverne . . .

The major's teeth gnashed against a large morsel of ham. *Hell and damnation,* but life was complicated! Oh, for the years on the Peninsula when his world was clear-cut in black and white.

A half hour later, Major Charles Tyrone stood, hands behind his back, gazing sternly at his youngest cousin. Lady Vanessa stood with him, shoulder to shoulder. "Now," the major declared to the wide-eyed boy, "what is this I hear about your refusing the Bath chair? I must inform you a very clever friend of mine built this one especially for you. It is smaller and lighter than the more ponderous vehicles one sees on city walkways, and it is in the new style where it may be pushed rather than pulled. You have only to grab the handle over the front wheel and steer."

Julian, looking chagrined, failed to raise his eyes above

the major's waistcoat. If he had, he would have seen that Charles's face revealed nothing more than amusement, tinged with gentle teasing. "And yet what do I discover upon my return—when I expected to find you tootling about the house, enjoying a reunion with your grandfather, perhaps even venturing as far as the garden? I hear, instead, the chair is gathering dust in storage. So kindly explain to me how the Julian Tyrone who refused to die when all the supposedly wise heads said he would has suddenly turned coward in my absence."

"Unfair!" Julian cried over Vanessa's squeak of protest at the major's harsh words. "If you could have heard Cousin Ambrose and Lady Horatia prosing on and on about that chair—about the accidents I could have. The front stairs, the back stairs, the terrace . . . even the river. They nattered on until I couldn't stand it. They called it an infernal contraption and acted as if it would fall apart at the first roll of the wheels."

"And you believed them." The major's voice was perfectly even.

Julian flushed, hung his head. "It's not that I don't know Lady Horatia always has a bee in her bonnet about something," he mumbled, "but Ambrose . . . he's the *vicar,* you know. How could I ignore him?"

"How, indeed?" Charles murmured. "Even when he alleged that I wished to kill you?"

Julian's head jerked up. "No!" he protested. "I never believed that. Never! You wouldn't; you couldn't."

"Then why would you not use the chair?"

"Stop it!" Vanessa exclaimed. "He's ill and he's frightened. I told you how it was. It is not easy to fight someone of Lady Horatia's determination and, most particularly, it is not easy to fight one's vicar. Julian and I took the cowardly way out. We waited for you to return and make this decision for us."

Slowly, Charles nodded. "Alas, I seem to have left my white horse and shining armor in Scotland."

Nearly identical sighs of relief echoed from Julian and

Vanessa. Charles was no longer furious with them. "That is quite all right," she assured the major. "We are convinced you do not need them."

The major was sorely tempted to seize her hand and kiss it. Instead, he made a brisk announcement. "Very well, we have work to do. Simmons," he called, "bring it in."

The door opened, held in place by Corporal Hart as Sergeant Simmons pushed the specially constructed Bath chair into the room. Made of wood with brown leather padding on the seat and back, it had two large rear wheels, the body tapering to a single small wheel in front, rather like the pointed prow of a ship. Rising above the small wheel was a rod with a handle with which the invalid might steer. Truthfully, it was a doubtful-looking conveyance, and Vanessa could not fault Julian for his reluctance to ride in it. Reason scolded that her doubts were fanciful, yet she had not had the courage to face this moment alone. This moment when something might go wrong, and Charles Tyrone would not be there to pick up the pieces. Long hours of reflection during these weeks the major had been gone had forced Vanessa to admit even the most conscientious caregiver could sink into depression and fearfulness. She, Lady Vanessa Amelia Courtney Rayne, now found herself dependent on a lowly engineer.

"I have checked every last piece of it personally," the major was saying to Julian, "and had Simmons and Hart go over it as well. I guarantee this chair will not break, even if your cousin Ambrose should sit in it, and it will scarcely notice a wraith like yourself." Charles paused to appreciate the slight smile his attempt at humor had coaxed from the boy. "Will you trust me to pick you up?" he inquired blandly.

The young viscount eyed the chair with obvious misgiving. "I daresay grandfather would like to see me," he ventured.

Vanessa echoed her agreement, then swiftly closed her

mouth, hoping she had not overdone her enthusiasm. Boys could be so difficult. Undoubtedly practicing to be men, she thought darkly.

"Oh . . . very well," Julian muttered. Charles swept back the bedcovers, then with a gentleness no one could fault, lifted the fifteen-year-old into the Bath chair. Corporal Hart swept a wool blanket over the boy's lap, tucked it in around his ankles. At a nod from the major, Julian grasped the steering handle, and Sergeant Simmons started the chair rolling. The rug did not make their task easy, nor their unfamiliarity with the vagaries of the strange three-wheeled machine. Their turn, on the far side of the room where Nanny Vance sat watching with some trepidation, was awkward, involving a bit of backing up and considerable use of the sergeant's strong muscles. But once they ventured onto the wooden floor of the hallway, Julian's frowning concentration transformed into a glow of satisfaction and finally into a grin. He waved an imperious hand toward his grandfather's room. Like a general signaling a charge, Vanessa thought, stifling a chortle. They'd done it; they'd actually done it. The young viscount was off to see the grandfather who had not laid eyes on the boy since he had returned to Eton after the Christmas holidays.

They made quite a cavalcade as Julian Tyrone, newly made Viscount Sherbourne, progressed toward the earl's wing of the Abbey—the boy in the rolling chair steering, Simmons pushing, Hart hovering at their side; Lady Vanessa Rayne following behind, nearly dancing with joy; Major Charles Tyrone bringing up the rear; and in their wake, Sally Vance and Peter Fielding creeping along, unwilling to miss a jot of this historic moment.

Chapter Twelve

*I*n the end, everyone cried: the old man, who beamed through his tears; Julian, who had not been prepared for his grandfather's frailty; Vanessa, who had feared this day would never come; Will Jarvis, the earl's faithful valet, who was so overcome he bolted into the earl's dressing room to hide his crumbling emotions. Major Tyrone and Sergeant Simmons blinked rapidly, even as Corporal Hart wiped a sleeve across his eyes. Out in the hall, where they had been peering through the open door, Peter Fielding offered his handkerchief to Sally Vance.

When the reunion was over, the earl lying back exhausted on his pillows and Julian safely returned to his bed, Vanessa flew to her room, crumpled up on the window seat, and burst into a waterfall of tears. It was some time before a semblance of rational thought returned. When it did, sensible girl that she was, she fumbled for a handkerchief, wiped her eyes, blew her nose, and attempted to face reality. Until this morning's milestone had been reached, she had not fully realized the depth of her emotions, the insidious nature of the tension she had lived with for so long. No wonder she had merely blundered on, doing what had to be done, her mind capable of functioning only in slow circles, never seeing the larger picture of what was happening at the Abbey. It had taken Charles Tyrone arriving fresh from the outside world, a man accustomed to dealing with adversity, to see what she might have seen for herself if she had not been so close—

Unfair! She could not have been expected to see villainy where only tragedy appeared to exist. Perhaps . . . perhaps Charles was mistaken? About fresh air, possibly, she conceded. About attempted murder, no. Violence was the major's area of expertise. She had no choice but to take him seriously.

Lady Vanessa continued her grave reevaluation of life at the Abbey while eating luncheon on a tray in her room. Then, having doused her face several times in cold water and dried it carefully on an embroidered linen towel before applying a dash of powder beneath her eyes and on her suspiciously red nose, she set off for the lower regions of the house. She was Lady Vanessa Rayne, chatelaine of Wyverne Abbey. This was her home; the people in it, her family. No harm would come to them on her watch.

With the major's return, the tempo of life picked up at the Abbey. At the dinner table, indulgent smiles greeted Arabella's happy chatter about her shopping excursion with her brother. Laughter rang out at Sir Godfrey's witty remarks rather than the polite quirks of the lip which had frequently greeted his sallies in the past. Even Miss Halliwell ventured an occasional remark. Charles contributed to the general bonhomie by announcing that Julian would soon be strong enough to join them at table. He also made a point of insisting Vanessa take some time for herself. Go riding, go shopping, buy something frivolous, he told her.

Since Vanessa was well aware her fear that the Abbey walls might tumble down without her constant presence was totally irrational, she found herself assuring the major she would follow his suggestions. What all were too polite to mention was that the absence of Ambrose Tyrone and Lady Horatia for four full days had contributed greatly to the lightening of the atmosphere at the Abbey. In truth, it began to seem as if murder and false accusations had never reared their ugly heads.

So when Charles noticed that Vanessa had been disappearing for an hour or more each afternoon—riding, he assumed—he was pleased, rather than concerned. Until one day when he thought to join her on her ride, then entered the stables to discover her favorite mare happily snuffling hay. Charles flicked his eyes over the other stalls. Not a horse was missing. The gig, which Vanessa occasionally drove to town, was also in its place. A flash of alarm surged through him.

No need to get in a pelter, Ned Burley responded to the major's anxious question. Lady Vanessa was most likely at her fav'rite spot. Hadn't had a chance to shoot her bow in ages, she hadn't. If the major took the path behind the maze, through the woods a mite—

Charles took off at a near run before the groom had finished his sentence, leaving Burley to come to his own conclusions. After a moment of scratching his head, the earl's head groom broke into a broad grin. Now, *there* was a match he'd like to see. Didn't seem likely though. A nice girl, Lady Vanessa, but uppity. Very uppity.

The path eventually brought Charles to a sheltered glade where an archery butt had been set up. Vanessa, surprisingly clad in an unadorned gown of dark green in some sturdy fabric, her ensemble completed by a leather arm guard and an archer's glove, was calmly nocking an arrow, her eyes fixed on the distant target. The major paused in the shelter of the trees and watched. She was good, he noted, as four of six arrows hit the bull's-eye; the other two, just outside it. But of course Lady Vanessa Rayne would be expert; she was expert at everything. A paragon of all virtues. Miss Nose-in-the-Air, the personification of Perfection.

Charles sighed.

Only when Lady Vanessa had put down her bow and

was returning from retrieving her arrows did she see him standing there. She stopped stock still, the arrows dropping from her hand. Charles, apologizing profusely, rushed to help her pick them up. As they walked back to the archers' line, he attempted to recover the ground he had lost by startling her. And instantly made matters worse.

"You are very good," he told her heartily. "A veritable Robin Hood."

Vanessa swung round to stare at him. "You were watching me! How dare you stand there and say nothing?"

Charles gulped. Better an entire regiment of Boney's lancers than this. "I didn't want to upset your aim," he protested. "Truly, I did not wish to intrude." *Liar!* He'd been enjoying the view. The role of Diana the Huntress suited her.

"Then you should have stayed at the Abbey." She strode off, leaving Charles standing alone near the middle of the glade, feeling the perfect fool. The women in Lisbon had never acted like this. Nor the ones in Spain. Or Paris or Brussels.

The more the fool, he, to think a lowly engineer and Her Arrogant Ladyship could reach some kind of rapport.

And what was she doing now, the little termagant? Holding out the bow, a quiverful of arrows? Head high, body radiating defiance. Damned if she wasn't offering him a challenge.

How many years had it been since he'd held a bow? Well over a decade. He had been a callow youth enjoying the long summer vacation with friends. When they'd grown bored, they'd set up a practice butt in a fallow field. In truth, he wasn't certain if he could hit the side of a barn, let alone Vanessa's target, which was set a good sixty feet from the archers' line. Oh, very well, Charles groaned. If a man was idiot enough to convince himself he was pursuing a rose instead of a gilded cabbage, he should not be surprised when thorns got in the way.

Pursuing? Where had that thought come from? He was not pursuing Lady Vanessa Rayne. He was merely doing his duty and keeping an eye on her.

She was still standing there, holding out the bow and quiver. Charles was close enough now to see the rather nasty gleam in her eyes. No ice princess today, she was closer to Vesuvius. He accepted the bow, slung the quiver over his back, slipped on the leather arm guard she thrust at him. *Hell and the devil, but the chit was difficult!*

His first arrow went sailing into the woods; the second caught the edge of the target butt, quivered an instant before falling to the ground. Charles refused to look at Vanessa, but was certain he heard a rather inelegant snort. His third arrow hit within a foot of the bull's-eye; the last two whanged into target dead center, so close together the one arrow nearly split the other.

"You are a fast learner," the lady murmured without inflection.

"Engineers must have a good eye."

"Of course."

"I believe it is nearly tea time," Charles said, equally bland. "May I carry these things back to the house for you?"

By the time they found the arrow Charles had sent into the woods, both tempers had flared still higher. Their return to the Abbey was marked by a silence which seethed with unspoken thoughts. Unfortunately, to add to their difficulties, as they approached the house three people were seen entering a carriage, then driving off down the driveway. Two of them the major did not recognize, but one rang a very sour note.

"What is that *she-devil* doing here?" Charles burst out.

"I gave her permission."

"You *what*?" The major's shout startled a group of pigeons into instant flight.

"I cannot keep her away, major," Vanessa explained, with considerably more patience than she felt. "Nor Ambrose either. They are family. Lady Horatia wrote a very proper note asking if she might bring the squire's children for a visit. Julian has known Benjamin and Sarah Yardley all his life. I thought they would be good for him. And for Arabella as well, as Sarah is only a year or so younger than she."

"And you never thought to mention the matter to me," Charles riposted in ominous tones.

"It never occurred to me," Vanessa replied in all honesty.

The major glared. "From this moment on," Charles decreed, "not a single soul enters this house or grounds without my approval. Is that understood?"

"How could two children be a problem?" Vanessa countered, having had quite enough of Major Charles Tyrone for one day.

"Is. That. Understood?" The glare never wavered.

"Yes, sir, Major, sir," Vanessa mocked, imitating Corporal Hart to a T. She even managed a stiff salute.

"You're not too old to paddle."

Vanessa gasped. "Try it and I'll have your liver and lights."

"I'd wager you don't even know what *lights* are," Charles drawled. "And, believe me, you don't want to."

Vanessa did the only thing a well-brought-up lady could. She turned on her heel and stalked off. She should have known there was no way to get the upper hand with Charles Tyrone. But it rankled, indeed it did.

And just when she had thought they were . . . friends.

How two children could be a problem became apparent ten days later when Vanessa was awakened in the middle of the night by Hugh Davies, the youngest of the major's guards, pounding on her door. Julian, it seemed, was taken with a high fever.

"Measles," Dr. Elijah Pettibone declared an hour later. Seeing Lady Vanessa draw breath to protest, the doctor drew himself up to his full five feet six and growled, "I may not be one of your Harley Street set, but you can't fool an old country doctor about the measles. Thought it was a damn fool thing for Lady Horatia to bring the Yardley brats for a visit when the younger ones were all broken out as red as lobsters. And, sure enough, the older ones succumbed the next day. So no need to look for where the boy got it. Plain as a pikestaff. *Measles!*"

When Lady Vanessa covered her mouth with her hand, staring at him in horror, Dr. Pettibone lowered his voice, hastily adding, "Won't tell you it's not serious, but the boy's got the best care. With luck, there'll be no complications. But there's no denying he'll be sick as a dog. Got to keep the room dark, watch his eyes. Plenty of liquids." Since Lady Vanessa still looked as if she were personally responsible for making the viscount ill, the doctor added, "Better he should get it over with now, my lady. Measles can be the very devil for a man. Causes steri—ah, that is, makes 'em very sick, don't you know. Not good for a grown man, the measles." Awkwardly, he patted her shoulder. "No need to fret. You've been through it before, girl. Armageddon is not at hand."

"I said they might come—the Yardley children," Vanessa murmured blankly, speaking to the air. "It is *my* fault. I thought it would be a special treat."

"Oh, Doctor, thank goodness you're here," cried a voice from the doorway. Mrs. Meecham, obviously as newly aroused from her bed as Lady Vanessa, was addressing Dr. Pettibone. "Miss Arabella's maid has come to me saying that miss seems feverish—" She broke off, eyeing the flushed face of young Lord Sherbourne. "Merciful heavens," she moaned, "have they *both* been poisoned?"

"Measles," Elijah Pettibone barked. "I suppose Miss Arabella was with the Yardley brats as well."

"Measles," Mrs. Meecham echoed. "Who ever would have thought? And at their age, too. Poor lambs. The older you are, the harder it is."

Job's comforter. As Vanessa scowled at the retreating backs of the doctor and the housekeeper, a large body suddenly blocked her view. A large comforting body. She came dangerously close to throwing herself into Charles Tyrone's arms.

When the major had heard the whole, he turned to Nanny Vance, asking the obvious. "How serious is it?"

Sally Vance wrung her hands, a warning sign neither Charles nor Vanessa missed. "The illness lasts up to a fortnight, sir," she told them in hushed tones. "Besides the fever, which runs high, there's many another thing can happen. Lung fever, brain fever, weakened eyes, a fearsome cough, and there are some whose skin turns yellow—"

"Enough," Charles hissed, holding up his hand. For the first time since he had known Lady Vanessa Rayne, she looked as if she were about to faint. He put an arm about her waist, but refused to overlook one last question to Sally Vance. "Is it sometimes fatal?"

Nanny Vance looked him straight in the eye. "Yes." Charles felt, rather than heard, the sob Vanessa quickly repressed.

"Thank you, Mrs. Vance," Charles nodded. "I do not know how we would go on without you. After I have spoken with the doctor, I will remain here through the night. You may tell me what I must do."

"I, also," Vanessa added, still sheltered in the circle of the major's arm. "Nanny, you must return to your bed. For we still need your good services with Julian's meals. Never fear, we will send Davies for you if there is a problem."

When Charles had seated Vanessa in the chair by the bed in which she had spent so much time in the past, and after they had both listened with care to Sally Vance's instructions, he excused himself and went in search of the doctor. When he returned, his face had gone from grim to furious. Grabbing Vanessa by the arm, he hauled her to the far corner of the room near Nanny Vance's favorite window. "The Yardley children had the measles," he ground out.

"Yes, Dr. Pettibone told me."

"And did he happen to mention that the three younger children all had the measles when Lady Horatia brought the older ones here?"

"Yes."

"Well?" the major demanded, gray eyes glittering.

"It was deliberate," Vanessa intoned. She had come to that conclusion not a half hour since. "Lady Horatia exposed an already sick boy to a serious childhood disease with malicious intent." Vanessa stuck up her chin and glared at the major. "Is that what you wished me to say?"

Charles braced one long arm against the wall between the two front windows. He leaned in, only inches from her face. "God help us, yes. That's exactly what I wanted you to say. I thought perhaps I had gone mad. *How could she?* How could anyone—particularly a mother—deliberately expose an already sick child to the measles?"

"She will say she assumed Ben and Sarah had already had the disease. Or that she was certain Julian had had the measles as a child. And there is the additional problem that Mrs. Yardley allowed her children to come, knowing full well they could be carrying the disease to Julian, for everyone knows childhood diseases jump from one child to another as if by magic."

"Perhaps she thought the measles would not dare enter the residence of the Earl of Wyverne," Charles suggested dryly.

"More likely, she—poor soul—like everyone else, could not say no to Lady Horatia."

Their colloquy was cut short by Julian erupting into a

hacking cough and querulously demanding a glass of water. It was the beginning of a highly unrestful night. When Sally Vance returned shortly after dawn, with Sergeant Simmons hovering at her side, the major and Vanessa were more than ready for their beds. And even then, the ugly word *propriety* failed to rear its ugly head. No one in the Abbey seemed to find it odd that Major Charles Tyrone and Lady Vanessa Rayne had shared a nighttime vigil at the bedside of a fifteen-year-old viscount.

Chapter Thirteen

*L*ate the following afternoon, after noting Lady Vanessa's absence at tea, Charles tracked her down in the Ladies' Parlor, which overlooked the gardens. She was stretched out on a sofa, reading a well-worn copy of *Pride and Prejudice*. Gowned in one of her more attractive almost-black dyed muslins, she made a charming contrast to the red upholstery beneath her. A small tea tray, with only one remaining tart, lay on a low table at her side. Obviously, Lady Vanessa had enjoyed the solitude of a private tea.

"I envy you," Charles said, without further greeting. "If I had known how comfortable you were here, I should have joined you. But then I suppose you preferred your solitude."

"I preferred not to discuss Julian and the measles," Vanessa replied firmly.

"You also preferred to have your feet up," Charles speculated, seating himself in an elegant satinwood side chair positioned so he could see her face. "I must say poor Miss Halliwell was quite disconcerted to find herself having to pour."

"Cruel of me, was it not?"

"Assuredly," Charles agreed easily. "Tell me," he continued, almost without pause, "do you think Cousin Ambrose has had the measles?"

"I have no idea."

"Yet he did not come with Lady Horatia when she brought the children. I find that very interesting," the major mused.

"Charles . . ." Vanessa warned, "you cannot be thinking what I—"

"Why not?" he countered. "I think we should invite our dear vicar to say special prayers at the boy's bedside."

"That is diabolical!" Vanessa exclaimed, sitting up abruptly. "Dr. Pettibone says the disease can be quite serious for a man—"

"And possibly lethal for a fifteen-year-old invalid," the major pronounced, without an ounce of sympathy.

Vanessa swung her feet over the edge of the sofa, placing them firmly on the floor. "The matter is moot, for his mama will never allow it," she asserted.

"He is as old as I," Charles barked.

Vanessa shrugged, drawing her index finger in idle circles over the page of her book. "You believe Ambrose is behind the acci—the—ah—incidents we've been having."

"Who else?" the major retorted. "Godfrey would never expose his precious sister to the measles, I simply don't believe it."

"Speaking of Godfrey," Vanessa continued, seizing the diversion, "his behavior this past Season in London was most odd. I can think of no reason for it. He has never been in the petticoat line, yet he followed me around like a puppy. It seemed at times I could not move without tripping over him. I even went so far as to ask Neville if Godfrey had lost his money. Neville merely laughed and told me Godfrey was simply practicing flirtation on a member of the family." Vanessa frowned. "Truthfully, his arrival here caused me considerable qualms. Yet he has been as good as gold. Nothing more flirtatious than an occasional raising of his brow. Do you think Neville had the right of it and Godfrey has had enough practice?"

The question took Charles by surprise. Yet, upon reflection, he had to agree that he had seen no sign of Sir Godfrey Tyrone attempting to fix his interest with the heiress. There were, however, other reasons his effeminate cousin might flaunt a *tendre* for Lady Vanessa Rayne. Some he could not discuss with her. But if Godfrey had wanted an excuse to be close to the Wyverne Tyrones, to be intimately aware of their comings and goings . . .

The major swore under his breath. What a coil!

"I heard that," Vanessa accused.

"You couldn't have."

"I have excellent hearing," she huffed, then spoiled the effect by giggling. "If you think I don't know Godfrey is what's termed a man milliner, you are much mistaken. I suppose both you and Neville think he was using me."

"I think this is a subject best left untouched," Charles, at his most repressive, replied.

"It is odd about Ambrose as well," Vanessa said. "I would have said he has absolutely no ambition beyond Archbishop of Canterbury."

"That's *all*?" the major asked faintly.

"I believe he would settle for York," Lady Vanessa conceded.

"Rather a large ambition for a village vicar, is it not?"

"You forget—he is related to the Wyverne Tyrones," Vanessa intoned, with a quirk of her lips.

"An heir, in fact, if several bodies removed," Charles agreed, a responding gleam in his eye.

"Really, Charles," Vanessa countered, suddenly sober, "Ambrose can be obtuse at times, and his sermons tend to be twice as long as one could wish, but I truly think he cares not a fig for the title."

"Fine," Charles declared, standing up. "We shall see just how dedicated he is to his profession. I'll send round a note immediately, inviting him to evening prayers in Julian's room." As the major strode out, Vanessa looked after him with some considerable misgiving.

But the stalwart vicar surprised them both, descending on the Abbey within an hour of reading the major's note. "Nasty business, the measles," he pronounced. "Suffered, I tell you. Only nine at the time. Mama assures me I nearly died."

The vicar of Lower Wyverne slipped into the place at table which had been hastily laid for him. After flipping his napkin open with the enthusiasm of a good trencherman, he made an effort to put on a solemn face even as his eyes gleamed at the sight of turtle soup. "Poor dear Julian," he said in sepulchral tones. "He has endured so much. Pettibone fears for his life. That is why I have come to you so quickly."

Then why, if Ambrose was so concerned, Vanessa thought crossly, was he sitting down in obvious anticipation of a meal of several courses?

"I stopped to see Pettibone on my way here, you see," the vicar continued. "Felt it only right to verify my mother's memory. Naturally, I must think of the entire parish. Can't have the vicar laid low by a childhood disease, now, can we?"

Vanessa kept her temper only because of the warning glint in the major's eye. She supposed she should be grateful that her emotions were reviving from the terrible lethargy which had seized her during Charles's absence. But it was difficult to be grateful for anything when Julian was once more struck down, struggling for his life.

The strangest moment of the day, however, was yet to come. When the imposing figure of the Right Reverend Ambrose Tyrone entered his young cousin's room, he seemed to don some invisible cloak of spiritual office, his prayers and words of comfort so sincere even the major had difficulty maintaining his cynicism. But if the villain was not Ambrose Tyrone, then who? Charles had considerable difficulty visualizing Sir Godfrey engaged in mass murder.

Yet, someone was trying to kill Julian. Every instinct the major had honed so finely during seven long years

of war insisted he was right. There could be no doubt,
of course, about Lady Horatia arranging the measles incident. She might even have arranged Julian's poisoning,
he conceded, for poison was a woman's weapon. But
Neville's murder in a village outside London—if it was
murder—that was man's work. And his own ill-fated encounter with the ha-ha? He had thought he understood
that one, for it was a resentful James Prentice who had
sent him down that path. But now . . .

As all around him murmured, "Amen," the major
scowled at the tips of his shoes. A London dandy, an
ambitious clergyman, a vitriolic mother, a jealous secretary who had nothing to gain but fleeting revenge . . .

A boy who might die.

Charles thought longingly of the fresh cool air of
Scotland.

It seemed to Vanessa that one moment she was talking
quietly to Nanny Vance, worrying what more they could
do for Julian's high fever, and the next she turned around
to discover his face looking like a splotchy painting displayed on a nursery wall. Gasping, she rushed to the bed.
He looked ghastly!

Irritably, Julian waved away her concern. "Stubble it,
Ness. Act-u-ally"—he paused to assess his condition—
"actually, I feel better. Do I look like a lobster?" He
sounded almost hopeful.

She would never understand the male of the species,
Vanessa decided. "A half-boiled one, perhaps," she
told him.

"The rash will spread," Nanny Vance decreed, "but
that's to be expected, and, in truth, we can be grateful
for it. It means your fever's days are numbered."

But after they had given Julian a drink of lemonade
and smoothed out his covers, Mrs. Vance spoiled the
cheerful effect of her words by indicating she wished to
speak with Lady Vanessa out in the hallway. "There will

be another day or so of fever," she said, "and now is the time we must be doubly watchful for complications."

"Is there nothing we can do to prevent—"

Sally Vance patted Lady Vanessa's hand. "We are doing all we can, my lady. We can only deal with the symptoms as they occur. *If* they occur. Mayhap the boy will recover without any further reason to worry. 'Tis said the Yardley children have naught but the simplest form of the disease."

Only slightly heartened, Vanessa started down the hallway to visit Arabella. She was some ten feet short of Miss Tyrone's door when a shriek echoed down the corridor. As Vanessa burst into the young lady's room, her feet crunched against something on the carpet. Startled, she found herself standing amidst jagged slivers of silver. Further examination revealed an ivory frame and carved handle, the remains of a handmirror. And to top this indication of raging temper, not to mention bad luck, Miss Arabella Tyrone—propped on a pile of pillows in her four-poster bed—was in the throes of a full-blown case of hysterics. Wrenching sobs filled the room, even as her arms flayed and her feet drummed up and down beneath the covers. She could not be as ill as Julian, Vanessa decided, or the girl could not have had the strength for such a display.

There was, of course, little need to ask what had set Arabella off. The mirror told the tale. Vanessa took two careful steps closer to the bed, nodded sagely at the sight that met her eyes. She had not thought it possible for anyone to look worse than Julian, but Arabella had managed it. Yet, while Julian seemed to consider his rash something of a badge of honor—undoubtedly, full-blown red would have pleased him better than splotchy patches—Arabella Tyrone was taking the fully female point of view. She looked hideous. She would never be beautiful again. The world had come to an end.

Ordinarily, Lady Vanessa Rayne was not above treating a case of hysterics with a good hard slap. She had had a certain amount of experience with Lady Kitty. But slap a young lady broken out with the measles? Impossible. As she approached the bed, Vanessa summoned her long line of ducal ancestors to march with her.

"Arabella," she announced, "if you keep this up, you will make yourself so ill you will be in bed an extra week." Miss Tyrone howled all the louder. "Stop this nonsense at once!" Vanessa roared over the girl's screams. To no avail.

"I can't do anything with her, my lady," declared Emma Trout, the woman Lady Vanessa had hired from the village to nurse the only female Tyrone cousin. "It's like she's never been crossed before in her life. Thinks she's too good to get the measles, she does."

Vanessa sighed. "I fear she has been indulged too much, Mrs. Trout, but truly she is a delightful young lady most of the time. We are seeing her at her worst." Thoughtfully, Vanessa looked at the still sobbing girl. "I was correct, was I not, when I said she was making herself more ill?"

"Aye, m'lady. She'll pay for this, she will. Higher fever, more days in bed."

Lady Vanessa strode to a nearby dresser, picked up a neat stack of linen towels and, lips thinned by determination, handed them to Mrs. Trout. That lady gasped, one hand flying to her mouth, as she watched Lady Vanessa pick up the porcelain pitcher of water which was sitting in a matching basin on the same dresser, walk to the bed, and dump the entire contents over Miss Arabella Tyrone's head.

Vanessa wiped her hands on her serviceable poplin gown. "I will send two maids to help you clean up, Mrs. Trout." With a regal nod, she headed for the door. Behind her, the room was plunged into silence.

The tension at the dinner table that evening was palpable. On this, the fourth day since Julian and Arabella had been taken ill, the fourth night Charles and Vanessa would share a vigil at the viscount's bedside, they each had assumed the animosities over the advent of the measles had already been aired: Vanessa's feelings of guilt, Sir Godfrey's anger at her hand in exposing his sister to the Yardley children, Charles's frustration that there was so little to be done to help the two sick youngsters. The major had even sent for a London doctor, only to have that gentleman confirm what they already knew. Measles. There could be complications, but with good care . . . The doctor shrugged, accepted his fee, and returned to town. So now, in addition to all else, they had managed to offend Dr. Elijah Pettibone. But more was yet to come. Since Vanessa had gone to bed after her morning encounter with Arabella and slept through teatime, she was completely unprepared for Sir Godfrey's attack as the soup was being served.

"You might have killed her!" Godfrey accused from his place at Lady Vanessa's right. "She will suffer a lung fever. My poor Bella, lost to us forever." He flung a dramatic hand to his brow.

"Cut line, Godfrey!" the major barked from his end of the table. "The chit's hysterics were doing her worse damage. She had to be stopped."

Vanessa hung her head. Dear God, Charles had already heard the tale.

"She was soaked," Godfrey proclaimed. "Soaked, I tell you." He glared at Vanessa who was still contemplating her plate. "If she gets brain fever and dies, it will be all your fault."

"Your sister," Charles declared, "has been greatly overindulged, besides being as empty-headed as any other chit of sixteen. Lady Vanessa did what had to be done."

"Lady Vanessa," Godfrey countered roundly, "is a high-handed termagant who thinks she has the right to play God—"

"Lady Vanessa," Charles proclaimed in a voice all the

more deadly for the softness of it, "has been the savior
of the house of Tyrone. I will hear no criticism of her,
do you understand, Godfrey? None whatsoever. You
should get down on your knees and thank the good Lord
she has been here to preserve both Wyverne and Julian.
And your sister as well."

Vanessa, the levelheaded. Vanessa, the Arrogant Aristocrat. Vanessa, whose emotions had not been entirely
stable since that fateful day of Neville's accident, pushed
back her chair and rushed from the room. Into the ensu-
ing hush, Sir Godfrey drawled, "Perhaps you would care
for a fencing lesson after dinner, Cousin?"

"Gladly," Charles snapped.

Miss Tabitha Halliwell stared for a moment at her rapidly cooling bowl of soup, then fluttered to her feet,
Charles jumping up to pull back her chair. With a swish
of her voluminous silk shawl, she followed Lady Vanessa,
leaving James Prentice goggling from Sir Godfrey to the
major and back. That the London dandy had been guilty
of an outrageous breach of manners at the Abbey table
and then added to his faux pas by challenging his host
to what gave every appearance of a duel was quite the
most stimulating happening at the great house since one
or two of Neville's more memorable moments. James
Prentice felt a surge of excitement and anticipation. Sir
Godfrey had whiled away a number of hours at the
Abbey, practicing with his foil on the smooth expanse of
the ballroom floor, his movements a symphony of fluid
grace and elegant style which had drawn many a secre-
tive eye. There was no doubt Sir Godfrey Tyrone was a
master of the art of fencing. James Prentice bent to his
clear summer soup, hiding a smile. That great lunk of a
major, who so enjoyed casting his weight about the
Abbey, was in for a rude surprise.

While the ladies dined on trays in Vanessa's room, the
chandeliers and wall sconces were lit in the ballroom.
Charles Tyrone stared at the foil in his hand with rueful
interest. He had studied fencing nearly as long ago as he

ad handled a bow. The biggest question, however, was
not his skill but the intentions of Sir Godfrey Tyrone.
Had this impromptu fencing match been engineered so
his cousin might kill him? Or, more likely, to reveal him
as the awkward ox Godfrey thought him to be?

With a sigh Charles moved toward the center of the
ballroom, where his London cousin awaited him. No matter their foils were buttoned, the major did not care for
the look in the younger man's eyes.

"En garde!"

Hell and the Devil, Charles groaned. He was about to
be trounced.

"My lady, my lady," Alyce Downes cried, bursting into
Vanessa's room in a manner much at odds with the
proper behavior of a haughty London dresser, "Meecham says you must come at once. They are killing
each other!"

Vanessa's tray clattered to the floor as she sprang to
her feet. "But surely they are using buttoned foils,"
she cried.

"I know nothing," Downes declared. "Only what I am
told. You must come." Indeed, this was nearly the last
straw for Alyce Downes. Dressing her mistress in ugly
mourning gowns and clothes fit only for the sickroom
were not at all what she had expected when accepting a
position with the daughter of a duke.

The sight that met Vanessa's eyes when she opened
the door to the ballroom took her breath away. Nearly
every male in the Abbey ringed the walls, eyes fixed on
the center of the room. Clustered near the rear door,
which was the servants' entrance, was most of the female
staff as well. No wonder there had been no handy footman to open doors for her.

At the moment, thank goodness, Charles and Godfrey
were doing nothing worse than breathing hard, circling,
looking for an opening. There was little doubt they had
been at it for some time. A surprising development, as

Vanessa had seen Godfrey fence, and she would have expected his skill and agility to have bested the major in a trice.

And where had an engineer—a man beyond the outermost fringes of the *ton*—learned such an old-fashioned gentleman's skill as fencing?

And when would she stop expecting Charles Tyrone to be so much less than he was?

Fascinated, Vanessa concentrated on the combatants. For years she had heard the major's military history flaunted by the earl, his son, and grandson. But until now she had not truly thought Charles Tyrone dangerous. Nor had she ever been able to rise above the thought that Godfrey was a gnat, flitting about with his long slim foil, attempting to prove he had at least one manly skill. But now, as their lithe bodies—the one so much larger than the other—suddenly moved in a series of lightning-quick thrusts and parries, she saw a whole new facet of their personalities. Stripped down to white shirts, form-fitting black jersey pantaloons, stockinged feet, and grim expressions, they could only be called menacing. Barely civilized. Beyond logic or reason . . .

Godfrey lunged; the crowd gasped. A trickle of red appeared on the major's white shirtsleeve.

"No!" Vanessa cried. "Where is his button?"

"Whacked it off, my lady," said Sergeant Simmons. "Furious 'e was when the major got a hit."

"They must be stopped!"

"Can't, m'lady. Distract 'em and someone's like to get hisself killed. Including," the sergeant added pointedly, "the person what's trying to stop 'em."

Another wave of sound from the crowd. A streak of red blossomed on Godfrey's cheek. Sergeant Simmons grunted his pleasure. Vanessa realized Charles also must have rid himself of the guard on his foil. *Insanity!* She considered sending Jenkins and Fisher for buckets of water. After all, that ploy had worked once that day. But, no, it was doubtful they would return in time. And besides . . . she would not have been a proper chatelaine of Wyverne Abbey if the fate of the ballroom's exquisitely parqueted floors had not been of some concern. After all, she assured herself, the cousins could not actually be bent on killing each other.

Over the measles.

Charles's arm was bleeding sufficiently to drip blood onto the floor. It was his misfortune to be the one whose feet eventually encountered the slippery surface. His attempt to regain his balance while parrying a thrust from Sir Godfrey resulted in a hard fall straight onto his back. A general gasp went up around the room as the point of Godfrey's foil trembled at the major's throat.

Sergeant Simmons's hand closed around Lady Vanessa's arm, preventing her from running forward. "They 'ave to settle it, m'lady. And that there London dandy ain't goin' t' kill 'im in front of all of us, never fear."

Charles stared up at his cousin, his sangfroid firmly in place. "I am amazed I lasted so long," he declared. "You are indeed a master swordsman, Godfrey."

The glitter faded from the slighter man's eyes. "You are more competent than I expected, Cousin. Perhaps if we practiced together, I might be able to give you a pointer or two." After a deliberate flourish of his slender foil, which drew a shocked gasp from his audience, Sir Godfrey flicked his blade into a formal salute, then reached down a hand to help the major up.

A great sigh rippled around the ballroom. Just wait, Vanessa thought grimly. Just wait until the two men were cleaned up and bandaged. Just wait until she and Charles were alone on nightwatch in Julian's room . . .

Chapter Fourteen

*L*ater that night, after Elijah Pettibone had stomped out of the house, grumbling about the ways of the quality and remarking rather loudly that even the Earl of Wyverne couldn't get a doctor all the way from London in the middle of the night—and all this in spite of noticeable largesse from the major's own pocket—Charles took courage in hand and entered Julian's bedroom. In no mood to have his hair combed with a joint stool, he was of the opinion he'd rather go another round with Godfrey than take on that Arrogant Aristocrat, Lady Vanessa Rayne.

"Charles!" She bounded to her feet, eyes wide but unreadable in the dim light of a single candle flickering on the small table between the windows. "You should not have come. I can manage well enough alone for one night."

"A merest scratch," the major said, dismissing his injury. "And I thought it best to get your scold over with tonight, thus clearing the air for another glorious day at Wyverne Abbey."

"Sarcasm does not become you," Vanessa chided. "For heaven's sake, sit down. I shall ring for tea."

Charles groaned. "I have been plied with lashings of tea for the past hour, so unless you wish some yourself, pray be seated and tell me what part of a flea-brained idiot you believe me to be." He waved his good right arm toward the two comfortable chairs placed near the window. He could only hope his left, confined in a sling, made him look properly pathetic.

"Begin!" Charles intoned, as soon as they both were seated.

"It is plain," Vanessa told him primly, "that you are already aware of the outrageous nature of fighting a duel with a guest in your own household—"

"*My* household?" Charles murmured, raising his brows.

"I concede you are master here," Vanessa pronounced grudgingly. "Therefore it was your duty to put a stop to Godfrey's nonsense, preferably before it began. Certainly after he was so foolish as to have struck the button from his foil." Lady Vanessa drew a sharp breath and continued inexorably on, obviously having had some time to build up a torrent of rebuke. "You are no longer Major Charles Tyrone. You are, in effect, Wyverne and all that implies. You do not need to prove yourself against some man milliner who uses fencing to demonstrate his masculinity."

"Ah-h . . . but you make no allowance for temper," Charles told her softly. "Nor for a soldier's pride. Indeed, for any gentleman's honor. No man could have resisted Godfrey's challenge and been able to look himself in the mirror the next day."

"Nonetheless—"

"Nonetheless, it happened," Charles responded brusquely. "Right or wrong, it is over. And there's an end on it. I could say I hoped to discover something more about Godfrey in the course of our little contretemps, but, truthfully, I was too bullheaded to resist his challenge. You are right, and I was wrong. Enjoy this moment, my dear, for it's a rare day you'll ever hear those words again."

She could not stay angry with him, of course. Peeping from under her lashes, Vanessa could see he was watching her steadily, curious no doubt as to why her scold had been so mild. How could she tell him that, as she waited, her anger had dissipated in fear for his safety? In totally irrational terror that he would succumb to his "merest scratch" and be lost to all those who had come to depend on him. Including herself.

"I do not intend to scold you further," she told him in remarkably even tones. "Go to bed, Charles. It will not be the first time I have kept watch in this room alone."

"A soldier never deserts the field of battle. And besides"—Charles settled his shoulders into the high-backed chair—"I long ago learned to sleep anywhere. Wake me if you need me."

And with that he was asleep. Vanessa stared in amazement. Soldiers were indeed a strange breed.

The candle flickered, sending shadows over the major's face. He was more handsome asleep, she decided. More vulnerable. The hawk faded, dissolving into softer, telltale signs of the carefree young man he had been before going off to war. And, yes, she felt the magic of that evening in the maze. The infinite attraction of the kinder, gentler Charles whose gaze had stopped her heart, whose lips had bent to kiss her . . . on the cheek. Did he perhaps care for her a little, and not just for her manor and pounds sterling? Or did he care only for the Tyrone Company of Engineers and returning to his lowly position in *trade* as soon as possible?

Enough! Lips quivering, Lady Vanessa Rayne stood and walked to Julian's bed, gazing down at the restless boy, whose rash now covered half his body. Her loyalty must be to Wyverne Abbey and all those who had sheltered her for so long. Perhaps, if she were very fortunate, a solution would present itself to their present imbroglio, and she would be free to decide what course her life might take.

She must have acquired a touch of Julian's fever! Since when was a female ever allowed to decide her own fate?

She would, Vanessa vowed. She and Charles would solve the Abbey's current problems and then . . .

And then . . .

Automatically, Vanessa dipped a cloth in water and sponged Julian's fevered face and hands, carefully patting him dry with an embroidered linen towel. One thing at a time. One hour, one day, one week, one month. She would survive. But not in some blind cocoon, as she had before. In order for *all* her loved ones to get through this ordeal, she would have to be more vigilant, more assertive. More *masculine*. Vanessa had a strong flash of Lady Kitty turning over in her grave. Her own mother as well. And very likely Neville, who had flirted with only the most feminine of women. Ninnies all.

It had been such a temptation to let Charles Tyrone sap her of her strength, enticing her to be dependent on him. And, indeed, she had no intention of eschewing the comfort of his presence. But her moment with Arabella and the pitcher was a turning point. If the Abbey Tyrones were to survive, she must forget some of the rules by which she had been raised.

As Charles had done when he fought a duel against a man who was his cousin, his guest, and three stone lighter in weight.

Vanessa looked back at the sleeping major. After pulling up Julian's covers, she found an extra blanket and tucked it in around Charles. His right arm sneaked out, seized her wrist, the inside of which was suddenly, inexplicably, touching his lips, receiving a butterfly kiss so light she thought she must have dreamed it. Lady Vanessa snatched back her hand and stood, arms akimbo, glaring at the major. But he was sleeping peacefully, that naughty right arm now innocently clutching the blanket.

Thoughts awhirl, Vanessa sank down into Sally Vance's favorite chair. Although it was one of Julian's quieter nights, there was no question of catching a few winks of sleep. The major's kiss was still burning her wrist when dawn streaked the early morning sky.

All fifteen stone of the Right Reverend Ambrose Tyrone quivered with righteous indignation, looming over Lady Vanessa like the wrath of an Old Testament prophet. With warm memories of his prayers for Julian, she had rushed to the drawing room to greet him, moving forward with both hands outstretched in welcome. But her footsteps slowed, the glow faded from her eyes as she caught the bristling expression on his face. "Merciful heavens, Ambrose, what has happened?" Vanessa cried.

"Mama!" he spat out, turning on his heel for one more round over the path he had been wearing in the Abbey's fine Axminster carpet. "I tell you, my dear, I do not know my head from my heels. I honor her, I truly do, but there are times . . ." The vicar paused some twelve feet from Lady Vanessa, hands clasped behind his back. He drew a shuddering breath, obviously determined to calm his temper.

Vanessa, not for the first time, felt sorry for him. Ambrose should have married and rid himself of his mama long since. "Won't you sit down, Ambrose? I shall ring for tea." Lady Vanessa seated herself on the elegant Chippendale sofa Lady Kitty had had done up in leaf green satin brocade.

Although he refused the tea, Ambrose Tyrone walked slowly to an exquisitely needlepointed armchair and sat down, where he promptly leaned forward, his head bent nearly to his knees. The incongruity of it suddenly struck Vanessa. Before her was this giant of a man who was a mouse to his mother's cat. And in stark contrast was his cousin Godfrey, the seemingly effeminate exquisite who was a master fencer and who had not knuckled under to his invalid mother's whining demands in all the time she had known him.

"Mother is right about one thing," the vicar declared

at last, sitting up and placing his hands decisively on his knees. "We must be married at once."

"Ambrose"—Vanessa did not bother to stifle her groan—"you know quite well I will not marry you. We are not suited. I cannot imagine myself as a vicar's wife, a bishop's wife, nor even an archbishop's wife. I am totally unsuited for such an honor. Believe me, Ambrose, there are a great many good women out there who would be delighted to have you. I fear . . . I *know* I am not one of them."

"But you *must,* you see," Ambrose declared. "I am perfectly aware the timing is poor, Nessa. I planned to avoid the issue until all was right and tight with Julian. Hence, my annoyance with mama. But you must admit she has her ear to the village gossip. And she tells me you have been hopelessly compromised, my dear, and must be married immediately."

"How so?" Lady Vanessa demanded.

"It is bad enough you have been living under the same roof with the major," the vicar intoned, "but now we hear you have been spending the night with him in Julian's bedchamber. Shocking, Vanessa. Totally shocking."

"Good God, you cannot possibly—"

"The entire village is abuzz with it. There can be no doubt Lower Wyverne is shocked to the core."

"Fine," she heard herself say, though in scathing tones. "Then it seems it is the major I must marry."

Ambrose Tyrone shot to his feet. "Oh, no, no, no, my dear. Never think it. You have not heard the whole."

The whole? Vanessa clamped her jaws tight and waited for enlightenment.

The vicar resumed his pacing, head down, hands behind his back. "This is not fit for your delicate ears," he muttered, "but I suppose I must, stubborn chit that you are." When he reached the fringe of the Axminister, he turned abruptly and came back, his scowl deepening with every step. He paused in front of her, staring down with such disapprobation Vanessa could only wonder what more she had done to incite his ire.

Ambrose Tyrone's lower lip was close to a pout before he finally said, "You recall Betty Miller, the little seamstress who helps Mrs. Blythe?" Vanessa nodded. Betty Miller was a mousy little thing who wouldn't say boo to a goose, a young woman of limited intelligence who had been fortunate to find a position with the local mantua maker, for it was doubtful she could ever manage a household on her own. "Well," Ambrose huffed, "it seems she is in an—ah—delicate condition." He paused, eyed Lady Vanessa with some trepidation.

"I am sorry for it," she said, considerably puzzled, "but what can this possibly have to do with me, other than giving the village another topic of conversation?"

The vicar cleared his throat, assumed his most lugubrious expression. "It is said Major Charles Tyrone is the father."

Shock was followed seconds later by hilarity. The vicar stared in amazement as Lady Vanessa Rayne laughed until tears ran down her cheeks. Ambrose spluttered, attempting a few words over her laughter, then comprehension dawned. The poor girl was hysterical. He proffered his handkerchief, then rang for Meecham, demanding Lady Vanessa's maid. No sense trying to pursue his interest with her at the moment. He was, nonetheless, well satisfied with his efforts at the Abbey. After uttering a few more platitudes, to which no one paid the slightest attention, Ambrose took himself off. Vanessa was still wiping her eyes when Charles thundered full tilt into the drawing room, having been informed that something queer was going on there. Waving Downes away with a look which sent the dresser scampering out of the room, Charles sat down next to Vanessa. Taking both her hands in his, he urged her to tell him what was wrong.

Which sent her into another fit of the giggles. Dear God, his eyes were so full of concern, he looked . . .

adorable. Vanessa blew her nose, peeped at him from under her misted lashes. "Charles, as much as I am enjoying your solicitude, I must tell you I am laughing."

"You're *what*?" He jerked her closer, peering into her reddened eyes.

For a moment her head reeled, then Vanessa drew back, settling her hands primly in her lap, and the whole tale came pouring out. "If it had been anyone else," she concluded, "I might have considered the possibility. But poor Betty Miller? Never! I suppose Lady Horatia was forced to take advantage of the only young woman available in that condition—which means that Betty must certainly be increasing and will need help, for she cannot manage on her own," Lady Vanessa added as an aside to herself. "But imagine the dashing Major Tyrone with Betty Miller I could not."

"But if it had been Tess Tanner, you would have boxed my ears?" Charles inquired blandly, naming the buxom tavern wench at the Bull and Bear.

Vanessa shrugged. "I was raised, however negligently, by Neville and Kitty Tyrone. I have few illusions."

"For your information," Charles declared most awfully, "I do not bed tavern wenches, even ones as inviting as Tess Tanner. And, no," he added, holding up his hand as Vanessa opened her mouth, "do not ask me the obvious, for I shall not answer it."

Lady Vanessa subsided into silence, ruthlessly forcing her thoughts back to the problem at hand, for she discovered there were certain things she truly did not wish to know. "That awful woman," she muttered. "What will she think of next? Truly, I begin to wonder if her eccentricity is not leaning toward madness."

Glad enough to escape the murky waters into which they had ventured, Charles took his time in answering. "There is one thing we cannot question," he conceded. "Lady Horatia wants you to marry her son. The combination of your ancestry and your wealth would ensure him high advancement in the church. We also know she brought those measle-ridden children to visit Julian. I cannot credit that as a coincidence—"

"Lady Vanessa . . . Major." Poised just inside the drawing room door, Meecham—his face even more inscrutable than usual—cleared his throat and announced, "Lady Clorinda Tyrone and Mr. Bertram Taggart."

Stunned by the sight of Lady Clorinda, the self-professed invalid who could seldom be coaxed to leave her townhouse on Portman Square, Vanessa did not at first notice that lady's companion, even though the mother of Godfrey and Arabella required his arm to lean upon as she made her way into the room, obviously exhausted by the long journey from town. Yet, in spite of her claim to invalidism, Lady Clorinda Tyrone maintained her reputation as a picture of classic English beauty, so much a feminine version of her son's exquisite features that she could easily have passed for his elder sister. Vanessa recalled hearing Lady Kitty once complain, rather spitefully, that Clorinda seldom left the house because of the trouble it took to turn her into the girl she had been at twenty.

For traveling from London, Lady Clorinda wore a startlingly inappropriate gown of peach silk, with alternating flounces of silk and lace, decorated by long thin trails of white satin ribbon. Her décolletage, dipping to an expanse of bosom usually found only in the ballroom, or perhaps the boudoir, was partially concealed by a white shawl shot with silver. Yet, Vanessa had to admit, Lady Clorinda's attire admirably set off her blond beauty and dainty figure while enhancing the ethereal aura she cultivated so carefully.

As Lady Clorinda tottered toward the sofa, guided by the stout arm of her male companion, Vanessa stood speechless. She was quite certain she had managed words of greeting for the unexpected guests, but she had no recollection of what she had said. Or of jumping to her feet, vacating the brocade sofa for the alleged invalid's use. She did, however, have a sharp vision of the major's eyes narrowing in sudden avid speculation. What did he see that she did not?

Lady Clorinda sank onto the couch. "My vinaigrette," she gasped, raising her eyes to her companion. "No, no, Bertie, perhaps my hartshorn," she amended in fading accents. "Dear, dear Bertie, so good," she murmured, as Mr. Taggart swiftly produced both of the required items. "So-o fatiguing," Lady Clorinda sighed, when she had had recourse to both restoratives. "I cannot believe I have actually journeyed so far. But my poor dear child, my precious Arabella—how could I allow her to suffer without her mama at her side? So I have come," she added with a dramatic flourish of her hand, raising her wide blue eyes to Vanessa. "I knew you would be happy to have my support, my dear."

Polite manners demanded that Vanessa return a socially acceptable response. Unfortunately, she was not at all sure she could manage it. And, far from giving her support, the major was, she suspected, fully occupied controlling either his laughter or his outrage. For no one in their right mind, even someone unacquainted with Lady Clorinda Tyrone, could possibly assume she would go anywhere near her daughter's sickroom. They were, in fact, being forced to add one more invalid—not to mention a perfect stranger—to a household already teeming with disaster.

Lady Vanessa pasted a smile on her face, said the necessary words, accepted her introduction to Mr. Bertram Taggart with her slightest, most regal, nod. Charles— infamous traitor that he was—stepped forward with a ready will to bow to Lady Clorinda and offer Mr. Taggart a firm handshake. Could he not see these people were not wanted? Could he not speak the magic words sending them back to London? Certainly there were enough evil spectres in the house—measles, poison, apoplexy, unexplained accidents—to frighten off a regiment of cavalry.

Lady Vanessa gritted her teeth and took herself in hand. Neither Charles nor she could turn a mother away from a sick child, even if it was doubtful Lady Clorinda would come closer than peering through the doorway of Arabella's room. And Bertram Taggart? While Charles assumed the conversational burden, Vanessa studied the stranger. As far as she could tell, he was simply another in a long series of men attracted to Clorinda Tyrone's helplessness, beauty, and remarkably generous widow's portion. Lady Clorinda was well known for having cicisbeos in an era when such platonic gallants had gone out of fashion. That she chose masculine men, consistently the opposite of her son in looks, build, and temperament, was one of London's most delicious *on dits*. As was the intriguing tidbit that she was inclined to choose as her companions gentlemen closer to her son's age than to her own. Mr. Bertram Taggart was no different, Vanessa speculated. Perhaps a bit more carelessly dressed than Clorinda's usual escorts, a bit sharper of face, his dark hair and tanned skin making an intriguing contrast to his companion's pale loveliness.

Vanessa could not, however, approve of the gleam she thought she caught at the back of Mr. Taggart's dark brown eyes. This was a man who might not wish to drift off into the pale when Lady Clorinda tired of him. Certainly, there was enough wealth in the London Tyrone family to make the widow an enticing attraction. Vanessa, who had had little opportunity to be a country innocent, could not help but wonder if this was the man who had finally gotten beyond Lady Clorinda's bedroom door.

Unfortunately, at that moment she glanced at the major, only to discover his all-knowing gaze fixed on her. Certain he could read her far-from-maidenly thoughts, Lady Vanessa Rayne was caught by a furious blush. After mumbling some inanity about how hot the day was, she suggested Lady Clorinda might wish to retire to her room for a rest before the ordeal of viewing her only daughter struck down by the measles. Perhaps a tray of ratafia and biscuits to further her recovery?

Charles neatly stepped in, offering Mr. Taggart something stronger if he would care to step into the study. Vanessa did not appreciate his gesture. Gracious hospitality was not the approach she would have preferred for Mr. Bertram "dear Bertie" Taggart.

Chapter Fifteen

*T*hen *it seems it is the major I must marry.* Impossible as it seemed, those words had actually issued from her mouth.

Vanessa sat beneath the scantily draped Venus in the center of the maze, her chin resting on fingers so tightly clasped her knuckles showed white. Humiliating, that's what it was. Ducal daughters did not marry men who earned their own living, even if caught in flagrante delicto. Compromising situations were smoothed over with copious lashings of money. The encroaching pretender discreetly disappeared, and the lady's reputation was somehow miraculously restored.

Alas, there was no way Lady Vanessa Rayne could fit Major Charles Tyrone into this classic situation. So far from encroaching was he that he gave every indication he could scarcely wait to regain his freedom, to go jaunting off to whatever project would offer to pay him for his services. She shuddered.

And what was so shocking about a man earning his living? Vanessa glanced accusingly at the statue, for surely the voice echoing through her head could not be her own. Was a clergyman's office not called "a living"? Soldiering was an acceptable occupation, and they, too, were paid. And many a younger son worked in government or the law.

Yet even in the army, she knew, engineers were merely

tolerated by the fighting regiments, always well down on the social scale from the officers of the cavalry, even the infantry. And to work as an engineer when a *civilian*, to exchange one's labor—however skilled—for pay was to engage in trade. For all his prestigious ancestry, Charles Tyrone was a *cit*. And mockery of cits was an art long practiced in the Tyrone family. Neville, Kitty, Godfrey, Lady Horatia, even Uncle 'Vester on occasion, were particularly adept at it. Vanessa had never questioned their point of view, as it was as pervasive among the *haut ton* as the smug certainty that the British upper class was just that much better than the wealthy and powerful of other countries.

But what if Uncle 'Vester agreed that she had been compromised? What if he insisted on her marriage to Charles?

Vanessa very much feared she would go, smiling, to her fate.

There! She had admitted it. Dratted man. If only she could cure him of his love for building things. Convince him that life at Beechwood with her would be enough to fulfill his dreams . . .

"Ah, I thought this might be where you'd hidden yourself." The object of her thoughts appeared in the opening of the dark green boxwood and rapidly closed the short distance to her side. Impeccably dressed in a claret-colored jacket and buff pantaloons, Hessians shining, sun-kissed hair gleaming, and his sling now relegated to the drawer, Charles Tyrone was, Vanessa had to admit, breathtaking.

Without so much as a by-your-leave, he seated himself beside her on the marble bench. Vanessa fought a moment of pure panic. Whenever he was this close, her brains became as scrambled as her morning eggs. "Needed to escape, did you?" the major continued. "I could not agree more heartily. Yet I believe you agree we cannot rid ourselves of the woman . . . nor of her companion."

Three eventful days had passed since Lady Clorinda's arrival. As expected, she had cooed to her poor dear Bella from the doorway of the bedchamber, then wavered off, supported by Mr. Taggart, in search of a restorative. Fortunately, however, both measles-ridden youngsters seemed to be on the mend, none of the feared complications having reared their ugly heads. "Almost out of the woods," Nanny Vance had chortled an hour earlier. Sergeant Simmons had flashed an enormous smile. Was it possible, Vanessa wondered, that the Fates were smiling on the Tyrones at long last?

"I believe we may readjust our sleeping habits," Charles ventured. "It would seem Fielding should be able to handle the night watch from now on. And I'm told Arabella's maid has a good head on her shoulders. We may cut back some of the extra help, I think." He raised his brows in polite query.

Vanessa offered him a smile of pure camaraderie. They had endured much together. "Though it is midafternoon and I have just finished breakfast," she admitted. "I look forward to returning to my bed in darkness." And then her well-bred "stiff upper lip" crumbled. For a moment she looked away, tongue-tied by the emotions which coursed through her. Joy, relief, triumph . . . and some nameless thing she very much feared might be love. "We've done it, Charles," she declared. "I do believe we've done it."

"I think . . ." Charles murmured, leaning close, "a small celebration is in order. Do you not agree?"

He could not possibly mean what she thought he—

But his lips were coming closer, so close they filled her world. The scent of him—exotic and indefinable—filled her mind, overwhelming her senses. At first his lips were as gentle as the butterfly kiss he had placed on her wrist, but, perhaps when he discovered so willing a partner, the pressure increased. In truth, the major seemed to put his whole soul into that kiss, one arm creeping around her waist, the other more possessive, encompassing her shoulders and drawing her close.

But how could she believe him? A tiny thread of Vanessa's previous thoughts forced its way through the dizzying pleasure. Head reeling, she broke away. "Have you decided to find the heiress appealing after all, Major?" she inquired. *Dear God,* how could she have said such a thing? Yet she had never been a beauty, and most of the time she had spent with Charles Tyrone she had been a bedraggled wreck, rushing between three sickrooms, falling into exhaustion, and snapping at everyone in sight. He could not care for her. It was impossible.

And, besides, he was quite, quite ineligible.

For the better part of a minute, Charles remained frozen to the bench. Then, slowly, with a grace a king might have envied, he got to his feet. "I may decide," he intoned, looking down his rugged nose, "that the difficulties at the Abbey have rendered your brain as topsy-turvy as our days. Then again, I may not. Good day, ma'am." The major turned on his heel and stalked off, quickly disappearing among the tall boxwood hedges.

An hour later Lady Vanessa Rayne still sat beneath the shadow of the goddess of Love. Too devastated to cry, she sat with bowed head, contemplating what appeared to be her enormous sins. She sat through teatime, through the dressing bell for dinner—even when Meecham brought a large Chinese gong outside and gave it two sharp whacks, obviously intended just for her.

She had just ruined her life, and she doubted the Rayne pride was going to allow her to do anything about it.

She was a fool. And would continue to be one. For there was no way she could convince herself Major Charles Tyrone had an interest in anything but her dowry.

Eventually—well aware that Meecham would soon instigate a search party—Vanessa was forced to leave the maze. After a cold collation in her room, she sat on her window seat, opened the mullioned casement window, and gazed out over the darkening landscape. Only the chill of the deepest part of the night brought her to a realization of the time. When she sought her bed at last, her mind was still as numb as it had been when she had broken away from Charles's kiss. It had been necessary, of course . . . but surely it was quite the worst thing she had ever done in her life.

"Glum as a smuggler down to his last keg," the Earl of Wyverne declared, eyeing the major with something close to his former shrewdness. "What's toward, boy? Clorinda putting on too many of her die-away airs? Come, come, where's the smiling face I saw only yesterday? Horse go lame? Horatia join the menagerie below?"

Shaking his head, Charles proffered a rueful smile.

"Well, boy," Sylvester Tyrone barked, "you'd best tell me, else I'll fidget m'self to death wondering what you're hiding. Just because you humor an old man by *consulting* with me every morning don't mean you're doing more than being kind. So out with it! What ain't you telling me?"

For a long moment Charles sat, head down, hands dangling between his knees. After forcing himself to look up into the gray eyes so like his own, he asked softly, "Do you truly wish a match between Lady Vanessa and myself?"

The gray eyes widened. "I do," the earl declared. "Making things difficult, is she?" When the firm line of the major's lips did not part in reply, Sylvester nodded. "Afraid of that," he admitted. "Came here, a princess born, and I did naught but encourage her."

"You'd think I was her bootmaker!" Charles burst out. "The second footman . . . or a groom. And to top it all, the lofty chit seems to think I'm after her dowry!"

"Well, ain't you?" the earl demanded. "Demmed fool if you're not!"

Charles groaned. "That's just it, my lord. When you first mentioned marriage, it was easy enough to fling the dowry back in your face. Then I met Vanessa,"—Charles ran his hands through his hair—"I thought her plain, unappealing, and the most arrogant woman I'd ever met. We fought over Julian, over the running of the Abbey like cat and dog over the last scrap of meat." The major paused, shook his head. "And then, almost insidiously, I began to see her worth. Worse yet, she even began to appear attractive. That's when I told myself it must be her dowry pulling the wool over my eyes, making me see what wasn't there."

"True," the earl sighed, " 'tis hard to separate the girl from what goes with her. But that's what marriage means in our class, boy. A man must always keep an eye on what will line his pockets. Never forget duty to the family, to those who come after. Love flies off, don't y' know, but land and money in the funds will see your sons and your sons' sons live the way gentlemen should."

"My lord, I was once a cynic about love," Charles returned quietly. "I now look back on that time with something akin to nostalgia. Halcyon days, indeed. I fear they are gone forever."

"Ah-h, that's good, then," the earl breathed.

"Good?" Charles roared. "Are you mad?"

"She's a fine girl, Nessa. Just needed the right man to appreciate her. One strong enough to keep her from ruling the roost. You'll do, boy, you'll do. Whatever you've quarreled about will pass. In time she'll come to appreciate what she has in you."

"She does not have me," Charles declared through clenched teeth.

The old man chuckled. "Fortunately, you are both fixed under this roof for some time to come. Propinquity, boy. Propinquity. If you can't beat out an ox of a clergy-

man or a wisp of a city dandy, then you must have left
the Charles Tyrone I thought I knew back on the
Peninsula."

The major grumbled a few Spanish curses beneath his
breath, which only caused the Earl of Wyverne to grin
more broadly. "Love is a damnable thing," the old man
declared, "but sweetened by land and money, it's like
the scent of honey to a bear. Be reconciled, Charles. You
can't escape your fate."

The major shot to his feet, performed a stiff mockery
of a bow. "My lord." The earl was still chuckling as
Charles shut the door, none too gently, behind him.

In the wee hours of the following morning Peter Fielding—Neville Tyrone's former valet who had so kindly
offered his services to the deceased Viscount Sherbourne's only son—got up from Nanny Vance's comfortable chair in Julian's bedchamber. Quietly, he opened
the casement window, then retrieved a rope which he
had hidden earlier beneath the bed. After firmly at-
taching the rope to one of the tall posters, he ran it
across the floor and dropped the remainder out the open
window. Then, with great stealth, he picked up one of
the armchairs and propped it against the door. It
wouldn't hold for long, but long enough was all that mat-
tered. If there had been a key, he would have taken a
chance on Corporal Hart hearing the *snick* as he locked
it. Unfortunately, Major Tyrone—blast him—had pock-
eted the key the night the boy was poisoned. Julian Tyrone should have died that night—hadn't he given him
enough arsenic to kill a horse?—but the major and that
miserable chit, Lady Vanessa, with the aid of that old
witch, Sally Vance, had made mincemeat of his plans.

Boy had more lives than a damned cat. Should have
died in the wreck like his pa. Or of the measles. Or
something. Killing Julian Tyrone with his bare hands was
not what he would like, but nothing else seemed to work.
Well, tonight there'd be no doubt. He'd finish the boy

off right and tight and collect his pay at last. Off on the next ship to the Americas, he'd be. With money in his pocket, he'd have the world by the tail.

Fielding eyed the jumble of pillows on Julian's bed with sudden interest. He should have thought of pillows before. No marks of strangulation round the boy's throat. He might even be able to pass off the death as natural, a sudden succumbing to the many trials which had beset the lad. Yes, the pillow was a fine idea. That way he didn't actually have to touch the boy. After all, he was not unaware of the enormity of his betrayal. But gold in his pockets and a chance for a new life were more temptation than most mortal men could bear. Peter Fielding, having reasoned himself into a killing frame of mind, picked up the plumpest goose-feather pillow.

Out in the hallway Corporal John Hart was growing bored. He and Hugh Davies had alternated night duty for weeks now while Luke Simmons snored, taking full advantage of his rank. During the many nights the boy was truly ill there had been a good deal of coming and going, enough to stave off boredom. But in the past few days, with the major and Lady Vanessa sleeping the night through in their own beds and nary a sound from the bedchamber, the hours passed slowly. Once or twice, he'd almost caught himself asleep on his feet. A shooting offense if he'd been caught thus on picket in the Peninsula. Corporal Hart squared his shoulders, patted the deep pocket in which he kept a pistol and a knife, and strained to stand taller than his best height which brought the top of his head only to the major's shoulder.

At first he thought nothing of the faint sounds from inside the bedchamber. Being accustomed to people moving around, he only noticed them because it had been perfectly quiet so far tonight. Odd sounds. Grunts? An exclamation of some kind? For a moment Corporal Hart stared at the solid oak door. He put his ear to it. A faint thud, as if some object hit the floor. A stifled cry. John Hart grabbed the doorknob and pushed. The door opened only a crack. Putting his shoulder to it, he shoved with all his might. The door ground back, something large slowing its progress.

Later, he would tell an avid audience in the kitchen that the sight which met his eyes fair froze his bones. Julian lying limply on his bed, the window wide open, a stout rope, and that villain Peter Fielding disappearing like a puff of smoke. But at the time, after one swift glance round the room, he had gone straight to the bed where Julian had cast aside the pillow and was struggling to sit up.

"Damn him!" the young viscount cried, gasping for breath. "Tried to kill me. Fielding. After him, John!"

But when the former corporal looked out the window, there was no sign of anything except the rope slowly swinging in the breeze.

"If y' hadn't been strong enough to fight him off—" the corporal began, then thought better of it. Bad enough he'd have to tell the major the boy had nearly died on his watch. If Julian hadn't fought back, attempted to cry out, knocked his ever-waiting mug of water to the floor, there would have been no sound. And Corporal John Hart, blasted idiot that he was, would still be standing in the corridor, guarding a dead man. The thought was enough to turn his blood to ice.

Well, he wasn't such a fool he'd leave the boy while he went to fetch the major. Corporal Hart took a deep breath and set up a holler that soon roused the house. By the time the story was told, it was generally agreed both young men were heros. And Major Charles Tyrone felt the most incompetent ass in the history of the world.

Lady Vanessa Rayne was inclined to agree with him.

Chapter Sixteen

Major Charles Tyrone, arriving at The Bull and Bear some thirty minutes past the appointed hour of his assignation, turned Rojo over to the ostler, tossed a friendly nod to Jed Tanner, the publican, and headed straight toward a private dining room at the rear of the inn. As he opened the door, his cousin Ambrose bounded to his feet, in full cry against the major's tardiness.

"It is about time you showed yourself, Major," the vicar intoned. "I wish you to know I am unaccustomed to cooling my heels in such a fashion."

Charles raised his brows. "Did Jed Tanner not see you had all you wished to eat and drink?"

"Ah, indeed he did," drawled Sir Godfrey from a small settee on which he was comfortably sprawled, idly twirling a snifter of brandy. "So much so, I wondered if you were waiting for us to mellow into proper malleability."

Charles removed his beaver, stripped off his gloves, carelessly tossing them, along with his riding crop, onto a serving table. "Perhaps I simply enjoy making a grand entrance," he murmured provocatively, as he poured a measure of brandy from the decanter arranged invitingly on the central dining table.

"You're not Wyverne yet," Ambrose declared with considerable heat, "and why we should be gudgeons

enough to meet you here just as if you had the right to
send for—"

"Sit down, Ambrose!" Godfrey snapped, his customary lazy mockery gone in a flash. " 'Tis plain enough why
we're here. Who but the eldest Tyrone cousins should
our dear major call to a council of war?"

"By what right—" Ambrose sputtered.

"By every right," Godfrey told him. "And try not to repeat
yourself. This is not Sunday morning, dear Cuz, and you have
no license to maunder on, belaboring a point long past its
prime. I have spoken with Wyverne. Our cousin Charles acts
in his name, not solely by the old man's decree but by virtue
of legal papers, properly signed and witnessed. If you had an
ounce of gumption, you would have made inquiries yourself. To all intents and purposes, he *is* Wyverne."

"Mother says it cannot be so," Ambrose countered
pugnaciously, "that he tricked Wyverne into it, and
therefore the papers cannot be legal."

"Don't be any more of a fool than you already are,"
Godfrey sighed. "Be a man, Ambrose. Sit down, be
quiet, and listen."

Charles, who had followed this exchange with considerable interest, murmured his thanks to Sir Godfrey before seating himself in a comfortable armchair placed at
the head of the dining table. The vicar, finding himself
the only one standing, eyed the door, but both his cousins
knew he was merely posturing. There was no way the
vicar of Lower Wyverne was going to leave the room
without finding out why they were there. With an audible
sniff of dissatisfaction, Ambrose Tyrone finally lowered
his bulk into a wingchair near the settee.

Charles took a sip of brandy, never taking his eyes off
his cousins. Now that the moment had come, he could
better appreciate how Wellington must have felt just before a battle. All the old clichés milled through his mind.
Had he bitten off more than he could chew? Had he
jumped feet first into a quagmire?

The major settled his snifter onto the stout pine table.

"There can no longer be any doubt," he pronounced. "Someone is trying to kill Julian. I also have reason to believe Neville's death may not have been an accident. Word has come that the man involved in driving the pig into his path left the village that same day and has not been seen since. And, given the enormity of the disaster and the earl's deteriorating health these past few years, his apoplexy was almost a foregone conclusion."

"I take it Fielding has disappeared?" Godfrey interjected.

"Gone on the wind," Charles ground out. That the thrice-bedamned villain had gotten away, and all his knowledge with him, was the darkest point of what was turning into very dire mystery indeed.

"And you wish our help in apprehending the villain?" Ambrose said with some alarm. "Not really my line of work, Major, I assure you. Wish to help, of course, but I was never good at puzzles, don't you know. Mother says—"

"Stubble it!" This time Sir Godfrey was close to shouting.

Silence vibrated. The vicar's jaw quivered. The major took another swallow of brandy. Thank God for French vineyards and English smugglers.

"We are here tonight," Charles continued softly, "because logic dictates that one of the three of us is guilty."

Ambrose stared. "Guilty of what?"

"Murder," Godfrey told him.

The vicar sat as if stunned. Though far from unintelligent, he could not seem to take in the major's words. "*Impossible!*" he whispered at last. "You're mad, the pair of you. Fit for Bedlam."

"I think not," Charles said, watching both his cousins with extreme vigilance. "We three are the only ones with sufficient motive. I've seen men killed for a shilling. Wyverne is a very wealthy man, and the title is both ancient and honorable. A prime plum for someone with ambition and no scruples."

"*You* are closest to the title," Ambrose crowed. "Why look any farther?"

"Because I happen to know I didn't do it," Charles replied evenly. "Therefore . . ." He allowed his voice to trail away, opening a Pandora's box into which no one really wished to look.

"And I know I did not do it," said Godfrey. "And, as much as I would like to believe this great lummox of a cousin a betrayer of his cloth, I'm inclined to doubt his guilt as well. Therefore, my dear Charles, we have a dilemma. If not we, then who?"

"As if declaring your innocence were enough!" Ambrose Tyrone roared. "A murderer can scarcely fall back on the word of a gentleman." Godfrey's feet hit the floor as he sat upright on the settee. The vicar came half out of his armchair.

"There *is* another possibility," Charles ventured. Both men subsided into their respective seats, eyes fixed on the major in cautious interest.

"Our mothers," Charles murmured, so softly both men had to strain to hear him.

He and Sir Godfrey tensed their muscles, preparing to spring out of the way of the vicar's bull-like charge. To their surprise, Ambrose hung his head. In the silence the cheerful sounds wafting from the taproom seemed incongruous.

"The measles," Ambrose moaned. "You are thinking of that disaster with the measles."

"You cannot doubt it was contrived," Charles told him.

The vicar shook his head. "I—I know I have overlooked many things simply because she is my mother. I know 'tis said I'm under the cat's paw, but I swear to you, on this matter I remonstrated with her at some length. She swears she had no idea Julian had not had the measles, but I confess I cannot find her motive pure. I am sorry . . . so very sorry."

"And the rest of it?" Godfrey prodded. "The poison, the accidents?"

For a moment the baronet's glance caught the major's, acknowledging that he had indeed been busy asking questions since his arrival at the Abbey. If, of course, Charles mused, Godfrey did not have more sinister reasons for knowing about the incidents.

The vicar's head flew up, his broad shoulders straightening in indignation. "Out of the question!" he declared. "Mama is a difficult woman, but she would never stoop—"

"Anyone who would stoop to giving a sick boy the measles would stoop to anything," Charles declared, his tone menacing enough to send a shiver down his cousin's spine.

Godfrey, who had been looking more and more thoughtful, spoke up. "I suppose you're thinking of Taggart," he said to the major.

"The thought crossed my mind."

"But he has no reason—" Godfrey mused.

"He does, if he is acting at your mother's instigation," Charles pointed out.

Godfrey didn't move a muscle except to say, very quietly, "You wish another fencing lesson, cousin?"

"Indeed not," the major replied easily. "I am merely indicating all the possibilities in this Gordian knot of disasters."

"What about *your* mother?" Ambrose Tyrone demanded. "You are closest to the title."

"By all means, let us not leave my mother out," Charles agreed, all amiability. "She was widowed quite young, I fear. And shortly after I joined the army, she married the scion of a banking family who was being sent to Canada to set up a branch of the business in Toronto. I think we may safely say she is well out of this discussion."

"If only that dastard Fielding had not got away," the vicar sighed, stating the obvious.

"You have given us considerable food for thought, major," Godfrey admitted. "Either one of the three of us is a murderer. Or Ambrose's mother. Or mine. A sobering prospect."

"If you can think of anyone else with a motive, I should be glad to hear it," Charles said.

"Amen," intoned the vicar.

Lady Vanessa Rayne nocked an arrow, raised her bow, pulled the bowstring back past her nose, and let fly. The arrow whanged into the outermost circle of the target butt, drooping slightly, as if mocking the lack of force in her release. The next one fell to earth at the base of the target. The third sailed off into the woods. In a fit of temper, she got off three more in rapid succession. None came within a foot of her customary bull's-eye.

Slinging her quiver to the ground, Vanessa stalked back to a wooden bench at the edge of the clearing, her bow clattering as she tossed it down beside her. Just when she had thought the sun was shining on the Abbey once again—when Julian and Arabella showed strong signs of making a complete recovery and even Uncle 'Vester was much more akin to his former self—they had been given notice that Julian was well and truly under attack. His danger was not a figment of their overactive imaginations, but a dire problem requiring immediate solution.

And now—when she most needed to confer with Charles—the entire household had become aware she had not traded more than an absolute necessity of words with the major for the past three days. And last night the three cousins had sneaked off to the tavern, deliberately excluding her from whatever occurred at such an extraordinary private conference. They had to have been discussing Julian, of course. Yet, always before, Charles had conferred with *her*. Even when their words were heated, she and he had dealt with the Abbey's problems together. Now . . . now Julian had suffered a direct attack, and she was shut out. Relegated to a woman's world. Unfit to partake in "men's affairs."

You wanted no part of Charles's world, Vanessa reminded herself. Indeed, she had made that all too clear when he had kissed her in the maze. Yet here she was, brooding about Charles Tyrone when she should be concentrating on a way to save Julian. Life with Neville, Kitty, and an indulgent Uncle 'Vester had not prepared her for the vicissitudes which had come upon them. Charles said she had done well, but Julian had now narrowly escaped death four times—if one counted the measles, which she surely must.

Undoubtedly, she should have managed better.

Charles should have managed better.

Oh, very well, she knew he was devastated by the latest incident. He put forth a face of stone, but Vanessa never doubted he blamed himself. *Fielding.* Of all people, Peter Fielding, Neville's trusted valet. She still had difficulty believing it.

"Go away," Vanessa declared without looking up as her bow moved and a large body took its place.

"In the house you flit from room to room, perpetually surrounded by a bevy of people. The only way I can speak with you is to track you down in the wild like a hunter intent on his prey. "

"I am no one's prey," she replied with asperity.

"Of course you are not," Charles soothed with suspicious humility. "I have erred, as usual. I beg your pardon."

Vanessa sniffed. "As long as you are here, you may tell me what was discussed at the Bull and Bear last night."

"Bothers you, does it?"

"You have a private meeting with the two men most likely to prefer Julian dead, and you think it should not bother me?"

"You feared for my safety. I am touched."

"I did not—" Vanessa broke off, realizing that fear

for his safety was indeed a goodly portion of her turbulent thoughts.

"In truth, that is why I'm here." With rapid clarity, Charles summed up his meeting with Ambrose and Godfrey.

When he was finished, Vanessa nodded slowly. "I can believe Lady Horatia capable of anything," she told him. "But how . . . ?"

"There's the rub," Charles agreed. "Unless she has some dirty dish relatives on her side of the family whom she has enlisted in her machinations, I cannot picture how she might have arranged Neville's accident."

"Fielding could not have managed it?"

"From what you've told me, Fielding was hired after Sherbourne went back to town. Lady Horatia never met him until after the accident, when he came to the Abbey with Julian."

"As far as we know," Vanessa muttered darkly. "So," she ventured after a few moments of cogitation, "Lady Clorinda is a more likely suspect because she has Taggart."

"Exactly. Taggart has attached himself to a wealthy widow, one capable of financing his every vice in return for . . ." The major broke off, strawberry red suffusing his usually stoic features. "That is—ah—he wishes to please her . . . would do anything for her."

"Even murder?" Vanessa inquired softly, rather charmed by his discomfort. As if she were too innocent to know that, on occasion, wealthy women were exceptionally generous with the younger men they took to their beds.

"Even murder," Charles agreed. "Like Cassius, he has a lean and hungry look."

The thought that Lady Clorinda, the languid invalid who had never showed an interest in anything beyond her own comfort, could manipulate a lover into murder—even for the sake of her son's inheriting an earldom—

was too much for Vanessa's credulity. "You do not think Ambrose or Godfrey—"

"I fear I must assume them all guilty until proven otherwise. Along with anyone else whose services might be bought." Charles sighed, his voice changed timbre, becoming low and intimate. "Vanessa?"

"Yes?" Her head whirled, her stomach muscles quivered. If only she could show him how much she regretted her reaction in the maze. And, no matter the cold dictates of society, Vanessa regretted it bitterly.

"We must declare a truce, I think," Charles said. "If we are to save Julian, we must work closely together, for you are truly the only family member I can fully trust."

"Of course," Vanessa heard herself say.

"We'll have much to say to each other when this is over," Charles told her. "And it *will* be over, Nessa. I promise you we will discover who the dastard is. And settle this matter once and for all."

He wasn't going to make another attempt to kiss her. She had hoped for a second chance, but why should he when she had treated him so badly? Ducal daughters were not the only ones with pride.

"Truce," she agreed. Lady Vanessa Rayne stood up, reached out a hand. "My bow, if you please." Solemnly, Charles gave it to her. Walking to the archer's line, she picked up her quiver, slung it over her back. She selected an arrow, nocked it, and let fly. It twanged dead center into the target. Head high, lips curling into a proud and haughty smile, she nocked another arrow. It struck hard, cheek by jowl with the first.

Major Charles Tyrone had confided in her. He trusted her. He would have much to say to her when they had safely passed through this ring of fire. Well and good. She would have a good deal to say to him as well.

Unfortunately, she was not at all sure what it was going to be.

*   *   *

Lady Horatia Tyrone maintained a stately pace behind Meecham as he led her to the Blue Parlor, a relatively small ground floor room which overlooked the rolling green park abutting the spinney and the infamous ha-ha. The vicar's mother wished she might have thought of that particular trick herself. Of course, the major had to have been wool-gathering or he would not have missed it. Which proved he was not infallible. A thought which gave her considerable comfort.

Meecham threw open the parlor door, announced her, bowed, and departed, his shoulders even more rigidly correct than usual. Lady Horatia swept into the room on a swish of stiff burgundy silk. She removed her black gloves with ostentatious deliberation, practically waving them in the face of Lady Clorinda, who lay stretched upon a sofa of dark blue velvet, presenting an exquisite picture of a society matron at ease in her own home. A gown of primrose georgette trailed over an undergown a shade darker. Tiny rosettes of the darker color were sprinkled over the georgette, culminating in a band of closely spaced flowers some twelve inches above the hem. Below the band the gown burst into an enormously full flounce which trailed over the edge of the sofa and onto the carpet. It was decadent, Lady Horatia decided. Thoroughly inappropriate for a matron who had seen thirty some years since her come-out. And not a sign of black gloves, not so much as a black velvet ribbon in token of poor Neville. Though no better than he should be, Sherbourne *was* family and should be shown the proper respect. Particularly here in his own home. Since Lady Horatia Tyrone throughly enjoyed being outraged, she chose not to make allowances for Clorinda's well known eccentricity.

Truthfully, she was already incensed by Lady Clorinda's summons. How *dare* the woman invite her to a meeting in the Abbey as if it were her very own home? As if Lady Horatia had not lived in Lower Wyverne for years and run tame at the Abbey?

"You wished to see me?" Lady Horatia demanded.

Lady Clorinda waved a languid hand toward an armchair. "Merciful heavens, Horatia," she sighed, "I only wished a comfortable coze. We have not seen each other this age."

"If you had come for Christmas, we might have," Horatia declared. Her tone quite clearly implied, "as you should have."

"Ah, but you know how I am," Clorinda murmured faintly. "To come so far in the midst of winter . . ."

Lady Horatia, whose health was as stout as that of her son, had had enough. "I swear you cannot be as weak as you claim, Clorinda, if you are able to deal with that Taggart person. I have heard all about him, you know. 'Tis not as if you could keep such a thing quiet."

Lady Clorinda did not rise to the bait. "Ah, dear Bertie," she smiled. "Such a fine stalwart gentleman. He treats me like a princess, you know."

Horatia resisted a surge of nausea. She had been faithful to her dear Clarence in marriage and in widowhood. Though she and Clorinda had taken each other in dislike years earlier on first acquaintance, Horatia's distaste for this cousin by marriage now began to escalate. "Our sons are in deep difficulty," she pronounced. "I believe the major wishes to see one of them hang. And I fear he is not particular about which one."

Clorinda's shriek was satisfyingly anguished. Horatia sat back and watched her fumble for her silver gilt vinaigrette, throw her head back against the pillows on the couch, flail her hands dramatically over her heart.

"Well done," Horatia commended. "You have been performing that little drama for so long you have it down to perfection. Though I hear Godfrey turned his back on your theatricals long since."

"At least my son had the sense to do so," Clorinda gasped, before she could think better of it. "He does not cling to his mama as close as a piglet to a sow."

Lady Horatia drew a deep breath, well aware that her

countenance now matched her burgundy walking dress. "My son," she intoned, "will marry Vanessa and become Archbishop of Canterbury. What chance have you for Tyrones of your blood?" she taunted. "What tragedy, my dear Clorinda, to have produced only girls."

Clorinda sat up with an abruptness which would have astonished her other acquaintances. "Godfrey and Vanessa will produce beautiful children," she declared, with an almost fanatical gleam in her eye. "After all, he is handsome enough for both of them. Your great ox of a son does not stand a chance with such a sophisticated woman. You are a fool to even consider such a match."

"She'll take the major over both of them," Horatia countered, so far gone in anger that reason triumphed over her fantasies.

"The major must go," Clorinda declared, without the slightest echo of her customary die-away airs.

"Agreed," Horatia snapped. After long seconds of scowling at the rolling green lawn outside the windows, she strode to the bell pull. "We will need refreshment," she declared, "if we are to concoct a scheme."

Chapter Seventeen

"You must not let him go!" Miss Arabella Tyrone declared with considerable heat, having had her previous protestations totally ignored by the crowd hovering around Julian's bed.

"Stubble it, Bella," Julian ordered. "I ain't seen the sky in months. And anyone with eyes can see the sun is out. As fine an August day as one could wish."

"It is cruel. Unfeeling!" Arabella wailed. "We are barely recovered, you and I. Who knows what pestilence might be on the breeze outside?"

Julian groaned. "If you think I wish to play one more game of draughts or spend another useless hour trying to teach you piquet, you are fair and far out. You may stay inside if you wish. *I* am going out."

"But—"

"Vanessa," the major snapped, "you will kindly keep the chit quiet. I swear she's as fainthearted as her mother." Dutifully, Vanessa took Arabella aside, whispering what she hoped were comforting words, although, in truth, she had her own personal qualms about Julian's proposed expedition.

Amidst exhortations of "Careful now!" and "There's the lad!" interspersed with grunts, anxious mutters, and an occasional gasp from Vanessa and Arabella—all overridden by sharp orders from Major Tyrone—Julian's Bath chair, followed by Julian himself in the arms of

Sergeant Simmons, made it down the broad staircase to the ground floor of Wyverne Abbey.

As soon as the young Lord Sherbourne began to recover from the measles, Charles had instituted a regimen of leg exercises and massages. Tom Jenkins had been promoted to valet and attacked his new duties with vigor. If moving a boy's legs up and down was not a normal part of a valet's daily routine, Jenkins was far too pleased with his promotion and devoted to the Tyrones to consider it anything but an honor. Luke Simmons himself, with his huge powerful hands, provided the thrice daily massages. With Sally Vance still keeping an eagle eye on Julian's meals and every inhabitant of the Abbey, from the major to the lowest tweeny, keeping watch, it was hoped they had weathered the worst of the crisis.

Charles, however, could not be easy. While keeping a particularly sharp watch on Bertram Taggart, he continued to castigate himself for allowing Fielding to escape. Without the blasted valet, they might never know who hired him. The true villain remained an unknown menace who might act in the next instant or, frightened off, bide his time for weeks or months, waiting until vigilance inevitably wound down, leaving the road to murder and mayhem free and clear. Charles's lips thinned in disgust, even as his glance swept the entire garden area from the rear terrace to the formal flower beds to the long slope of lawn leading down to the stream. On the left was the tall dark green facade of the boxwood maze. All quiet. Yet what a perfect hiding place the maze would make if the villain were suddenly to change his tactics to overt violence. A thought which came a bit late, Charles amended. Fielding's act might have been stealthy, but it was well and truly an overt act of hostility.

Deciding he had played the mother hen enough for one morning, the major stood back and let Sergeant Simmons direct the placement of the Bath chair on the smooth brick walkway while Vanessa hovered, looking as if she were ready to bite her tongue in half. *Good girl,* Charles mused. She was learning when to keep her mouth shut.

Fortunately for the progress of the Bath chair, the primary branch of the Tyrone family had never suffered a deprivation of wealth. Any addition or renovation desired at the Abbey since its creation in the time of Henry the Eighth had been as easy as the current earl saying it should be done. Therefore, for the past fifty years, the Abbey had boasted brick pathways instead of the more customary pebbles. Lord Sherbourne had only to grasp the steering handle, shout "Tally Ho!" and he and Luke Simmons were off on an exploration of the gardens. Responding to a brisk wave of the sergeant's hand, John Hart and Hugh Davies sprinted to the fore, nearly decapitating several fine dahlias in their haste, though it seemed doubtful the stalwart sergeant was apt to lose his precious burden on the gentle slope of the garden toward the river. Since Arabella had decided she could not miss this grand event in spite of her misgivings, she and Vanessa strolled along behind, with the major bringing up the rear.

It was a fine August day, with perhaps a hint of autumn in the air. The kind of day where it was almost impossible to believe that evil lurked around them. The Abbey household had survived so much, Charles thought. The death of the heir, the earl's much beloved only son. Julian's serious injury, the earl's apoplexy, poison, measles, asphyxiation. And yet the sun shone, the fountain tinkled, fat fluffy clouds skidded across a cerulean sky. Birds twittered, the stream gurgled, and life went on.

If he could just keep it like this, Charles groaned. Suddenly, the burden seemed overwhelming. It was as if the enemy were coming at him from every side, from behind blind turns and twists and smiling faces. At least, on the Peninsula, he had always known who the enemy was.

When the cavalcade came to a halt down near the river, the ladies seated themselves on marble benches placed for the pleasure of those who enjoyed contemplating the stream, which was nearly large enough to be called a river. Deep enough for both swimming and fishing, its current was not as strong as in the spring, but the sound of its passing over a natural waterfall of tumbled granite just upstream was soothing to the ears. Charles's lips curled into a smile as he recalled the fat trout he had caught on a visit to the Abbey in his youth. How very easy it would be to be lulled into thinking there was no danger. That life at Wyverne Abbey was as idyllic as it looked.

The path, which ran from the Abbey terrace straight down to the water, ended in a large bricked circle, broad enough to provide space for three red marble benches which blended surprisingly well with the brick. Beyond the circle was a strip of grass, perhaps four feet wide, and then a steep mud-covered bank plunging down to the water.

Charles looked down at Vanessa. He might as well try his luck, he thought. Belatedly, he had caught her disappointment at the archery field. Unexpected, but a balm to his wounded pride. Undoubtedly he was a slow top, his knowledge of females regrettably confined to women who had chosen to express their emotions rather than repress them. Further fence-mending was in order. And, besides, he liked being private with the Arrogant Aristocrat. She was a delightful challenge. When he wasn't being inspired to wring her neck.

"It is a fine day," Charles remarked, seemingly casually. "I have discovered Neville's old curricle, which has been gathering dust in the stables. I would be pleased if you would join me for a drive this afternoon."

Vanessa was not surprised by this revelation. Some fifteen minutes after the major gave the order for the old curricle to be cleaned and polished, Vanessa had been informed of Charles's resurrection of the vehicle Neville had left behind in order to buy a spanking new one for the London Season. Truth to tell, she had been hoping for an invitation. Though, naturally, she would never allow him to see her eagerness.

"Thank you, Major," Lady Vanessa nodded coolly. "That will, I am certain, be most enjoyable."

It was an exceedingly merry cavalcade which trooped back to the house, even though John Hart occasionally had to grasp the handle of the Bath chair, helping Julian steer as they pushed back up hill over an occasional brick, off kilter from years of frosty winters. Charles was close to breaking into a grin. It was a beautiful day, and all *would* be right in his world. He would make it so.

Vanessa kept a carefully demure face. Inside, her heart was pounding. A drive was so much more intimate than a ride. She and Charles had ridden together on numerous occasions, a companionable venture, but not at all the same as sitting hip to hip in a curricle. She would wear something not so . . . well, buttoned up. She would wear a fetching bonnet . . .

Vanessa heaved a sigh. She would do her duty and wear one of the two conservative black bonnets she had worn for months now. Her feet kept walking, but her spirit drooped. And yet . . .

Truthfully . . . truthfully Neville would *hate* seeing her in black. Neville would be the first to ridicule the conventionality of her mourning. Perhaps if she wore a black gown, she could venture out in a more frivolous bonnet . . .

Not unless Charles planned to drive on roads where they would not see a soul. The residents of Lower Wyverne would never forgive her. *Six months,* Vanessa vowed. At six months she would go into half-mourning. She was quite certain Neville would cheer her on.

From behind thick undergrowth at the edge of the park, Peter Fielding peered at the procession returning to the Abbey. Since he had failed in his mission, he had not been paid. Although terrified of the consequences, he was stuck here until the deed was done. But today, at last, he had been visited by inspiration. He was now almost certain he had discovered a way to ensure the blasted boy met a speedy end.

For all her rebellious thoughts, Vanessa succumbed to the dictates of convention for her drive with Major Tyrone. A last disgusted look in the mirror revealed a crow-like figure, head to toe in black, even though she had put on her Sunday-best bonnet with a band of jet beads, the inside ruched in black silk. Her nose, she decided ruefully, even rivaled a crow's beak, seeming to grow larger and longer with each moment she gazed into the tall pier glass. So be it. Charles had invited her. He would have to take her as she was.

More's the pity. With a pronounced lift to her chin, Vanessa donned her spencer of quilted black muslin, pulled on her black gloves, picked up her equally black reticule, and exited from her bedchamber.

The afternoon continued the fine promise of the morning. Vanessa had to make a severe effort not to show her enthusiasm as Charles helped her into the two-wheeled open vehicle. As they bowled down the driveway, she sat back and absorbed the wonder of it all. She was *out.* She was not driving to the village to attend church or match embroidery silks for Tabby. She was driving out, with a gentleman at the ribbons, for the sheer pleasure of it. She could look at the soft greens of the Cotswold trees and shrubbery, the gentle undulations of the hills and valleys, the golden glow of the fields being harvested, the mellow stone of the houses and barns, and come to the full realization that her world did not begin and end within the walls of Wyverne Abbey.

It was glorious. Even if she had alienated Charles by rejecting his embrace . . .

Even if he had not kissed her at the archery field . . .

Even if she looked like a crow . . .

It was a glorious day, as long as she shut away Julian's danger. Which was, of course, quite impossible. Vanessa's smile faded. Assailed by guilt, she turned her head straight forward, contemplating nothing more than the steady gait of the fine pair of bays.

As if reading her thoughts, Charles said, "I've given orders that Julian is to go outside every day. The fresh air and sunshine will do him a world of good."

"What if it is a gray day?" Vanessa instantly countered.

"My dear, this is England, not Spain," Charles told her, none too gently, "If he did not go out when it is cloudy, he would scarce be out at all."

"But he might—"

"He's going out, Nessa," Charles interjected, totally intransigent.

"What if it is raining?" she challenged.

"Don't be ridiculous. Of course he shall not go out if it is raining."

"Mizzling?" Vanessa demanded.

Charles groaned. "Do you number me among those who wish him ill?"

"No, of course not," she murmured, turning away so her face was completely hidden by her bonnet.

"Then let us cry friends and enjoy the afternoon." Charles's words were conciliating, but his voice held a hint of steel.

How fortunate he could not see her rush of tears. And how very lowering to discover her emotions were becoming as volatile as young Arabella's. Lady Vanessa Rayne was torn in so many directions, she did not know which way was up. Indubitably, it was very poor spirited of her.

Charles eyed a fork in the road a half mile ahead. "The village or Houndstooth Hill?" he inquired.

"Houndstooth Hill," Vanessa responded instantly, the mist in her eyes evaporating into genuine enthusiasm. "I have not been there in an age. The view is breathtaking."

"Houndstooth Hill it is," the major agreed, and turned the pair of bays toward the left fork.

They had gone no more than a mile when Vanessa realized just how foolish it was to deny herself a full view

of the beautiful Cotswold countryside. The broad rim of
her Sunday-best bonnet was fine protection against prying eyes attempting to discover if she were paying attention to Ambrose's interminable sermons, but today it was
nothing but a blasted nuisance. With a defiant gesture,
she loosened the shining silk ribbons which held it in
place and shoved the offending bonnet back behind her
neck. Her rebellion not yet finished, Vanessa began to
remove the pins from her tightly controlled coil of hair.
With each one she slipped into her reticule, she felt
stronger, freer, more determined to be herself, not what
others thought Lady Vanessa Rayne should be.

She shook her head, and her long straight brown hair
swirled round her face, blown on the wind created by
the swiftly trotting team. *Wonderful!* She looked up, suddenly shy, to discover Charles grinning at her.

"That's my girl," he approved. "Shall we go back to
the village and let Ambrose get a good look? Perhaps
he'd stop making you offers."

A scowl chased away her gaiety. Did she truly look so
hideous? Yes, very likely—

"Nessa!" Charles said with a considerable edge.
"Smile, foolish girl. I was not insulting you. I *like* the
way you look. You do not, however, look like a proper
vicar's wife. More like a runaway wood sprite."

Though somewhat mollified, Vanessa found she could
not look at him. Would it always be thus? They simply
could not be together without misunderstandings or out-
right quarrels. It did not bode well for any kind of a
future—

A moot point. They had no future.

In order to enjoy the view from Houndstooth Hill,
which encompassed a goodly portion of the spectacularly
lovely Cotswold countryside, it was first necessary for
their team to climb the hill. "Highwaymen used to lie in
wait behind those trees over there," Vanessa said. "Even
coaches with four horses slowed to a crawl when climbing

the hill. It was the perfect spot for an ambush. Coaches traveling this road always went well armed."

"Does it not happen any more?" Charles asked.

"We have become quite civilized in recent years," Vanessa replied primly. "One robbery, as I recall, in all my years at the Abbey. Both miscreants were promptly tried and hanged."

"An outcome bound to discourage imitation," the major agreed, lips twitching.

The sweating bays had made it to the top of the hill. Charles walked them down a well-worn sidepath to a popular lookout point, where he pulled them up for a much deserved rest. As he swung Vanessa down, his strong hands about her waist, she was startled by the surge of attraction which shook her. She should have known better than to drive out with him. She and Charles Tyrone should never be alone.

But they had arrived at the viewpoint they had come so far to enjoy, and all else paled before the beauty of the Cotswolds. The rolling hills, the fields, the clusters of darker green along unseen meandering streams, church spires marking the location of villages tucked into sheltered valleys. Vanessa wished to capture the moment forever, keep it in her heart. A treasure to light the way when her path grew rough and slippery beneath her feet.

Charles remained strangely silent. Again, he did not kiss her. Although she had thought that, surely, this time he would. But before they declared a truce, she had dealt his pride a severe blow. And perhaps—though highly unlikely—his heart as well. It was too much to expect he would once again open himself to her contempt. Yet here they were, all alone . . . .

It seemed a terrible waste.

They stood for some time in silence, absorbing the beauty of the moment, then Vanessa allowed Charles to walk her back to the curricle. Out on the main road, at the top of the precipitous drop, Charles paused the team to allow one last view of the panorama below. Then, cautiously, he began the descent, one hand on the reins and one on the brake. Vanessa assured herself she trusted the major completely, that she could not be in better hands. Yet as she looked down and down and down, her heart was in her mouth. Had the view truly been worth these moments of abject terror?

Everything would be fine. People did this all the time.

But, suddenly, the curricle began to wobble, the wobble became a lurch. Charles jammed the brake handle hard, but they were picking up speed. The lurch increased, throwing them both from side to side. And then it happened. A wheel went flying off. Charles shouted for her to jump. In the seconds she flew through the air, Vanessa prayed she would hit the grassy verge rather than the rock-hard road. A sickening thud, and air whooshed out of her lungs. A sharp pain, and the world went black.

Chapter Eighteen

$\mathcal{L}$ ate that afternoon, Ambrose Tyrone waited impatiently for his mother to return from her weekly round of visiting the sick and needy in the surrounds of Lower Wyverne. Although few parishioners would say they garnered warmth or comfort from Lady Horatia's visits, none would dispute the value of the foodstuffs which came with her. And, as one frail and elderly maiden lady once said, "If you have not spoken with a single soul the whole week long, even the devil's handmaiden has a certain appeal."

Since the living for the church at Lower Wyverne was almost inevitably held by some scion of the Tyrone family, the vicarage was spacious and well appointed. The drawing room might have been acceptable in any manor house of modest size. Ambrose had been happy here. Even his mother seldom complained of her accommodations. But, now . . . now fear struck him to the core. His cozy world was teetering on the brink of annihilation. Word of the curricle accident on Houndstooth Hill had sped through the village like lightning, as bad news always did. The summoning of Dr. Pettibone was said to be urgent. Frantic. The major badly injured, the residents of the Abbey in fear for Lady Vanessa's life.

Vanessa. Who should have been his bride. Vanessa, whom he had known since she was a gallant twelve-year-old, trying to cope with the loss of both parents and with guardianship by a man she scarcely knew. Vanessa, who had made it infinitely clear she would not have him.

It seemed impossible she could prefer a rough engineer to a man of the cloth. But, with the help of his faith, his pride would weather the storm. Yet Ambrose feared—he very much feared—his mother might have been tempted to stronger action. Not that business with Neville. No, indeed, he would not believe it. But the measles? She was guilty as sin, he had no doubt. And today's incident on Houndstooth Hill? Somehow he had no difficulty believing his formidable mama capable of arranging such an accident. But fate had intervened in a cruel manner, putting Vanessa beside his cousin at the fateful moment. Vanessa, for whom he truly cared, even if he would never have considered her as a bride without her magnificent dowry.

As he heard the sound of carriage wheels, the click of the housekeeper's feet in the hall, the opening of the front door, the Right Reverend Ambrose Tyrone sternly reminded himself he had been a dutiful son through thirty-one years of his life. But now the time had come for him to remember he was a man of God. He must stand up and be a man.

When he told his mother about the accident, he saw it. Beneath the shock of hearing about Vanessa, he saw quite clearly the guilt, the horror—the anguish. Not because Lady Horatia truly cared about Vanessa, he realized, but because she had possibly ruined forever her son's chances of marrying a ducal daughter with a fine manor house and fifty thousand pounds.

When Vanessa's eyes inched open, the world was still dark. Wonderfully so. For surely heaven would be filled with shining light and not look and feel so remarkably like the shadowed confines of her tester bed in her very own room. And if her soul were fated to go the other way—which she certainly felt she did not deserve—then why was she so very comfortable, resting on what was surely her exceedingly inviting goose-feather mattress?

After a single infinitesimal attempt to turn her head, Vanessa discovered she was not so comfortable as she had thought. Pain pierced her skull, shot down the length of her body to her toes. Agony, sheer agony.

No complaints! If she could feel pain, she was alive. And . . .

Charles! The horrible scene on Houndstooth Hill came back in a rush. The curricle's erratic jouncing, Charles's vain effort with the brake, the wheel flying off, Charles shouting, her sudden flight through the air. Oh, dear God, what had happened to Charles? Vanessa struggled to sit up. She must find someone, must ask . . . The room whirled around her. With a moan—part pain, part frustration—she fell back onto her pillows.

"Nessa? Nessa?" A cherished voice. Gentle fingers touched her cheek. Was it her imagination? "Nessa, confound it, speak to me," the major ordered. "I swear I saw you open your eyes."

That was more like it. Vanessa smiled to herself. She was rather inclined to think she wasn't dreaming. Charles had been sitting there beside her all the time. She was going to be vastly disappointed if she discovered otherwise.

"Are you hurt?" she asked, without opening her eyes.

His reply was delayed by a heartfelt sigh of relief. "A sore shoulder, a slight limp, a great many scrapes and bruises, but I shall do."

"But you were on the road side," she murmured.

"I've had prior experience jumping from moving objects. Horses, carriages, wagons, artillery limbers. Stationary ones, too. Men who blow things up have to be agile, you know."

Vanessa's lips curled into a tiny smile. Convinced she wasn't dreaming, she opened her eyes. Leaning over her, his face not a foot from hers, was Major Charles Tyrone.

In the pre-dawn light filtering into the room she could see him quite clearly. He looked . . . beautiful. Her very own guardian angel.

"I am so very sorry, Nessa," Charles said. "I never thought he'd try the same trick twice. It never crossed my mind I might be endangering your life when I took you for a drive."

It took a few seconds for his words to filter through the haze of Vanessa's headache. When she realized what Charles was implying, she was very glad he had found one of her hands and was clasping it tightly. "You think it was deliberate . . . that someone was trying to kill you," she whispered.

"I've had all night to think on it, and I'm close to certain of it. Though I'll admit there's no way anyone could have known I would drive to Houndstooth Hill. Even you and I didn't know until we were on the road. So I presume someone merely loosened the wheel, hoping it might be enough to do the trick. Not a thorough or professional job of assassination, as was the trick played on Neville," Charles mused. "Nor could he have known you would be along. That, I imagine, came as quite a shock."

"Are you talking about Peter Fielding?"

"Possibly. Though Taggart is another I suspect is capable of anything."

Charles suddenly straightened up. Giving her hand a firm squeeze, he said, "I'm a fool to be talking of such things when you need your rest. You may not have noticed, but Emma Trout is back with us, asleep in the chair in the corner. Though I've no doubt she'd be awake on the instant if you should need her. Or," the major added, leaning back over Vanessa, one eye snapping shut in a salacious wink, "if I should do something outrageous."

His lips brushed her forehead, then he disappeared from her line of sight. No matter. He was here. Vanessa snuggled into her pillows and promptly fell asleep.

*   *   *

Over the next two days Vanessa had no difficulty recognizing the warm glow that suffused her mind, even as her body developed remarkable shades of black, blue, green, and yellow to match her all-pervading aches and pains. Charles *liked* her. He cared about her. She was almost certain of it. Her dowry had not inspired him to sit by her bed all night. Nor that special something which suffused his voice when he spoke to her.

This morning, after Luke Simmons brushed the major aside with a gruff, "I'll take the lady, sir. Ye'll put your shoulder out again," the former soldier had scooped her up as easily as Julian and brought her to the cheerful Ladies' Parlor overlooking the gardens. She was ensconced on the chintz-covered sofa, with a choice of books and a pot of chocolate within easy reach. A wool throw, knit by Tabitha Halliwell's own hand, covered Vanessa's lower limbs. Both Tabby and Emma Trout had arranged themselves nearby, ready to jump up and be of service on a moment's notice. Mrs. Trout appeared, as ever, complacent and relaxed. Miss Halliwell kept raising her head from her embroidery to cast fearful glances from the hall door to the floor-to-ceiling windows leading onto the terrace. Just as if, Vanessa sighed, the poor dear expected someone to burst in and attack them at any moment.

She would not think on it! Other, more delicious thoughts, filled her mind. What if . . . what if Charles really did care for her? And if he were Wyverne, would she truly object to a marriage between them? Honesty forced her to admit she would not. She was nearly twenty-one, and Major Charles Tyrone was the first man who had ever been able to make her heart feel as if it had been struck by an earthquake. Truthfully, he had become so much a part of life at the Abbey that she could not imagine her small world without him. The scant three weeks he had been gone to Scotland had seemed interminable.

But he did not want to be Wyverne. Indeed, *she* did not want him to be Wyverne. For that would mean both Uncle 'Vester and Julian were gone. And even if Charles acted for Julian until he came of age, the time would come when . . .

Ah, yes . . . as she had long recognized, the time would come when she would have to adjust to Charles Tyrone's life, instead of he to hers. Lady Vanessa Rayne steepled her hands in front of her face and closed her eyes.

"Have I come at a poor time?"

"Not at all." Vanessa smiled up at Godfrey, whose voice she had instantly recognized. "Please join me. Tabby and Mrs. Trout are quite worn out trying to amuse me." She flashed both women an apologetic smile for maligning their many kindnesses. A distinct huff was heard from Emma Trout. Miss Halliwell bent her head still lower over her embroidery frame.

Sir Godfrey, as perfectly dressed as if he were paying a morning call in Mayfair, seated himself across from Vanessa. He looked a good deal more solemn than was customary. "Are you all right, Nessa?" he inquired anxiously.

"I will be," she assured him. "It is kind of you not to mention how perfectly dreadful I look."

"It *is* daunting," Godfrey conceded without a smidgeon of mockery. "I am appalled at the evidence of how close you came to death."

Good God. She had never seen him like this before. It was as if someone had taken a cloth and wiped away the supercilious but sharp-tongued Godfrey she had known. Even the hot-headed Godfrey who had fought a duel with Charles over the measles. Outwardly, he was still Sir Godfrey Tyrone, London exquisite. But within . . . Vanessa was unsure quite what she was seeing. Very well, she would be blunt. And watch closely for his reaction.

"Charles believes the accident was planned, as was Neville's. He believes himself to be the target this time."

Taking a leaf from the former Godfrey's book, she added dryly, "I fear the major will not take me driving again."

Showing no appreciation for her attempted humor, Godfrey began to fidget. Before Vanessa's incredulous eyes, Sir Godfrey Tyrone, the darling of London society, twisted his legs, put a hand over his mouth, chewed his knuckles, flicked a glance out over the terrace, eyed askance Vanessa's two companions, shifted his shoulders as if his coat were too tight, and generally committed every solecism of an unusually gauche young man on his first foray into the social world.

"Vanessa," he declared at last, leaning forward so his words would reach her ears alone, "would you consider becoming betrothed to me?"

Vanessa, once a sophisticated member of the *haut ton,* realized how far her conduct had deteriorated when she blurted out the first thing that came into her head. "Godfrey, you know quite well you do not wish to marry me!"

He glanced swiftly round, making certain Miss Halliwell and Mrs. Trout were not privy to their conversation. "You and I know that," he hissed, "but that's not what I asked. I was—um—thinking you might be safer if you was spoken for. I mean"—he leaned closer still—"we don't know why someone tried to kill Charles, but it is possible there is more than one villain in all this. More than one motive as well. If you was engaged to me, then no one need kill the major just because he might be the one to gain your dowry."

Vanessa stared. "That is very generous of you, Godfrey," she murmured, stunned by the self-sacrifice his offer entailed. She could be confident he did not need her wealth because Charles had had Silas Ellington investigate the matter. Sir Godfrey Tyrone had even deeper pockets than anyone had suspected. "I believe," she said carefully, "that someone wishes to be rid of Charles because he stands too close guard over Julian. Or possibly because he is Julian's heir. I doubt any of this involves me at all."

Godfrey shook his head. "I cannot be comfortable, Nessa. The veriest idiot can see Fielding did not act on his own. So it seems certain someone in the family hired his villainy. Yet we cannot be certain it is he who loosened the bolts on the curricle." Sir Godfrey placed his long slim fingers over hers. "I can do little for Julian, Nessa. Charles won't let me near him. But I *can* protect you—if you will allow it."

"Godfrey, I—" She had no idea what to say. *No,* certainly. The thought of Charles's reaction if she accepted Godfrey as her betrothed was enough to make her want to scurry back to her room and pull the bedcovers over her head. But, merciful Heavens, he was so earnest. So gentle. So kind. So un-Godfrey. Words failed her.

In the end, she managed it. She hoped she managed it well, although admitting to the reality of it shook her to the core. Lady Vanessa Rayne rejected Sir Godfrey Tyrone by telling the truth. Or what she hoped was the truth. She and Charles had developed a *tendre,* however tentative, for each other, she told him. She could scarcely be expected to damage this uncertain relationship by becoming betrothed to another man.

Sir Godfrey sighed, nodded as if he had feared as much, and took himself off. For the remainder of the morning Vanessa lay on the sofa and contemplated his extraordinary offer. Would Godfrey have offered for her if he himself were the villain? Possibly—if a second and unknown assassin had suddenly popped into their midst. Or was Godfrey exactly what he appeared to be—a very worried man, who feared the villainy lay in his own family?

Vanessa considered the problem. Perhaps the accident which befell Neville and Julian was genuine, and the murderer had merely been inspired to take advantage of the Tyrone family's run of misfortune. Although Charles, as heir to Julian, she conceded, had the most obvious motive, she could not believe he wished to be Wyverne, particularly not enough to kill for it. If he had, she was quite certain Uncle 'Vester and Julian would have joined Neville in the crypt long since.

Peter Fielding could have been hired by anyone. But since it was known that Lady Horatia had not left Lower Wyverne in well over a year, that connection seemed unlikely. The vicar's mother could have managed, however, to subvert Fielding to poison and the pillow, even the damage to Charles's curricle, but Vanessa doubted it. Yet Lady Horatia had most definitely been responsible for the measles.

Ambrose? The vicar had enough of his mother in him to be ruthless in his ambition. Yet Vanessa was almost certain he would consider being Earl of Wyverne a liability rather than an asset.

Godfrey? Vanessa suspected Godfrey had a great deal more of the Tyrone steel in his constitution than she had previously realized. If he had a powerful and unnatural urge to be Wyverne, he was certainly capable of arranging it. Yet, though beset by a few nagging doubts, Vanessa did not believe he had done so.

Which left the impossible—that languishing invalid, Lady Clorinda.

Impossible!

But Lady Clorinda had Bertram Taggart, who, Vanessa was convinced, would stoop to anything to please his ladylove. Or avoid losing his means of support. And if Clorinda were a doting mother far more passionate about seeing her son Earl of Wyverne than anyone had ever dreamed?

Dear God, was it possible?

Sergeant Simmons was in for a busy day. Only an hour after receiving an abrupt order to return Lady Vanessa to her room before nuncheon, he was carrying his daily burden of Viscount Sherbourne down the stairs to the waiting Bath chair. With the major and Lady Vanessa still resting from their ordeal and Miss Bella currently at outs with his lordship over a game of cards which had

ended with Julian's young cousin bursting into a flood of
tears and running from the room, they were a small
group for the viscount's regimen of fresh air and sunshine. Just Julian, Corporal Hart, and the sergeant himself. But both men were armed, and Simmons had rigged
a canvas haversack to the back of the movable chair,
in which resided a large and very obvious shotgun. The
sergeant had agreed, wholeheartedly, when the major decreed it was better to warn attackers off, rather than risk
a fight around a boy who could not move.

The garden was right fine, the sergeant had to admit.
He could recognize hollyhocks and marigolds, but he'd
had to ask the upstairs maid about some of the other
August flowers. Hy-dran-jah, she'd said. Hi-biskus, dal-
yahs, and the vines with big purple flowers were clemmy-
somethings. And she'd offered to continue his lessons
any time. As he pushed the viscount's chair down the
slope toward the stream, Luke Simmons's lips curled in
a reminiscent smile.

"Do you think we might bring a pole next time?" Julian asked, as the sergeant parked his chair on the brick
circle overlooking the stream.

"Well, now," Luke Simmons declared, regarding the
water with careful consideration, "I don't know as the
major'd like that. If you was to fish, you'd have to be
closer to the stream than a body could wish."

"Sergeant," Julian groaned, "I'm fair fit for Bedlam. I
must find something to do besides play childish games
with Bella or I shall surely go mad!"

Simmons shook his head. "I'll speak to the major,
m'lord, but I have m'doubts."

A long scream rent the air, continuing in a series of
high-pitched shrieks. The heads of all three males jerked
round, gazing intently back up the brick pathway to the
house. Corporal Hart had the best distance vision. "It's
that lady what has the vapors all the time," he said.
"Lady Clorinda. Shall I go to her, sergeant?"

Since the lady was still screaming, waving her arms,

and pointing toward one of the flower beds, Luke Simmons felt he had little choice. Though the major was surely not going to like it. He waved the corporal up the path.

"I think she's crying, 'Snake!' " Julian contributed. "Probably nothing more than a green garden snake, frozen to the ground by her carrying on."

"Aye," Simmons agreed. "Females don't much care for snakes."

With their attention fixed firmly on Lady Clorinda's wild gesticulations, neither Julian nor the sergeant heard Peter Fielding as he rushed out from the shrubbery some thirty feet away, striking Luke Simmons a stout blow with a cudgel before grabbing the Bath chair. With one hand on the steering handle and the other on one of the large wheels, he propelled it toward the river.

Peter Fielding was a strong man. Not only did Sergeant Simmons drop like a stone, but the former valet was able to develop enough momentum over the bricks to overcome the treacherous pull of the grass as they reached the riverbank. The chair crested the bank, tilted sharply, the wheels plunging forward, digging into the mud. A hard push from Fielding and Julian catapulted into the swift-flowing water. Sergeant Simmons, a bear of a man, staggered to his feet and lurched toward the bank. He was in time to see Julian Tyrone, Viscount Sherbourne, being swept downriver, only his head visible above the blue-gray water. He was also in time to catch Peter Fielding contemplating the results of his handiwork. Either Neville's former valet heard the sergeant coming or he was determined to make sure Julian went down and stayed down, for Fielding ran along the bank until he was opposite the place where the viscount was struggling to keep his head up, then plunged, feet first, into the water.

Sergeant Simmons, fearing the worst, pulled out his pistol and shot him dead.

Chapter Nineteen

*C*harles, alerted by Lady Clorinda's screams, burst
through the bookroom door onto the terrace and
reached the stricken lady almost as soon as Corporal
Hart. At the major's stern and totally unsympathetic
command for quiet, Clorinda's shrill cries dissolved into
a flood of tears. There was no sign of a snake. When the
sound of a pistol shot reverberated across the park, both
men sped toward the river, leaving Lady Clorinda standing amidst the flower beds, a faint malicious smile of
satisfaction illuminating her fragile, if somewhat damp,
features. She had done her part rather well, she thought.
Surely this time that idiot Fielding would not fail. For a
moment Clorinda allowed herself to picture her beautiful
son, resplendent in the full regalia of the Earl of Wyverne, participating in some great occasion at Westmin-
ster or St. Paul's. Ah, yes, her splendid Godfrey deserved
so much more than a mere baronetcy.

And poor dear Julian? She supposed she would have
to make a show of going into mourning. How fortunate
she looked so well in black.

Although her cheeks were still damp, Lady Clorinda was
smiling as she walked with dainty steps back to the house,
completely missing the continuing drama along the river.

"Can't you swim?" the major demanded of Sergeant
Simmons, who was standing calmly on the riverbank as

if enjoying the beauty of the day. "Here, you idiot! Help me with my boots."

Simmons laid a giant hand on his major's shoulder. "No need, sir. Take a look. The lad's saving himself. I say let him do it. Needs to feel a man again, he does."

Charles paused . . . and stared. As did Corporal John Hart. Julian, after recovering from the initial shock, had evidently discovered his arms and was managing to swim across the current. He was making enough of a success of it that he would soon come up against the leafy branch of a willow tree which was lying out over the water, within easy reach.

"Seems about time to scoop him up," Luke Simmons declared, as laconically as only a grizzled veteran of years of action may do. He and Charles exchanged a speaking glance. All three men grinned in unabashed relief. Then they loped along the grassy bank toward the willow tree.

A further surprise awaited them. As they hauled Julian up the bank, the boy's knees bent and his toes dug into the mud. After only a few seconds to catch his breath, Viscount Sherbourne chortled, "They moved. My legs, they moved! I was swimming, Charles, really swimming. And did you see me come up the bank? I was helping, was I not? I was. I truly was."

"Yes, Julian," Charles agreed in a voice far from his usual steady tones. "We saw. And your timing was superb, dear boy. You could not have picked a better moment." The faces of Luke Simmons and John Hart were a study in grown men struggling not to cry.

The Bath chair, tilted on its side on the muddy bank, was retrieved, and the cavalcade marched up the red brick path toward the house as jubilantly as if no one were trying to kill the young heir to the Earl of Wyverne.

When Vanessa finished what the major described as smothering Julian with her fussing, ordering hot bricks for his bed, hot soup, a tisane so close to the boil it burned his tongue (and all in August!), she and Charles

had stalked into the hallway and gone at it hammer and
tongs. At least that was the description the upstairs maid
reported to the staff at supper that night. "And when
she heard about them a-standin' there and lettin' that
poor boy swim to shore on his own," Bess Martin continued to her rapt audience, "you should have heard her.
Fair curdled, she was. And here we all thought she and
the major had come to terms. Blistered his ears, she did.
And can't say as I blame her," Bess added righteously.
"Imagine leavin' 'im in the river like that." She lowered
her voice. All heads around the long deal table leaned
in to hear. "When his lordship hears of it, I don't doubt
he'll have another attack," Bess hissed.

Meecham, belatedly recollecting his responsibilities,
called a halt to the conversation. "Mark my words," the
irrepressible Bess muttered to those around her. "Just
mark my words. The old man'll go off in a fit, right
enough."

But the conspiracy of silence around the frail old man
was iron clad. He never heard about his grandson's unexpected swim in the river.

The next morning Vanessa discovered she was not the
only person disturbed by Julian's close call. Or so it
seemed, when she saw Bella burst out of her young cousin's bedchamber and rush down the hall in a manner
which would have shocked her mama. Though, truthfully,
Vanessa did not care if Lady Clorinda was shocked or
not. There now seemed little doubt the mother of Godfrey and Arabella was involved in the attempted murders
at Wyverne Abbey. But what was to be done about it
remained unknown. The major had summoned all those
involved to a meeting after dinner that evening. Vanessa
offered a heartfelt prayer that this would make an end
to the long nightmare.

After arranging her face into what she hoped was a
cheerful smile, Vanessa said a bright good morning to
Hugh Davies, then scratched upon Julian's door. Imme-

diately, Tom Jenkins let her in. Viscount Sherbourne greeted her with a boisterous, "Good morning, Nessa."

The male of the species was so strange, she thought. Someone is trying to kill him, and one would think he hadn't a care in the world. "What did you do to Bella?" Vanessa demanded.

"Told her I was tired of her hand wringing and sighs. And her constant chatter. That if she wasn't careful, she'd end up like her mother."

"O-oh, Julian," Vanessa groaned. "That was unkind. I realize you have been under a strain—"

"Strain?" the viscount snapped. "Is that what you call it? Well, let me tell you, Nessa, it's considerably easier to deal with inept assassins than it is with Bella. Everyone keeps throwing us together. Thank God for the time we had the measles. Then I had a bit of peace and quiet. You know what Godfrey and Lady Clorinda want? You do, don't you, Nessa? They want me to marry the chit! As if I ever would. She's sixteen, Nessa. *Sixteen!* By the time I'm ready to take a wife, she'll have been married for years and mother of a hopeful family. Charles says a man must take his time, not marry until he's good and ready. And look at my cousins, Ness. Did they marry at eighteen or even twenty? Not they! So why should I? Charles says he is three and thirty and has not yet met a woman to whom he would be leg-shackled, so there's no way I'm going to marry Bella. And you can tell Godfrey and his mama I said so."

Vanessa reminded herself that she loved him. That he had been through an appalling series of ordeals. He was fifteen years old. Someone was trying to kill him. His father had been murdered. His grandfather could die at any moment, leaving him Earl of Wyverne. The strain—without the presence of Arabella Tyrone—had to be overwhelming. Therefore Julian could be mistaken. Charles could not possibly have said he had not yet met a woman to whom—

With a barely repressed sob, Lady Vanessa Rayne turned and ran from Julian's room.

*   *   *

"Thank you for coming." Major Charles Tyrone surveyed the solemn faces ringed round the drawing room that evening. Raising his brows over the empty chair to Ambrose Tyrone's right, he inquired, "And where is Lady Horatia?"

The vicar coughed, then straightened his shoulders and spoke directly to Charles. "She left for Abbington Grange yesterday morning, Major. That is one of her brother's properties in Northumberland. Pretty country, don't you know. I am certain she will find it quite peaceful." Ambrose folded his hands in his lap, gazed limpidly at the major, obviously having said all he intended to say.

"I take it this is an extended stay?" Charles inquired faintly.

"Indeed, cousin," Ambrose intoned. "I believe Mama had begun to find her parish duties onerous."

"Well, I say!" Julian crowed from his Bath chair, which had been thoroughly cleaned under Mrs. Meecham's gimlet eye before being allowed onto the drawing room's Axminster carpet.

"Julian!" Vanessa hissed, shooting him a warning glance. Though, truthfully, her spirits soared as high as his. Ambrose had freed himself from his mother at last. Even if Lady Horatia had not been guilty of murderous scheming, it was more than time she retired to a home of her own.

The major turned his gaze to Lady Clorinda, who had volubly protested this meeting over dinner but had now fallen remarkably silent. She gave no sign she was even aware that Bertram Taggart sat beside her. A cool façade, carefully contrived by two people who might well have souls as black as the devil's chimney. After several weeks of the nauseating sight of watching them sigh over each other and hold hands, Charles could only applaud the change. The cynic in him appreciated their performance. Or was Lady Clorinda a tool of her son, rather than of her lover?

Charles continued his survey of the room. Vanessa, of course, seated in a chair next to Julian. When his gaze rested on her, she put up her chin, assuming the Arrogant Ladyship pose he had thought gone forever. Inwardly, the major winced.

His regard moved on. Godfrey and Arabella were seated side by side, but almost as far away from their mother as they could get. Tabitha Halliwell and James Prentice completed the circle Charles had carefully arranged at one end of the vast room. In the background, Simmons, Hart, and Davies stood at attention at intervals around the walls. Even Arabella had noticed they were quite ostentatiously guarding the exits.

"I believe," Charles said, still on his feet though all others except the ex-soldiers were seated, "that we are all aware someone is attempting to do away with Julian—"

Lady Clorinda sparked to life. "And who's to benefit most?" she demanded. "No one but you," she accused. "Who else would wish the poor dear boy dead?"

"Which brings me to my second point," Charles responded calmly. "We seem to be dealing with a singularly inept killer—possibly even two. For no one who was seriously trying to cast the blame onto me would have damaged the wheel on the curricle in an attempt to break my neck." There was a general murmur of assent from his audience. Lady Clorinda sniffed.

"Do not attempt to place this on Mama," Ambrose cried. "I fear she knew of it—indeed I saw it in her eyes—but she could not have planned it. I won't believe it."

"Do not be a fool, Ambrose," Vanessa told him with disgust. "And just as I thought you had seen the light at last. If your mama were capable of ensuring that Julian and Arabella caught the measles—quite diabolically, I might add—she is capable of paying Peter Fielding or some other poor soul to loosen a wheel. I must tell you, Ambrose, your mama is not an upstanding person."

"We are not here to make accusations," the major interjected, earning himself a venomous look from the love of his life. "I merely wished to make sure you are all aware that I believe the person or persons responsible for these disasters is sitting in this room."

When the shocked gasps and whispers, punctuated by a satisfied chortle from Julian, had died away, Charles added, "For those of you who are not already aware of the situation, I believe Neville's accident was contrived." Bella gasped and clasped her brother's hand. Miss Halliwell so forgot herself, she began to chew on one of her knitting needles. James Prentice turned the color of chalk. Charles kept a surreptitious watch on Taggart, Lady Clorinda, and Godfrey. Neither of them moved a muscle, their faces betraying no more than polite interest. Ambrose's features were still pugnacious. The vicar might have sent his guilty mother away, but he was still willing to fight over her honor. After all, could the son of someone who had attempted murder become an archbishop?

In neat, concise phrases the major summed up the events of the last few months. The accident which had befallen Neville and Julian. ("He was so proud of that new curricle," Lady Clorinda sobbed.) The earl's collapse. ("Hear he'd been failing for a year or more," Bertram Taggart contributed.) Julian's brush with poison. ("Boys eat the strangest things," Ambrose pontificated. " 'Tis no wonder their stomachs rebel.") The calamitous bout with the measles. ("If you can explain that one away, cousin," Godfrey said to Ambrose, "then why send your poor old mum to Coventry?")

"Didn't," the vicar snapped. "Northumberland, I told you. Northumberland."

"Think I'd prefer Coventry," Godfrey mused, picking a speck of lint off a jacket the amber brown of fine brandy.

Charles mentioned his own accident at the ha-ha. "Embarrassing, yes," he admitted, "but I was deliber-

ately sent along that route, told it was a fine ride with
an excellent view of the abbey." (James Prentice went
from chalk to sickly green.) "Then," the major said,
"events became serious again. Peter Fielding attempted
to smother Julian with a pillow." Charles's gray eyes,
perfectly bland, swept over Bertram Taggart and Lady
Clorinda. "That was shortly after you arrived, I believe,"
he told them.

"Indeed," Taggart snapped, "but I assure you the
events are not related."

"Ah," Charles nodded. "Perhaps not. And then came
my accident in Neville's old curricle—"

"I say," Godfrey asked, "have you thought that perhaps the wheel had been loose for months? That someone tampered with it before Neville decided to leave it
behind and order a new one?"

A spark of appreciation lit the major's eye. "How . . .
enterprising of you," Charles murmured. "But I had
every inch, every strip of wood, every piece of metal, in
that curricle gone over with a fine tooth comb. Believe
me, before I let Lady Vanessa set foot in it, I made sure
it was in perfect working order." Godfrey, with a languid
wave of his hand, subsided into his chair.

"And then came Julian's near-drowning yesterday."

"Was not!" the young viscount burst out. " 'Twasn't
even close. Father taught me to swim in that stream
when I was five. Never in any danger. Not a crumb."

Vanessa reached over, patted his hand. "Yes, and
thank God for it," she told him. "But that does not
change the fact that Fielding tried to kill you."

"Exactly," Charles agreed. "And I want the guilty parties to know that I am convinced the perpetrators of
these events are right here in this room. He, she, or
they—very possibly with the aid of Lady Horatia—have
made numerous efforts to commit murder. That only
Neville and Fielding have died is nothing short of miraculous. And I"—Charles paused, once more slowly scanning each and every person—"I have passed from

righteous anger to the blood fury of battle. The line is drawn. The dying stops now."

"That's all well and good," Bertram Taggart taunted, "but who's to say you haven't maneuvered all this yourself? Ambrose, Godfrey, and I make good scapegoats, do we not? While you waltz off with the title and the heiress as well."

"As I determined to break my own neck on Houndstooth Hill," Charles drawled, dripping sarcasm.

"An excellent diversion—"

"By George, he's right!" Ambrose cried. "He's a military man. Knows how to plot so many dire deeds. And how to save himself."

"And while he's so busy diverting suspicion," Godfrey mocked, "he might as well kill the goose that lays the golden egg."

Charles shot him a surprised, and appreciative, look. Several others in the circle looked blank.

"He means," said Julian with all-too-obvious condescension, "that if Charles wished to stage an accident, he would not have been fool enough to take Nessa with him. And it ain't just her money," he added judiciously. "I rather think he likes her."

Miss Halliwell had not attempted to return to her knitting. But at this remark, she allowed herself a small, secret smile. Lady Vanessa's thoughts were unknown, as she never took her eyes from her hands, which were tightly clasped in her lap.

"That is all, actually," Charles told them. "You might call this evening a declaration of war. I *will* find out who is doing this. And I will see that he, or she, never sets foot in these isles again for as long as either lives. Or else I will see them dead here and now." The major lowered his head, his previous stance having been very much in the style of Wellington addressing his staff. "Ambrose, Prentice, Vanessa, I wish to speak with you privately. The rest of you may go. My thanks for coming."

Warily, the vicar rose from his armchair, eyeing his cousin with some trepidation. "I've told you all—"

"I trust someone is keeping an eye on your mother?" the major inquired. "Permanently?"

"Yes, yes," Ambrose assured him. "I was forced to tell her brother enough that he understands completely. He has vowed to see to it." Charles, after several moments of attempting to find the man of God behind the façade of the nervous vicar, slowly nodded. He could only hope Lady Horatia was one problem which had dropped off his horizon. The vicar made his farewells and left the drawing room.

"Prentice," the major murmured, "please tell me why you recommended the ride which comes to such an abrupt end at the ha-ha?"

James Prentice gave every indication of being a man who wished the floor to open and swallow him up. "I was jealous," he choked out, his face blooming from white to purple on the instant. "I had thought to handle the Abbey affairs—with Lady Vanessa, of course," he added, shooting her a mortified glance. "We did not want, or need, your interference. We were doing well enough on our own. But . . ."

"Yes?" Charles urged.

The earl's secretary put a hand to his head. He moaned. "I soon realized I was wrong. You were exactly what the Abbey needed. I think even Lady Vanessa came to agree with me."

James Prentice's voice had grown so soft, Vanessa had to strain to hear him. God forgive them both, but he was right. As much as she despised the major at the moment, they could not get along without him.

"Thank you, James," Charles said. "You may go."

The secretary's voice came small and dull from lips that barely moved. "I shall pack tonight and be gone in the morning."

"No need," Charles told him. "Your transgression was

a small one. And all too natural under the circumstances."

"Sir!" Hope blossomed in Prentice's middle-aged face. He tried to say more, but his lips quivered, inarticulate. With a groan he turned and dashed from the room.

"May I sit?" Charles asked, indicating the chair next to Vanessa.

"If you wish."

"Julian told me of his faux pas," he said. "He is at a difficult age, and life has treated him badly of late, but he is not so lost to propriety that he did not realize what he had done. Though, alas, not until after he had made his colossal blunder."

Blunder indeed. "I do not wish to discuss it," Vanessa told him.

"We agreed, I believe, to wait until this nasty business is over before we discuss our personal lives," Charles responded earnestly. "But I cannot let this pass, Nessa. I must explain."

"You may speak," Lady Vanessa conceded grandly. "But discuss it I will not."

Charles took a deep breath. Now was his opportunity, and somehow coherent words had fled. "Have you noticed," he blurted at last, "that Bella seemed to have a fondness for me? More so than for Julian? Although I worried about Godfrey and Clorinda pushing her on the boy, I was not truly concerned. Bella seemed as bored with Julian as he was with her. But just to make certain we ended up with no unnatural *tendres,* either between a child of sixteen and myself, or between a boy of fifteen and a cousin only a few months older, I did offer him some man-to-man advice. Or perhaps father-to-son would be more appropriate," Charles amended. "I wanted him to understand that a man was a fool not to sow a few wild oats. To see the world and sample its beauties before he settled down to being a married man. I wanted him to know that I, as his guardian, did not wish him to marry young. Perhaps I waxed too eloquent, but I truly had not seen a woman I wished to marry"—Charles's voice dropped to low and caressing, with a touch of the supplicant—"until I came to Wyverne Abbey."

"It is most kind of you to explain, Major," Lady Vanessa Rayne told him. "You have a generous spirit. And now . . . good night." She rose majestically, crossed the vast room, and exited with her head held high.

Stunned, Charles stared after her, gray eyes wide, mouth grim. The Arrogant Aristocrat had struck again.

Chapter Twenty

Sir Godfrey Tyrone cursed as his fencing foil, attached to a makeshift belt, caught on a rhododendron branch and stopped him in his tracks. He jerked it free on a particularly nasty epithet. If any of his London acquaintances could see him now, he would never live it down. His reputation as the *ton*'s premiere dandy would be utterly destroyed. The fine jersey of his yellow pantaloons, never intended for skulking in the shrubbery, was already snagged in several places. Ruined, totally ruined. His jacket of blue superfine, the latest of Weston's inimitable designs, was damp with dew; the lace trim on his shirt cuffs drooped limply, having already lost its starch. For a disconsolate moment Godfrey wondered about his sanity. What, indeed, was he doing out here, following a furtive shadow which darted in and out of the trees and shrubbery bordering the narrow road to the Abbey's home farm?

But for the past several days, even before his cousin Charles's grim meeting with the family, Godfrey had made it his business to follow his mother's lover. Not the most pleasant of tasks under any circumstances. But— his mother involved in multiple murder? The thought was past all bearing. If only Lady Horatia might be blamed for the whole . . . But common sense denied that hope. For who had been screaming so loudly in the garden, providing the perfect diversion for Fielding's dastardly deed? His mama was Taggart's dupe, she had to be. Otherwise . . . The alternative was too terrible to contemplate. The alternative was that his mother was manipulating Taggart.

Impossible!

But Bertram Taggart had no motive beyond pleasing his darling Clorinda. Godfrey winced, and suddenly realized his wandering thoughts had cost him his quarry.

Fortunately, his grace as a fencer stood him in good stead. Moving swiftly, with one hand clasped to his scabbard to keep it from snagging on every passing bush, Godfrey moved forward as lightly as a cat, eyes straining for a sighting of Bertram Taggart. When a dark figure suddenly loomed up, perhaps forty feet from where Godfrey stood, the London dandy was forced to dive under the nearest bush. He grimaced, even as he reminded himself he could well afford a new outfit. Taggart had looked . . . different. Godfrey frowned. How so . . . ? His quarry's outline—dark against the late afternoon sun filtering through the trees—had been . . . hunchbacked. With not at all the perfect symmetry dear Bertie had displayed when he started to wind his way through the woods. Godfrey risked a peek. Bertram Taggart was crouched behind a giant rhododendron just off the road to the home farm. On his back, distorting his shape, was a quiver. Vanessa's? Upright in Taggart's hand was a bow.

An ambush. Although Sir Godfrey Tyrone did not lack for courage, he had never before been called upon to make a decision of this nature. Accost his mother's lover now? Or wait to see what would happen? If the former, Taggart would insist he was merely indulging a taste for some old-fashioned hunting. Even as Godfrey stared, wondering what he should do, the clip-clop of a single horse was heard. *Charles!* Before Godfrey's horrified eyes, Taggart rose, his arm pulled back, and an arrow flew straight at the major. The arrow's flight was simultaneous with Godfrey's shout of warning.

Charles flattened himself over Rojo's neck. The arrow passed harmlessly over his head. "Here, over here!" Godfrey shouted, his foil flecking blood from Taggart's throat.

"Call him off!" Taggart gasped, flat on his back beside the rhododendron.

"Well, Cousin," Charles drawled, gazing down from Rojo's back, "it would seem you have solved our mystery. But don't kill him, dear boy, for I would very much like to hear the whole of it. If he is willing to enlighten us, we may even let him live."

"I'm not sure I can allow that," Godfrey said, quite evenly.

"Ah, the problem of Mama, of course. I should have realized," Charles sighed. He contemplated Bertram Taggart's prone figure with what appeared to be complete indifference. "Shall I ride off, then?" the major inquired. "His won't be the first death I've known outside the heat of battle."

"You can't!" Taggart screamed. "You're an officer and a gentleman."

"Really?" Charles said. "Perhaps you should remind my dear Nessa of that."

"For God's sake, Major, you can't let him kill me! He knows his mama put me up to it. It was her idea, every bit of it. Except what that witch, Lady Horatia, managed for herself," he added viciously. "Clorinda threatened to cut me off, refused to pay a penny of my debts, unless I rearranged the succession."

A small spurt of blood blossomed on Bertram Taggart's throat, where the tip of Godfrey's foil rested just above his Adam's apple.

"You know, Godfrey," Charles said conversationally, "I doubt you've killed a man in cold blood. Only murderers and sometimes spies can know that feeling. It is possible murderers enjoy it. I can attest that spies do not. I doubt you would wish to live with that burden for the rest of your life. So perhaps we can come to some other arrangement for Lady Clorinda. For even if you kill this vermin here and now, I must tell you that I will not allow your mama to return to the life she once led.

"Godfrey," Charles continued, as his cousin's foil toyed with Taggart's cheek, drawing a fine trickle of blood, "you have just saved my life. I am in your debt. Perhaps . . ." Charles thought for a moment. Somehow he, too, had pictured the satisfactory denouement of Taggart dead and Lady Clorinda banished in a fashion similar to Lady Horatia. However . . .

"Shall we say, our own private form of Transportation?" Charles suggested. "The two of them sent under escort to New South Wales? Personally, I think it's much too good for them, but family is family. And I have no wish to destroy either you or Arabella."

Godfrey considered his enemy, prone and at his mercy. Slowly, with careful efficiency, he flicked off each of the buttons on Bertram Taggart's waistcoat, then proceeded to do the same for his shirt. With each flick of Sir Godfrey's wrist, Taggart's eyes grew wider. He appeared to think each button presaged his last moment on earth. Godfrey cocked his head to one side, regarding the dark hairs on the chest of his mother's lover. When he had shortened a patch of those by a quarter inch, he gave a slow nod, flipped up his foil, and thrust it into the scabbard. "Oh, very well," Godfrey sighed. "He can live."

Vanessa had spent the afternoon engaged in a chess match with Julian. It was an excellent sign of his recovery that he had progressed past a simple game of draughts. His eyes were also back to normal. Although Julian swore he never wanted to read another Minerva novel, nor even any writings by that great gun Walter Scott, the fact that he could now read without difficulty was one more blessing Lady Vanessa could report to the eager ears of the Earl of Wyverne. Uncle 'Vester himself was, in fact, so much improved he had declared that by the time Julian no longer needed his Bath chair, he would be fit to leave his bed and ride in it.

"Need to see something besides your long face," the earl grumbled to the faithful Will Jarvis, as Vanessa listened. "See my Laura's portrait again . . . and see if her roses still bloom. And those demmed dahlias Kitty liked so well. Never could see it m'self. Big old things, fat as a dinner plate. Not like our dainty Kitty at all."

Vanessa had not reported this conversation to Julian. No sense reminding him he was an orphan. Outside of his grandfather, she and Charles were all the family he had.

Pain stabbed through her heart. She very much feared she was going to have to marry Charles even if he only cared for the luxuries which came with her. For he was the true Tyrone who must guard and guide Julian until he was grown. She had no rights here. If she felt compelled to watch over Julian as well . . . If she wished to stay at the Abbey beyond her majority, which was only a few months away, she would have to marry Charles.

Where was her arrogance? Vanessa asked herself. Where was her pride? On her twenty-first birthday, when she had access to her inheritance, she and dear Tabby should pack up and move to Beechwood. Acquire a cat or two and live out their lives in maidenly dignity.

But she loved Charles Tyrone. And he loved her money. By *ton* standards, it was a marriage made in heaven.

She should not mind so very much.

"Checkmate!" Julian crowed.

Vanessa frowned at the board, conceded without protest. She should, in truth, apologize for putting up such a poor game. "How many steps today?" she inquired with a smile.

"All the way to the window," Julian declared. "Simmons says I can try the hall tomorrow. A few days more, and I'll pop in on grandfather. Won't he be surprised?"

Vanessa squeezed his hand, leaned forward to kiss him on the cheek. No, she would not leave him. Eventually, of course, he would leave her, finding his own life. But they had been through too much, the ducal daughter and the bereaved boy, for her ever to leave him while he needed her. *I hope you realize that, Charles,* was Vanessa's grim thought as she left the room. *It's Parson's mousetrap for you, whether you like it or not.*

She paused before Lady Clorinda's door. For two whole days—since Charles's threatening words to the family—the door had opened only for Clorinda's maid. That did not take into account, of course, the inner door which connected—through a sitting room—to that of Bertram Taggart. Mrs. Meecham, having been well trained in the vagaries of country houseparties by the somewhat slippery morals of Neville Tyrone, had placed "dear Bertie" exactly where Lady Clorinda wanted him.

Today, however, it would appear Mr. Taggart's presence had done the lady little good. A wan Clorinda was tucked up in her huge tester bed, its aqua silk draperies boasting ruffles of white lace. As did the lady's dressing gown which drooped artfully off one shoulder as she held a crochet-trimmed handkerchief to her red rimmed eyes.

"It was Bertie!" she announced dramatically, as soon as Vanessa entered the room. "I cannot protect him any longer."

Such loyalty, Vanessa scoffed. Obviously, Lady Clorinda had decided to save herself.

The woebegone figure of Godfrey's and Arabella's mama hung her head, blew her nose. She heaved an enormous sigh. "Bertie wished to please me, you see," she declared earnestly. "He thought he had only to rid the world of Neville and Julian and, *voilà*, Godfrey would inherit Wyverne. I fear he did not know about Charles," she added on a sob.

"*You* knew about Charles," Vanessa countered swiftly.

"Charles," Clorinda spat out, her lovely façade suddenly fractured by a burst of temper. "Charles should have died in the war. Indeed, I was sure he had. Not one glimpse of him had I seen—" Lady Clorinda snapped her jaws shut. Vanessa watched in fascination as the older woman's features resumed her customary vapid innocence. "You cannot think . . ." she murmured dolefully, "you cannot imagine that *I* . . . ? It was all Bertie's idea, I do assure you. I would never—"

"Do not be ridiculous, Clorinda," Vanessa snapped. "Taggart did not do this on his own—he had no reason. He did it for love or money. Or both."

"Love!" Clorinda scoffed, her soulful blue eyes once again narrowing to mean little slits, her beautifully sculpted lips twisting into a snarl. "Bertie loves, indeed he does. He loves my paying his gaming debts and paying for his fine clothes. For his stallion, his curricle, and his pair of fancy high-steppers. And no doubt for his high flyers as well—the bits of muslin he visits when he tells me he's at his club."

Lady Clorinda's venom was so great Vanessa nearly took a step back from the edge of the bed. But she could not allow herself to falter now that the truth was being revealed at last. "The poison, Clorinda? Did Taggart do that too?"

"He gave it to Fielding. Stupid man! How could he be so close to the boy and make such a botch of it?"

Vanessa recalled the terrible scene as they poured soapy water down Julian's throat and held his head as he heaved up the contents of his stomach in agony.

"And to fail twice more!" Clorinda spat. "Couldn't kill the boy with a pillow, couldn't even drown him—when there I was, screaming myself hoarse so those blockheaded soldiers would leave the boy and come to my rescue. Why, I scarce had voice enough to scold Bertie for not doing the deed himself."

This time Vanessa obeyed the urge to step back. Not all the sturdy common sense she possessed could keep her from wondering what poisonous creature had taken

over the body of the once languid and lovely Clorinda
Tyrone. The lady was truly mad.

"Then you and Taggart killed Neville," Vanessa said,
her voice flat with shock. "And when Julian showed signs
of recovery, you set Fielding to finish the job."

"Yes, yes!" Clorinda spat out. "Bertie hired that
dreadful valet long ago, then recommended him to
Neville."

"Was it Fielding who caused Neville's accident?"

"No," Clorinda told her. "That was someone else.
Took ship to Jamaica, Bertie said. And a great shame it
was, he must have told me a hundred times. Nothing
went right after that."

A shiver shook Vanessa. *Nothing went right.* Everyone
lived . . . except Fielding himself.

"And the accident on Houndstooth Hill?" Vanessa
persisted.

"No, no, that was Horatia's idea," Clorinda burbled,
glad enough to have something for which she could cast
the blame elsewhere. "And that worked because Bertie
loosened the bolt himself," she added, with something
which sounded close to pride.

Vanessa had a horrid vision of the ground coming up
to meet her, vivid memories of pain which still attacked
her at odd moments. Undoubtedly, Transportation was
too good for Lady Clorinda Tyrone. Only for the sake
of Godfrey and Arabella would she fail to lay an information against this vile creature and her lover. But, perhaps, Vanessa thought hopefully, Clorinda and Bertie
would eliminate each other on the long voyage to New
South Wales.

"You will pardon me if I do not offer condolences on
the failure of your plans," Vanessa declared. As Lady
Clorinda drew breath for a fresh wail, Vanessa picked
up the tiny silver gilt vinaigrette from the dressing table
and tossed it onto the bed. "Charles and Godfrey will
decide what must be done," said the ducal daughter, with

all her long line of ancestors arrayed at her back. "I shall not visit you again."

For a fleeting moment Vanessa wished she could say the same for Arabella. *There* was a duty she dreaded to face. But Arabella would have Godfrey, and that was not such a bad thing.

That night, after Lady Vanessa Rayne had poured tea for those who remained in enough good grace to appear in the drawing room, Major Charles Tyrone asked Lady Vanessa if she would be kind enough to join him in the bookroom. Julian winked at Arabella. Godfrey smirked. James Prentice tried to appear indifferent and failed. Miss Halliwell's eyes lit with all the glow of romance which had never been her own. Vanessa tried to gain courage by picturing the time she had stalked into the bookroom prepared to do battle with the major over table leaves. She, too, failed. Charles was standing, politely holding the door for her. It appeared they were to have their long-delayed discussion of what he termed their "personal lives." Vanessa was very much afraid she might be sick.

"Did you think I would put this off?" Charles inquired, as he seated her on the burgundy leather settee, then sat down beside her, altogether too close for comfort.

Vanessa swallowed, struggled to find her voice which threatened to come out as a gurgle. Looking straight ahead, she announced, "I have decided to marry you. Julian needs me."

"No words of horror about my close call this afternoon?" Charles chided. "No, 'oh, dear Charles, when I nearly lost you, I realized how much I needed you'?"

"You know perfectly well—"

"I know nothing."

Vanessa's resistance crumbled. "When I looked out the window and saw Godfrey marching Taggart down the road, his foil to his back," she blurted. "When I heard what had happened . . ."

"Yes?" Charles encouraged.

Vanessa made one last struggle toward sanity. "Why?" she demanded. "Why on earth did Taggart use my bow and arrows?"

Charles chuckled. "Can you not guess?" Vanessa, scowling, shook her head. "The idiot knew—as did the entire household, I might add—that we were at outs with one another." Charles paused, waiting for the inevitable reaction.

Vanessa's deep blue eyes, by far her best feature, widened in incredulity. "He thought . . . he was mad enough . . . Dear God, he wished to blame *me*?" she gasped.

"There you have it," Charles said. "Just another coil in a massively convoluted and thoroughly incompetent plot."

"Except for Neville," Vanessa sighed.

"Except for Neville," Charles solemnly agreed.

"But that he should try to implicate me," Vanessa huffed. "That is outrageous."

Charles examined his fingernails. "Just so," he said blandly. "Truly, the man was singularly incompetent or perhaps merely unfortunate." Seizing his opportunity, as a good soldier should, Charles added softly, "Nessa, what if Godfrey hadn't been there this afternoon? Would you have cared?"

Cared? What a shallow, colorless word for what she had felt when she discovered how close Charles had come to death. "You are a monster," she told him. "You know quite well I love you and are torturing me to say it. Very well! I love you. I was in anguish when I heard Godfrey's tale. There now! Are you satisfied?"

"Not until you believe I love you and not your money," Charles declared.

"Impossible!" Vanessa snapped.

Charles found he could no longer keep a straight face. This was going to be easier than he had feared. "We soldiers are not much good with words," he grinned. "Perhaps a demonstration?" So saying, he took her in his arms and kissed her. So thoroughly, he not only banished his lady's doubts, but he vanquished forever all thoughts of the voluptuous and willing women of the Peninsular campaign. After all, he had known his goose was cooked since that evening in the maze when the plain ducal daughter had transformed into a beauty before his very eyes.

"You are so lovely," the major murmured into his beloved's ear, as the sheer need to breathe forced him to break off a second most satisfactory embrace.

Lovely. Vanessa smiled through tears of joy. If Charles thought her lovely, he must love her very much. For love transformed one's vision. Hers as well as his. Charles Tyrone—the man, the soldier, the engineer—would do very well for her. Very well indeed.

Epilogue

Charles Tyrone stood up to his waist in water, contemplating the elegant bridge which stretched across the swift-moving water in front of him. A good bridge, if he did say so himself. Even if this sojourn in Portugal's exotically beautiful Serra de Sintra had been planned more as a delightful vacation than for any monies it might add to the satisfyingly ample coffers of the Tyrone Company of Engineers. In less than two weeks they would be off to the south of France, where they would be constructing their largest project yet, a fine hotel overlooking the beach. But they would return to the Abbey to keep Christmas for the young Earl of Wyverne. As they had every year since that awful time so many years past. Fleetingly, Charles thought of the structures his minions had built (and built well) without his direct supervision during the summer months of Julian's six long vacations.

It had been worth it, however. Well worth it. He had gained a younger brother as well as a growing family. And three cousins he found he rather liked. If only Bishop Tyrone could be convinced to shorten his sermons.

A shriek from the shore. It had been some years since Charles was a soldier in constant fear for his life. Swinging around too fast, he stumbled and fell, finding himself floundering like a veritable lummox in water which was, thank God, considerably warmer than the water in that long-ago stream in Scotland. The Serra de Sintra, with the tumbling streams, jagged rocks, and gnarled trees that had inspired the opening passages of Byron's famed *Childe Harold,* was set in a climate far more mild than the Highlands of Scotland.

Feminine laughter and childish giggles met Charles's struggle to regain his footing. When he did, for a moment he simply stood and stared at his family. All was well, the shriek nothing more than childish exuberance. *His family.* Something he had once thought well nigh impossible for a man who planned to roam the world, creating structures wherever his skill was needed. How very fine it was to watch a creation come to life rather than figure how much explosive it would take to blow it up.

His family. Vanessa, who still remained as beautiful as she had appeared to him that night in the boxwood maze. Elizabeth, age five, who was so exquisitely lovely he already worried about that terrible year when she would make her debut in the *ton* and some young whelp would want to take her from him. Jeffrey, age three, who could count to one hundred and already knew his alphabet. And somewhere behind his wife's wonderfully rounded abdomen a third blessing, one more affirmation that love could grow on rocky ground and endure where no one thought it possible.

Charles slogged his way out of the stream, climbed the bank, thoroughly kissed his wife, then responded warmly to his children's cries of, "Me, me, me!" By what miracle had a soldier found his way to such love?

Vanessa reached up, wiped a tear which refused to stay put in a tough engineer's eye. "I love you," she whispered, smiling.

"Forever," the major returned.

"Papa!" Miss Elizabeth Tyrone tugged sharply on her father's dripping trousers. "Papa, I want to swim."

"Me, too," declared Master Jeffrey Tyrone.

Vanessa, shoulders shaking over this typical interruption of an intimate moment, laid her forehead against Charles's chest. All her fears had come to this. A loving husband who had never strayed and a burgeoning family who filled her heart with joy.

Yet, she had come so close to rejecting the life she now had. Charles still teased her sometimes, calling her His Arrogant Ladyship whenever she got up too far upon her high horse. To think, she had truly believed the daughter of a duke could not possibly wed a gentleman with no title at all. A man who actually earned his living. An *engineer*.

And she had thought the Ladies Horatia and Clorinda quite mad!

About the Author

With ancestors from England, Wales, Scotland, Ireland, and France, **Blair Bancroft** feels right at home in nineteenth-century Britain. But it was only after a variety of other careers that she turned to writing about the Regency era. Blair has been a music teacher, professional singer, nonfiction editor, costume designer, and real estate agent, and she has still managed to travel extensively. The mother of three grown children, Blair lives in Florida. Her Web site is www.blairbancroft.com. She can be contacted at blairbancroft@aol.com.

Allison Lane

"A FORMIDABLE TALENT...
MS. LANE NEVER FAILS TO
DELIVER THE GOODS."
—*ROMANTIC TIMES*

THE NOTORIOUS WIDOW
0-451-20166-3
When a scoundrel tries to tarnish a young widow's reputation, a valiant Earl tries to repair the damage—and mend her broken heart as well...

BIRDS OF A FEATHER
0-451-19825-5
When a plain, bespectacled young woman keeps meeting the handsome Lord Wylie, she feels she is not up to his caliber. A great arbiter of fashion for London society, Lord Wylie was reputed to be more interseted in the cut of his clothes than the feelings of others, as the young woman bore witness to. Degraded by him in public, she could nevertheless forget his dashing demeanor. It will take a public scandal, and a private passion, to bring them together...

To order call: 1-800-788-6262